La Rochelle

Michael Nath

route

First published by Route in 2010
PO Box 167, Pontefract, WF8 4WW
info@route-online.com
www.route-online.com

ISBN (13): 978-1-901927-43-6
ISBN (10): 1-901927-43-1

Michael Nath asserts his moral right to be
identified as the author of this book

A catalogue for this book is available from the British Library

Design:
GOLDEN www.wearegolden.co.uk

Printed by CPI Bookmarque, Croydon

Route is supported by Arts Council England

For Eric Nath 1938-2008

'He that seeketh victory over his own nature, let him not set himself too great, nor too small tasks.'
Francis Bacon, *Essays*

'We cannot look around our own corner.'
German proverb

'It is a general rule in medicine that rest and fasting are beneficial in fever cases. But it may be the wrong treatment in a particular case.'
Aristotle, *Ethics*

Monday

'You're like the man who was annoyed half his life by a creaking door, and could not come to the resolution of removing the daily annoyance with a few drops of oil. But so it is with us all! The darkening and illuminating of man make his destiny. The daemon ought to lead us every day in leading-strings, and tell us what we ought to do on every occasion. But the good spirit leaves us in the lurch, and we grope about in the dark.

'Napoleon was the man! Always illuminated, always clear and decided, and endowed at every hour with energy enough to carry out what he considered necessary. His life was the stride of a demigod, from battle to battle, and from victory to victory.'

So I was alone in the house with an old self-help book by a good old German that smelled of paper-lined old empty drawers. Was my problem no worse than the man with the creaking door? But it wasn't the door that was the problem was it? It was himself. No daemon to advise him. The daemon being equivalent to the good spirit, surprising as that might sound. Then what were leading-strings? Were they what toddlers have? Or hawks in training?

On television the members rose and clapped. They clapped as if Stalin's warm-up man had set them off, then they clapped an extra minute just for joy because they were quite free not to if they thought the speech sucked. They were all dreaming of the night anyway in their suits and little name badges, poor bastard in Baghdad quite forgotten. When the night came they'd be at it like beasts, for below the belt we're all...

My phone emitted a few bars of 'Where the Bee Sucks There Suck I'. Somebody told me that I ought to change that the other day, but I said so what if it makes me sound like an old fruit when it goes off in my pocket. Don't judge a bloke by the tune on his phone, all right?... Below the belt we're all a billion years old.

Assuring Master Edwards that I wasn't too bad thanks, I could hear myself with the waxy intonation of a new receptionist repeating a message. I'd been in clinic this afternoon. So what was I doing now? What I was doing now was reading, supine upon the settee. What about the weekend? Ah, the weekend – had he noticed darkness and light had become equivalent lately? He couldn't say he had. Well I'd had an abject one. Silence. You know, drunk a little too much, read a fair bit, tried on a nervous breakdown, just for size. He hummed. Could I go down this evening? I said that I *could* (for we both knew it wasn't orthodox, this calling on a Monday). He did not respond. I was going to be about forty-five minutes.

By the hall mirror with its slightly convex glass in which it was impossible to see yourself straight, I mounted the stairs to clean my teeth. The mirror was framed round with golden ripples of painted wood. Bending like a hag to keep the foam off my suit, I recalled humanised pictures of the sun with yellow hair from books of the past, blown upon by fat-cheeked winds. It was antique that mirror, pre-war. Passing darkly across its silver glass, I left the house for the High Road. Uphill by the cemetery and library then down to the underground, I made my way.

I would have had something to tell myself about this excursion, if I'd not now been counting stations like an addict. Highgate to Archway really stretched the patience. You could say it was 2 minutes 28. That did nothing to describe the sensation, of being in a hurry with a rotten conscience. I would have been telling myself I should have said no. Tufnell Park. Kentish Town. Their names were time. What I needed was will, iron will... Even then, could the iron refuse the magnet? If you'd excuse a venerable proverb. Fashionable Camden Town, where the arseholes gathered and the punks. That time we met in Camden, he looked like Mr Hyde. Yet the bigger problem was I couldn't say yes. Mornington Crescent: the famous game without rules. What the hell did not saying no matter, when you lacked the will to say yes? This had to be the issue. With a film crew and interviewer who crossed her legs, I'd go into this personally on the southbound Northern Line, my trouble with No and Yes.

Too passive for No or Yes. Fundamentally this was the problem: inability to be active. Goethe made a religion of it. *Activity*... Ah, I should still have been at home reading Goethe, down on the settee; not hurrying passively. Why could I not be active? Why couldn't I perform? Why could I not have a biographer? A book based on my life and times? Was this much to ask?... Why couldn't I be like Napoleon?

For the very good reason that that sort of greatness was dead and gone. What we had now was the 'heroism of modern life'. Fine phrase, though no one was at all sure what it meant, except it certainly didn't go on horseback.

Anyway I'd let him suggest a drink. He'd be wanting to visit his local, and I would see Laura for ten minutes before we slipped out. Worth coming for. Maybe she'd tell me something she'd just read in the paper.

Out on Warren Street I observed my face in a window, sniffed the air and for a moment turned to look behind me. If I wasn't mistaken, we were in for an equinoctial gale.

In the outer hall, letters for departed tenants collected in a chipboard rack. Here Ian Edwards greeted me with an attempted smile and took me in by the black hardboard door of the flat. At the end of his own hall, we hung about by the hanging jackets and doorless kitchenette. Her pink raincoat was there.

At last he patted the fridge. What would I have? He had beer and wine. I hummed and lowered my eyes. In the tone of a man answering an inspector, he told me the other drinks he had. He had raki, he had rum. I nodded officially. Last time we'd drunk raki, we'd discussed my passivity. Three or four in the morning, Laura sound asleep (it was to be hoped). The bedroom wasn't far from the living room. Evidently he'd started on a little session by himself, and wanted company. His session, my trial.

I said I'd have a cup of tea, actually. With the detachment of a nauseated man he set about making my tea; then he led me into the long living room, where cable news was on. The brother of the hostage was saying the Prime Minister's silence was the kiss of death. Standing ovation for the Chancellor at the party conference. As I sat on the short settee behind the squat Eastern coffee table, on which stood two opened cans, the members rose and clapped.

Across a narrow cobbled mews, the room faced an office building where young people involved in creative work were rising from their desks, hovering, departing. In the daytime, the office blocked the sunlight to this room, which surely couldn't suit Laura; though I'd not heard her complain. Ian drank from one of the cans. Nearly empty. She'd be on her way home. I wanted to smoke: a bad time for it. He should have been making her something to eat, not drinking cans. If I'd been him, that's what I'd have been doing, making her the sort of thing ladies like. With truffle oil.

'Something weird happened last night, Mark.' He backed towards the doorway as if he'd been warned to stay put in a painting, and was losing confidence in his first steps beyond the frame. Normally he had the poise of the character actor, the naturalness and reserve. I invited him to tell me what had happened last night.

He was going to get another beer first. Did I want one?

Yes. I thought I would. Pathetic. But what's the point of trying not to drink? It's so bloody aimless isn't it? He came back with a couple of cans of Holsten, bending to place mine on the low, squat table. Yellow-green aluminium skin: cold-sweat condensation. We avoided each other's eyes.

Laura's shown me photos of him. There was one in

which he was eating from a white bowl with such thoughtful elegance that he appeared merely to be sampling its contents while his judgement was awaited. Another in which he was standing on a cold beach. Behind him, embedded in the sand, was the wooden hull of a wrecked ship. And one in which he was writing (a postcard, as I remember) in an anorak, with moors in the background rising to a chilly bright sky. That was taken by Laura on one of their earliest holidays.

I cracked my can. Got me with the first taste, witch's brew. Never mind. I'd have none tomorrow, or Wednesday; I'd have none till Friday. No. Saturday... I swear.

'Woke about 2am.' He sat down in the armchair by the door. His movement was barely his own: in the way he lowered himself there was a trace of ataxia. It was the manner of sitting down of the Huntington's patient, as if in apprehension of the cushion of a prankster.

Well now, when he'd woken about 2am, he'd heard this music, seemingly coming from the street. Weird, very weird. A kind of music and singing at the same time, without being entirely one or the other. If anything, there'd been something German about it. Like Germans carousing in war films, in a bar in an occupied town. That was how it had been, passing in the street last night.

We had a little vision. Blond faces, barmaids, bodices, tankards. Oom-pah-pah, oom-pah-pah, that's how it goes! Scene: *Wehrmacht* carousing; location: Northern France.

Carouse and fall. I love the fall of the Third Reich. I know I shouldn't, know we should have forgotten by now – but I just can't stop loving it.

Anyway, this was what he'd heard. Straight up.

I was interested. Did he think we'd been invaded? They never got in here. *Take one with you!* God bless you, Mr Churchill. I have a shotgun in the shed.

He didn't know what he thought.

He was sure he'd heard it though?

Yeah. He'd actually got out of bed to look in the mews. But it must have been round the other side. Round the front. Then he heard a woman come out in the street and tell them she was trying to sleep. Whoever they were. That was when it stopped.

Could you actually hear the street from here?

He looked straight at me. No. Usually you couldn't. This was weird too. I thought of him returning to bed and Laura's sleeping face. The next impression he had was it had somehow broken off from a carnival in another place, and turned up in his neighbourhood.

Really?

Yeah. Then it had put him in mind of a kids' film.

Which one?

One where the kids got taken away, he advised me bleakly.

Ah… I began to wonder how many times he had seen Laura's face in the darkness. Thousands probably, lucky bastard. If he made sure he woke up often enough, how long before he'd seen her face a million times? That was one for the courtly poets. Arithmetical adoration. Say, one hundred times a night: twenty-five years.

'What d'you think it was, Ian?'

Now and then the three of us meet on a Saturday in the West End. I buy champagne to keep her there. But she notices the time; and as when winter begins on a September afternoon, in Archangel or Astrakhan, so she has to go. Why does she never stay longer? Because she does not love to drink, you fool. Grey-eyed: eyes like a sky that's going to break into light.

Ian stays on beside me when she leaves. This is what he wants, it's what she's happy with. I should persuade him to go with her, shouldn't I? But what if this thwarted his wish to have some time on his own. What if it thwarted hers? Or made it seem I wished to create a stir between them, one insisting the other resisting? Hands off, is the principle. Let them be. Whatever they do is what they want to do. However they are is how they are. Don't interfere with domestic relationships: you don't know what you are getting involved in; they have these traditions and arrangements and subtle unspoken agreements you'd only understand if you'd been there from the beginning. And to be there from the beginning, you'd have to be one of them. To interfere is impolitic. Particularly when they've no doubt got an arrangement concerning yourself.

When Laura gets home, let her phone to let us know – I always remind her. In the time it takes, I feel a wild, exquisite fear. I should have caused him to go with her, contrived it. Could have looked at my watch, feigned surprise: I had to be off as well alas! This would have sorted it without intervention, an elegant exit. But I had to want to stay for another. What's more, I did not want it looking as if she were what I were there for, she alone; for that wouldn't have been the truth... particularly if she'd been complaining about him.

She likes to walk. She certainly doesn't hurry. The night is full of alleys and men in cars; most people now won't help a woman in trouble. I see the eyes watching her like a wandering bobbing light. Rear door opens and slams. Down goes her bright head. The ride begins.

When I tell Ian my fear, with manly abbreviations, he gives me an old look. And then she rings. Let's drink to that! Let's drink to the end of fear.

Complaining isn't a habit of hers though.

★★★

'I think it was an omen,' he said now.

'Really? What of?'

'I don't know, Mark.' He wouldn't look at me. Your professors of body language say people who won't look straight at you are hiding something. Yes, they are hiding something – or contrariwise, they are not hiding something and would not have you see. Ha ha. Make your mind up, Prof. What about good liars who look straight at you?

'That's the thing about omens isn't it?' he murmured.

'Depends if you've got the art of reading them.' Like the priests who descried the lines the birds flew, or tossed entrails on the ground and made predictions from the patterns, when the world was young.

'I think it was an omen something bad's going to happen.' He looked straight at me. No doubt he too

15

knows what the professors say. Maybe we all do these days. We know it to be the shallowest kind of sense, but it makes us self-conscious. Self-conscious about levelling with each other, self-conscious about deceiving each other. We want to be honest but we look insincere. We want to lie but we look like a liar. What's the way out? Maybe the novelists could show us. They don't tell the truth and they don't lie either; they've found a middle way, the novelists have. We could learn a trick from the novelists, if only we weren't stuck here.

'Yeah? Something bad's always happening,' I muttered apotropaically… I may not like life, but that doesn't mean I'm not bothered if it gets worse.

'No. Something bad close to hand.'

'Get out of it!' I scoffed: he was making me anxious.

'Then something good.' He nodded at me.

'In that order?'

He hummed.

I didn't like the sound of this. I badly wanted a cigarette. Obviously, he didn't really mean anything; but I'm oversusceptible to the sound of other people's convictions. Something bad followed by something good? Well, it was the formula for a happy ending. But a bad thing could be losing your left leg in the gap between the tube and the platform, a good thing learning to appreciate life more after the accident, *strange as it may seem*. Or going to jail for a sexual offence you may not have committed and learning humility among the other jail folk, reading them *War and Peace* and sharing their golden rolling tobacco… Christ! There were millions of possibilities, weren't there? I needed another drink.

I needed a drink in a brightly lit establishment where a rude Scotsman and his woeful wife and straight and gay and office folk weren't worrying over omens, and three or four men in their fifties are playing the golf machine. Grey-haired to his collar and fish-eyed, their ringleader is whacking it. That's usufruct, that's his right of enjoyment. He's had his something bad happening, and now he's enjoying the good times. Some years ago he did a week on remand. I've heard him speak of it. One week of hell. He doesn't disguise how scared he was, and it was nothing heavy, just VAT fraud.

'Fancy going over the road?'

Ian shook his head. He did not know whether he wanted to visit his local. Now I'd thought that's what I was coming down for, for him to suggest a quickish visit over there. In truth, and regardless of all that fuss on the tube, it's what I'd wanted, to hang about in the hall chatting with Laura for ten minutes without threatening to establish myself semi-permanently, then leave with him and get moderately pissed, her image still with me. Wasn't counting on this talk of omens.

He was muttering something. He had to wait here; or wait to hear; or it may have been that he said he had to wait for her. 'Wait' snagged me: ominous word, compared to its partner, 'expect'. You expect someone at a certain time, don't you? We're expecting them about eight. She's expecting a baby in March. I'm expecting Laura in five minutes. You expect them without apprehension. But when we wait for them, it's because we aren't sure when they'll be back.

Women wait for guys who've gone inside. They bite

their lips at railway stations, at docks and airports, and say they'll wait for guys who may never come back. *Oh we don't want to lose you, but we think that you should go!* Fathers say, 'We're still waiting for her'; and everyone watching thinks, After all this time? Get real!

I settled back to wait with him and he gave me another beer.

★★★

His face reminds me at times of a Renaissance wiseguy, a Cardinal's secretary in a sort of flat velvet cap with a clipped beard. I think I've seen him in a painting. Clever white face. Those secretaries weren't just there to download the boss's Blackberry and book seats on Eurostar; their learning and their skill were great, as were their effects on the lives of people in the city states, since they were trained in the *ars dictaminis*, which taught you to write letters in such a way as to make things happen. This all started in Bologna about 1120; then the secretaries began to visit Paris; there they learned even more stunts from the ancient rhetoricians, which they took back to Italy. And this is what got the Renaissance going: letter writing – a skill in decline in our own time.

This evening, however, he looked less sure than usual. As if some trickery or sharp practice he'd been devising had now sprung to take its chance on Fortune's Wheel. Just for fancy's sake, say the Cardinal's second name is something like 'Caprice', which means the wiseguy might get hacked in half longways, ragged parts laid in the plaza for all to see in the noonday sun, as recommended by

Machiavelli; on the other hand, he might be rewarded with a vineyard and two hundred rich acres. That's where you are with Cardinal Caprice: on uncertain ground with respect to the appreciation of your secretarial efforts.

As I opened my can with a crack and little hiss, thinking to myself of Dukes and Cardinals, Guelphs, and gonfalons, a word that means less than it sounds, Ian was telling me something foreignly... Whose side were the Guelphs on?... He seemed to be telling me they'd been having sex the other day. I nodded in acknowledgement, bloke to bloke. Presently, he had another go: the two of them had been having sex the other day. Like a toothless ancient, in the interlude between this and what he told me next, I set my mouth, grinning as the Chancellor grinned, now he had been taught to grin. Then he said he thought she'd had a tear in her eye.

She'd been crying. Such words were a sign of crisis, and crisis-related privileges. Could I have an ashtray? He rose and fetched a small, heavy vessel that appeared to have been formed on a day when a potter fell nose-first into a lump of left-over clay which he contrived to pass off as an artefact once he'd sobered up, setting it on the low table. I lit a cigarette and drew until the end glowed like a tracer bullet with its little phosphorus coat. Radiant heat scorched my nostrils, hydrocarbon heat and hot monoxide burned my heart; it stopped me imagining them, and their legs.

She'd made out it was allergy. He looked at his hands. Affecting her eyes.

With a professional air, I said it could have been allergy this time of year... I was damned if I couldn't still see the both of them, two blonde seals ramping, on inhospitable sand or ice… Late-season pollen from one of the garden squares perhaps, or Regent's Park even.

He'd wanted to think it was. Or possibly dust.

I nodded. Could've been dust.

Maybe they'd thrashed so much they'd raised a host of mites and bugs and microscopic devils that came in at their eyes; the Lady Laura being of tenderer feelings had wept and wondered why she was sad. Fancy it. She'd have been on top for them to rise and enter. Uh-uh-ah. Just through there, through that wall in the bedroom. Makes me strange to myself to think of. What is wrong with me? I should get more involved.

'Laura hasn't spoken to you has she, Mark?'

'When?'

'Recently. Hasn't phoned you has she?'

'No. I don't even think she's got my number.'

He smiled. 'Does she mail you?'

'Never.' Why doesn't she? To keep it special!… Imagine if that was why, you great fool.

'Really?'

'I don't know her in that way, do I?' What was he trying to suggest? I felt compelled to dissimulate, though except for a strange and compound feeling of excitement and unease, I had nothing to hide. Practically speaking, there was nothing on my conscience. At no time recently had she confided in me about anything – categorically.

I declared that to be honest with him, I was surprised he'd asked me that.

He smiled again: 'It's only because I know she respects you, man; very highly.'

'Doesn't confide in me. Never.'

Touches me on the arm and stands close to me, that's what she does; sits close to me as well; though only when Ian's looking. When he goes to the Gents', she leans virtuously back. There is no come on with the Lady Laura. Of course, it may be she thinks I'm not up to it. She asks me about my love life: ah this is fantastic sport. It's something like an interview, if you imagine an interviewer who seems to have a vivacious rapport with you, perhaps for the sake of her institution's commitment to affirmative action. I don't tell her the truth; that would hardly be politic – or possible, I should think. Her questions can be pretty crafty; but I always know what she's after, being considerably craftier. I'm like an expert malingerer or work-shy scally. No one's tricking me into getting a job. Of course, it's all nothing more than a big tease; but I'm happy to play my part.

★★★

'What d'you expect her to have spoken to me about?'

As if it were a pet rat that didn't care for the light, Ian put his hand over his phone on the arm of the chair. 'Nothing.'

'Nothing?'

He was an odd distance from me for one man in conversation with another, as if phantom attendants were sliding back and forth his inner being. 'Or everything,' he made an effort to say.

'She hasn't spoken to me about nothing. Or everything.'

'I didn't think she had,' he said.

So that was that. I was now aggrieved, and apprehensive. Aggrieved about the pointlessness of this inquisition; apprehensive – well I am always apprehensive. With me, it's second nature, apprehension, as much a part of me as my height, and moderately northern accent. So I was apprehensive now because of his talk of omens, the light sweat on his face, his strange comportment, these questions such as he'd never asked me before about Laura. The whole arrangement was ominous… 'ominous' being the younger brother of 'omen', a sinister pair, two hooded lads.

'What about the future?' he suggested now.

'She has not spoken to me about the future.'

He finished his Holsten and said something about the weekend. Like a driver peering at road signs in heavy rain, which may have been wrenched up and re-pointed the wrong way by unhelpful sprites or activists, he wasn't giving conversation his best attention. Now he rose and away to the kitchen. Back with more cans.

What about the weekend?

They'd gone out for lunch. At the weekend. He pressed the sharp tabs of the ring-pull in his thumb.

Where had they gone? I screwed out another cigarette. It stood in the ashtray then drooped, like a Seger cone dilapidating in furnace heat.

They'd gone to Farringdon.

Oh very nice…

Fine train station, Farringdon. Notable for its high glass roof in the manner of the neighbouring meat market. Cowcross Street, Charterhouse Street, Smithfield Long

22

Lane: fine names. Why did he take her there? Maybe my influence. The first English domestic tragedy has a scene in Farringdon (known as 'Aldersgate' in those days). Nobody knows who wrote it. *Arden of Feversham*. Told him about it this summer, two of us sitting in Queen's Square on an evening when he had met me from work, at a wooden trestle table outside the Queen's Larder. I can remember what we were speaking of before as I can remember what we talked of after. Can even remember the date, damn it. 'You remember too much you do,' my mother once said to me. That was autumn thirty – no, twenty-nine – years ago. I'd have been recalling an incident which anyone else would have forgotten – any normal person.

They must have done the deed when they came back from lunch. A perfect day.

'She said something about old age.'

'Whose old age?'

'Ours.'

'What sort of thing did she say?'

'Ah – about when we were shrivelled. Me and her.'

***

In the Farringdon scene in the old tragedy, two hitmen come up from Kent for the husband of Alice Arden. Thomas Arden is in London on business. Since he's from Kent too, you wonder why 'Black Will' and 'Shakebags' didn't just do him there. Extravagant plotting. The more so because the hitmen are thwarted by a newsagent, the shutter from his booth felling the pair of them by accident

23

while they're setting their ambush. Ian opined that this didn't sound very tragic. It isn't. Yet it contrives to be a sinister play, because of Alice Arden.

Alice wants rid of her husband so she can get it on with her lover, Mosbie. The lengths they'd go to for a ride... And still the same isn't it? Still the same; but when you think of them doing the deed four centuries ago, what do you see? What do you *smell*? They were shrivelled early in life. They were fit for less than a decade, maybe six or seven years; then their beauty was gone, and their teeth, and their feet were black. Is that what you see? Cocks like organic carrots?

It does cheer me up when I think of books and plays and those who inhabit them. It's like going to the museum. There were millions here before us, millions and millions. We're just the tip or arrow point; and not long till all we millions fall back down the shaft from the present, into the trailing air.

★★★

'Did Laura use that word?' My friend shook his head. 'So you're having lunch and she envisages the pair of you in your old age. This is what you're saying?' He nodded and hummed. I could see it her way. 'Not in Britain probably. The Bay of Biscay, I fancy: that'll be where she wants you to end up, in a little French town. Little old couple, holding hands by the ocean. In the year 2044...' And I'll have long been dead. Hurrah.

Ian's thumb was bleeding neatly from the ring-pull. His face was horn white.

'What did you say to her?' I urged him.

'I said in my opinion we were old already. I said we were both already shrivelled.' His voice was low and definite.

'*You* used that word?'

'Yeah.'

They don't have that much money, the pair of them, so this outing would have been a treat, I fancy. I could see Laura's face. He says she doesn't know how to get angry. During her occasional attempts, she just turns pale pink and operatic, four or five minutes max. That is the best she can manage. Lovely.

'Well I hope she'd finished her sea bass before you started,' I said. I saw her walking on her own to the tube, everything ruined. *Oh what have I done to deserve this!* She'd have been in her pink raincoat. He really could be a slag. Twenty-four carat. 'What did you say that for?'... Must've been this she was crying about when they were having sex. How come he's surprised? *Thought she had a tear in her eye.* 'Thought'? I'll fucking give him 'thought'! He's bloody lucky she got down to it with him at all. *Shrivelled!* And still she gets down to it with him? Makes her cry and she still gets down? Slag.

I'd made myself feel like crying now. I could have kicked his slim face in, cracked it like horn: I'd made myself feel like that too, though of course I was as far from violence as a picture from an act it represents.

'She shouldn't have looked so far ahead, man,' Ian said with a kind of intensity. 'It's death that is.'

'Well what you did, pal, is you spoiled the present too. Ruined it. Why not let her look ahead for Christ's sake? Why not let her?'

He moved his tongue along his upper right molars as if feeling for a fragment of meat, or exploring new damage.

'Why do you not do things her way for once?' I was uncommonly peremptory this evening. 'Why not take her for lunch and say what she wants to hear? Hey? Why not take her for lunch and be sweet to her? Why d'you have to take her for lunch and existentialise?' Suiting my action to my words, I stood.

'Thanks for your advice, man.' Having finished with his teeth, Ian leaned back in his chair to let me through to the door. 'You're like the Coalition.'

'What?' I was past him now, out in the hall.

'You're like the British-American Coalition.'

'How?' I slowed to take an insult but I did not turn.

'You get off on telling other nations how cruel they are. You've got no idea what it's like inside them.'

'Well you bloody well asked me down.' I was now at the door.

'It was a mistake. I'll see to this on my own.'

Having made my exit, I hung around on the street for five minutes smoking a cigarette in a strange state of triumph. That little tear-up had been well out of character. I was surprised at myself. A fresh wet wind was blowing. One thing was already certain. I wasn't going home yet. I seemed to have a part to play in this.

The wind gusted, scattering a couple of drops in my face from a drainpipe or window frame. The street door opening, Ian appeared in a pale blue anorak; we were going along for a pint after all.

Ian's local was buzzing in what you might call a recommended manner, like a collaborative project of business-friendly government and researchers at the BBC. This wasn't to say the place was a mere simulation. The problem went a little deeper.

'I'm in for the bypass next week,' Mary told us as if we'd just appeared the other side of the garden fence. 'It'll be nae more of these.' She fingered the leather pouch that hung on a gold chain around her neck, where she kept twenty Regal. 'What're you having, boys?' I ordered a couple of pints of Stella, then we set out to find ourselves a table.

What I disliked about The Green Man – *one* of the things I disliked about it – was the apparent lack of proper corners. Somehow everywhere seemed to be in the middle. Where in God's name was the perimeter? You kept overhearing other people and their neurotic hedonistic conversations. Much of the time they were on their cellphones, telling their friends how to get there, telling their friends about the night before. As often as not, their friends had been with them the night before, but they wanted to be reminded of their own behaviour; certain tones of disapproval were prized. What had happened to privacy? It was even worse than listening to myself. Two or three tall tables with small circular tops had been installed recently to maximise throughput: no way could you slump at one of them with your beer for the best part of an afternoon. You'd fall off the tall stool like a coconut, and break your bastard neck.

On the wall to the left of the L-shaped bar, a new blackboard encouraged everyone to try a sausage. The baroque calligraphy couldn't be Mary's work, or Rab's; no doubt it had been pre-inscribed at pleasure HQ and sent with an operation manual. A trio of voluptuous specimens was represented in brown chalk, white steam rising; and here was a novel invitation: Ask for your *favourite*. Ready for you, 30 minutes max. Any flavour. Any flavour in the world. *Try us!* Strange how they insisted. Did they really give a damn? Strange... Very well. I want an owl sausage. No. Changed my mind. I want a snake sausage marinaded in Drambuie, and I want it fast... Who the hell went to the pub for a sausage? Yet the problem with this place was it was real.

Yonder the Remand Hero slammed the golf game, recoiled and pitched forward. Of anyone here, he seems to be furthest from the middle, the fish-eyed fraud. His crew recoiled and pitched with him, and Ian was doing something to his cuff and saying, 'She's gone, Mark.'

'In what sense?' When am I going to see her again?... Am I never going to see her again? For God's sake why does he not answer? 'I take it you mean Laura's left you?' Nine years they've been together. Still he hasn't married her. Why does he hold out on every damn thing? Why didn't he give her a kid? I'd have looked after it if they wanted a night out. I'd have read it poems and brought it Ribena. I'd have told it about pirates and constellations. They'd have trusted me.

And now she's gone, and we two are left like men of stone.

Oh, Laura! That was a tough school you worked in. Did you ever complain? Never. Laura, you were a diamond. A tough school and you always talked it up, God and Allah bless you. You told me humorous things about Amy and Zainab, Ilnaz and King, Brent, Vitas, Panayiota; you told me humorous things, but you never mocked them. You said the French you taught them was good for them because it gave them half an hour off talking patois. English was a challenge – but there were some poems they liked: you must have had skill to get them liking poems. How on earth did you do that? Did you give them simple ones? You'd have known how to do it, known how to be nearly as simple as your kids. Should have asked you which ones you gave them... '*I must go down to the sea again, the lonely sea and the sky*'... but I was ashamed... '*Do not go gentle into that good night, my father*'... I can't handle simplicity.

You said they enjoyed talking about films. Enjoyed talking about violence too, the girls as well. When you were teaching them *Macbeth* for their GCSE, they really got their heads down. How did that make the syllabus in the first place? He slits the rebel Macdonald open from his navel to his jaw, does Macbeth – and that's before he's gone to the bad. I don't think the examining boards really see what's going on in these plays. But the kids do; they asked you what the lines meant; they were as zealous to know as kids used to be about sex. Yet when you explained, they were quiet.

Ian told me your pupils sat in race lines and spat after

you passed their desks. He told me this in sympathy, outraged sympathy. But as the philosopher says, 'There are no moral phenomena at all, only a moral interpretation of phenomena.' This was his moral interpretation of what went down in your school; it wasn't yours, and you weren't deluded. The truth is what we make it... *'If you can bear to hear the truth you've spoken/ Twisted by knaves to make a trap for you'*... Maybe you gave them that. I don't have as much trouble with Rudyard Kipling as a lot of people. I'm not under the same obligation.

You got a sound degree at university. Never insisted that you almost took a first, like all the others who almost did. English and French – not a deep degree, but a wide one. You joined some clubs, you probably did one or two things for charity without being a fanatic about it, always gave your work in on time and you never needed counselling, never vomited over yourself at happy hour. You didn't try to be funny but you loved to laugh. You would not have been self-absorbed, unlike this egoistic bastard.

When you graduated, you went to work in France for a while, teaching English near Bordeaux. You had a lovely accent for French as you told me the place names, unself-conscious: *Quimper, Le Bouscat, Mirambeau*... You were like a singer with those names, smiling when you voiced them. (I'm sure this would have been how you smiled when you were teaching.) Then you moved down to Eastern Spain. I asked you why you'd left France. You couldn't really say. One day you just went. Maybe you'd been thinking there might be more kicks in Spain. In France, all you had was food and culture. You'd have been about twenty-two at the time. I still seem to want kicks. With you, it would have been a healthy phase.

I reckon you had a quiet, civilised upbringing; reasonable parents, strong conscience – no, a sound conscience. Maybe you'd done two or three naughty things in all the time before you left home; but I never heard you brag of your sins – unlike a lot of people I've come across... Christ, everyone's so bloody transgressive nowadays, the jails'll soon be full of Mormons in raincoats, girls in hijabs and the WI. The dominion of the naughty is upon us, the time of the hedonists is here. They'll bang up all the squares. Come to think of it, even the WI have been edging their way into *Fifty and Over* territory for a while now... But I don't think you really left one day in search of kicks. That wasn't the reason.

For down to the Costa Blanca you went with a guy called Norbert, a Spaniard you met up the coast from Bordeaux, near La Rochelle. God how I love that name. *Norbert.* Sounded like an anagram, or an error; with repetition it becomes preposterous.

Norbert. You trilled the *r* sounds, to show me how they said it where Norbert came from. Out of delicacy, I was careful not to laugh, thinking you'd been an item, Laura and Norbert. I asked you solemnly if he was from a good family, of diplomats or something of that order, fancying that 'Norbert' must be a grandee name from the nineteenth century. (I've got a complex of preconceptions about Spanish stateliness, narrowly confirmed on a conference visit to Madrid when I noticed that grown men wore long trousers and walked slowly in the shade – and no one of any age had a baseball cap either.) You

31

laughed at this. Your laughter made me feel old; or young – the wrong side of experience either way. Then you said, '*Eramos amigos nada más.*' I asked you what this meant, sucking my teeth slightly. It meant, 'We were only friends.' You knew Spanish too. Laura, you had many tongues.

Norbert got you a translating job at Jensen Wesley, a mighty inkjet and high-tech corporation. You must have had to say *Eramos amigos*, etc, quite a lot to Señor Norbert, that's what I was thinking to myself – and in the present tense too. Most guys when they sort you a job in a foreign land, it's a bar job if you're lucky; and a career in dick-sucking if you aren't. Must have been very solid – I was going to say 'connected' – Norbert, to get you a job with a big company like JW. Solid, though unlikely to have been a source of kicks I should have thought. But I reckon you weren't that much of a hedonist anyway, Laura, God bless you. Yet I could never work out why you just got up and went with him if it wasn't for pleasure, and wasn't for love. Maybe you were just very good at waiting, biding your time in the sun. That's something these days, it really is, amid the clamour for immediate satisfaction, the bawling for service and all the screams from the joy-wheel of desire. Almost takes genius, to sit and wait till what you want turns up.

Some of this you told me the first time I met you both; weeks later on a pavement in Camden, you elaborated.

***

I thought all that about her in less time than it takes the morn to slip o'er the meridian, or for summer to end at the latitude of Archangel. We'd hardly said a thing, Ian and I: he'd been fiddling with his phone. But I can do the same in busy conversation, scroll the memory down, and down and down.

Wish to God I'd told her about Goethe's 7th Roman Elegy, a song of the north v south. At the start, the poet is an egoistic bastard, caught up in himself like a man considering his reflection in a canal, catching sight of the shit and iron on the bottom. Then he travels south to the sun and cuts out the self-reflection. Knowing her made it mean something to me. If I saw her again, I would tell her.

Ian rose to visit the bar.

★★★

He made a trip out there himself at the time when going to Barcelona was still such a European novelty that the supplements of the swelling British newspaper of the early Nineties hadn't quite attained that sussed, slightly-naughtier-than-thou tone they settled into once the Oxbridge grads got their hands on the arts, lifestyle, food and travel pages. *What you must do when you arrive*. Well now, Minty advises you to stand on Avenida Xavier to watch the transsexual whores; and Heidi says you must try the pigs' balls – they come in a sort of savoury custard. The papers were still leaving you to your own devices when Ian made his trip. It was that long ago.

They were there for the stag celebrations of a young squire named Leo. Having arrived on Friday evening, by Sunday afternoon they had with them the spirit that takes young blokes after forty hours on the sherbet and pills in unaccustomed heat, with pussy on the brain. Sitting in a plaza in the Gothic sector, they were drinking beer and slammers, bothering girls with impunity. Then it came about that Ian was staring at one girl alone, so he found, *una chica*, over there. Her partner was a Spaniard, shortish in stature, dark, capable, dark hair neatly cut, in a shirt of small checks. (Sounds a bit like me, I was inclined to think when I first heard this, aside from the shirt; and depending what you mean by 'shortish' too for that matter. I am five nine. Used to be taller, but I've burned some of it off in the – ha! – furnace of experience.) He wasn't going to stand in Ian's way, if you were looking at the world with Ian's peculiar knack of looking, boosted as it was with the heat and the steady intoxication; no way was he going to. For Señor Check Shirt couldn't see what was doable in the situation. Ian could. The sky hazed over. The other squires were chortling and cracking in the tinny heat about something Leo had done with a dark Valencian in a narrow bed like a kiln ledge between 5am and sunrise. What Ian could see was that he could run rings around Señor CS in this situation. In fact he knew, with the way of knowing he has, that he could work magic. *La chica* was a curly blonde. He took it she was Spanish too: he'd seen others like her in the city. The dark Valencian had been Lita, he kept hearing the name. She would never appear again. Yet he could produce consequences round Señor and the curly blonde, could drop a stone and make ripples. Wouldn't be too much to say, he felt confident he could produce future.

He got up and made a pass of the table the girl and her partner were sitting at. She took notice of him in the way

34

someone waiting on a railway platform for a stopping train might when the second or third express roars past on the down line. Señor's eyes were on nothing. Her mouth was the thing about her, the fullness of it in her blonde face.

Ian crossed the plaza. On the other side of the road was a bookshop that seemed to be particularly busy, which he entered. Inside was a bustle of young people looking ardent, and rather mysterious, as if they were in on something. He felt them watching him, this foreign mage.

He knew what he was doing. As sure as Napoleon, the illumination was on him. From the shelf he picked a yellow book, which was an edition of Shakespeare's Sonnets. The poems had been translated, the English versions faced them. He bought the book and returned to the plaza.

The haze had gone and the sun was bright again. Its heat criss-crossed and crowded the air, like a magically erected maze of thick hedges. Marvellously, he could get through it; to him it yielded.

He says he had no sense of sound, only heat, as he found his way to that table and put the book in front of the girl. Señor recoiled in his chair as if the table were steadily accelerating. She said, 'Don't please, Norbert!' She didn't want trouble. But how much trouble was a fellow called *Norbert* likely to produce anyway? Here Ian realised she was English. Laughing he presented her with the book.

'I've got you this!' he told her.

Norbert took the opportunity to calm down and said, 'Do you know this guy from the UK?'

The girl was now taking notice of Ian the way someone waiting on a railway platform for a stopping train might the first express to roar past on the down line. He wasn't there for her; but at the same time he was, an image on the burning air. She said, '*No lo he visto – nunca antes*' and Norbert waved his hand like a hot man and said, '*Vete*'. Retiring to his table, Ian heard Norbert announce the words 'Fucking bastard' with placid competence. As the squires cheered, Norbert and the curly *chica* rose and walked away. More cheers for Ian. What a glorious defeat! But he'd written his name and number on the inside cover before he left the shop; and she had not left it behind.

★★★

And that was ten years ago. But a long time before, 400 years before, Don Quixote comes to Barcelona, where they make a great fuss of him and lead him a dance, as do certain lords and ladies wherever he goes. Tony Moreno shows him a metal head, cunningly forged, that gives answer to any question. So the Don asks if his beloved lady will ever be disenchanted, return to her proper form and belong to him. In a room beneath the head, Tony Moreno's clever nephew is giving all the answers through an arrangement of pipes. What do you think he says?

And Tony's men stick a label on the Don's back so everyone knows him and cries out his name as he rides about the city. He visits a printing house – this is very choice – where they are printing the book of his life; in this Don Quixote shows little pleasure – indeed, he manifests a kind of scorn. Then armed to the teeth he patrols the beach, to see who he can fight.

This was what I had to swap with my friend Ian when he told me of his visit to Barcelona. Something I had read.

★★★

Ian was turning to me now from a drooping hanger-on. On the table were more pints, and a couple of whiskies for the crisis. Incidentally, the knight Don Quixote fights on the beach in Barcelona is an acquaintance in disguise. 'She left a note,' he murmured.

Well here was something. She could have texted him, but she'd written a note. The hanger-on retired. What had she put on it?

That she'd gone away for a while. To think about things.

A while?... *While*. A word that slides about the spectrum of inexact time, that ancient, ever-new quantity, unknown to the trader in the city, the astronomer, the chief of staff, who can none of them be doing with *a while*: inexact time being human time, for lovers, and fathers, and aunts. So, the lover says, *I'll be back in a while, baby!* and her man says, *Jesus, make it soon!* Or the dad says, *I'll be home in a little while with your comic!* and the kid scratches at the door. Then the aunt says, *Come and sit with Aunty for a while, darling!* and the kid runs behind a tree... On the other hand, time of the inexact kind is for everyone who isn't all that bothered about the one they're addressing. So a colleague on the stairs says, *Haven't seen you for a while!* Or a plumber looks down at the handle that's rotating freely in the cistern and says, *It's gonna take a while to get another one of these*, because he has to order the replacement from Scandinavia believe it or not. And the secretary says, *He'll be back in a while*, the wind rattles in the forecourt, the secretary hasn't even asked your name, and you wish to God you hadn't taken a tip and come all the way down here to see a man who can give you advice.

On that spectrum, where does Laura's 'while' belong?

'What d'you think she means by a *while*?' I asked, as one with a technical interest.

He shook his head slightly like a chess player watching two others at play when they're missing the best moves. He wasn't seeing it as I was. The definition of *while* was probably of secondary importance where he was concerned. The going was the issue. She'd left him, to think about things between them. As I saw it, 'a while' could slide towards a maximum of a few months; or it could be over before the end of the week, if her thoughts were propitious. As the months passed, it might begin to mean 'forever'. Perhaps that's what it was already, a soft way of saying 'forever'.

What was I getting so worked up about? He swilled the middle third of his pint.

He was being a bit vague was he not, in the circumstances?... In truth he was being bloody casual; a blunter man would have told him so.

At the table just behind my shoulder, a girl was saying 'Graham is *so* cool!'

Well he'd taken four or five codeine tabs, he told me casually. No doubt this was why he seemed vague. Taken them when he'd got in from work.

Where had he got them from?

When he had that abscess. Dentist prescribed him a couple of strips. Time we met in Camden, last year, Midsummer. Left half of his face hardly knew the right...

They were 30mg tablets?

Yeah.

That, I opined, was a fair dose of codeine.

Yeah. Got rid of anxiety. Got rid of a lot of stuff.

That was on the way to a cancer dose. Had she said anything else?

She'd taken a week off work. She'd written that as well.

'So she's gone away for a week?'

He nodded, as new staff listening to instructions nod, whether they've taken them in or not. We had a think about this. It would be splitting hairs to separate a week from a while, for the time being. The whisky was Irish. Goes down too easily, Irish, with its catpiss aroma. They weren't doubles. Privately, however, I enquired into the equivalence of 'week' and 'while', which worried me. It suggested manoeuvring within time. With 'while' she might have been staying put somewhere; 'week' seemed to bring in a vertical axis of varying distances from home. I shivered. Jesus. She might be standing at the window laughing at us. I glanced casually over my shoulder. She wasn't at the window.

'What did she put at the bottom?' But what if she had been just before I turned to look, like a man checking whether rain has stopped?

'She put LOVE.' He was sweating, suddenly becoming remote. This had really got him, to come home from work and opiate himself. He'd be nauseous from the codeine. 'And her name.' Would have been the codeine affecting him when I arrived, moving round as if he scarcely knew himself. I wanted to ask him why he'd been waiting, why he'd insisted on it, if he knew she'd gone. But he'd have had his reasons. And the question would have sounded too hard-headed, too rational in the circumstances; though the truth is, I've always found it difficult to confront him.

I asked him where he thought she'd gone. To myself, I pictured her in France again, or in Barcelona, in the autumn sun. Then I asked him where her mother lived.

Her mother lived in Hove. As I knew already.

Did he think she was there?... He did have quite a constitution for a slim man, to sit and drink on top of that dose. Stronger than mine, as I've sometimes had cause to notice. To be honest, I've got the constitution of a woman – a pretty hard-living woman, but a woman nevertheless.

He didn't know. He couldn't ring anyway, could he?

In case she wasn't? Yeah. I did see what he meant... Privately I wondered how she could take a week off work. It was term time, late September. Could teachers just do that?... Obviously, I said to help him, he couldn't ring the school either, could he?

What should he ring the school for?

To find out where she'd gone, I equivocated swiftly.

He'd appeared to be recovering, but now shook his head nauseously: if he let the school know he didn't know where she was, it would be bad for her reputation.

I hummed and nodded. I felt I was learning the rules of the game. Not that this was any mere game – far from it. Only that every department of life is something like a game, and at the same time of course a bloody serious business.

He wouldn't want to be ringing her friends either?

40

No. He wouldn't want to be ringing them.

I could understand this... I was mastering the rule that a 'hands-off' attitude was required here, as indeed it was in the game of letting her go home before him when I'd taken them out to drink champagne. It was all about not-interfering-in-the-wrong-way.

'Thanks, man.' He watched me with the false concentration of the nauseous: 'Basically, I have to wait for her to ring me.'

'That's right.' I patted his hand. 'You've got to wait for her to get in touch.' I was about to say, 'Or come back.' Tact prevailed. Of course, he would be expecting her back; it had given him a jolt though, as it was no doubt intended to. And cunning of her to leave no clue where she had gone. A man of initiative might have made a trip up to Edmonton tomorrow late afternoon to hang around outside her school. Perhaps she would leave as normal (though did teachers leave in the throng of kids, or later, by a staff entrance? I had no certain knowledge of this). He would then make one or two deductions. Perhaps he'd follow her. Might even go right up and say hello! That man would be interfering in the wrong way. Besides, hanging round outside schools can give the wrong impression.

'Graham is the *lick!*' declared the girl behind me. A man yelped in approbation.

I went up to get more drinks. Stepping to my side, the Remand Hero acknowledged it was my turn; Rab served him first anyway. I was relieved to see Ian was feeling it, for I've wondered often how much he feels. The attraction, the interest, of the man is – well, it does seem to have had, always, something to do with what he doesn't show, with his reserve, his holding back, and I've been ravished by this, I suspect, though I know it's maybe only a fine thing, as opposed to a good one.

It must be this that's the attraction, since it's a quality I'm sure I lack; unless it's a case of our seeking out our own kind in our friends, as the wisdom of the world has it... But is my friend my own kind? How long would it take to recognise him as such? Would I know from the beginning, or not until the final moments? Surely, the essence of friendship is the leading of the ego to the mirror. If it won't be led, then it must be dragged. How like me is my friend? How like my friend is the dog-ear, the dirty page called 'I'? So we like such and such, hold such and such in contempt, seldom talk of music, and so forth. Does this truly bind us?... Or do we seek our opposite? 'Opposites attract.' That too is the wisdom of the world. This world is crammed with wisdom, is it not? Like a punnet of bleeding berries.

Either way it's his reserve that interests me, and also his timing, another quality I lack. When to do, this too he knows instinctively. Think of Barcelona. Combine the timing and the holding back and it's as if – as if what? As if everyone were about to start dancing or playing instruments, just as soon as he gave the signal?

Ah I dunno; but what I do know is where the verb 'to interest' comes from: it's formed from the Latin verb 'to be' and the word for 'between'. So, my friend is, or he exists, between me and... forget it.

'Couple of Stellas, Mary, please, and two Jamesons – large ones.' And a plutonium and Wensleydale sausage.

Maybe I'm just attracted because of what he tells me about Laura.

***

He came back from Barcelona. Nothing changed. Since he'd left university, he'd worked in a call centre, he'd done phone surveys for a social research organisation, he'd worked for an antiques dealer, mainly taking things out of boxes and putting them back again, he'd worked in another call centre; these days he was loading boxes for printers on a truck in Archway. Thus, he'd spent several years either on the phone or fucking about with boxes; but he was surplus graduate number five-five-five treble zero in late twentieth-century Britain, so he had to bite the bullet and take what came. Then again, he didn't have standard ambitions: promotion, property, kids, chino trousers in two to three different shades and a good strong brown leather belt. It might have looked like he didn't have ambitions full stop. But I fancy he would have told himself that he was out of the ordinary, and would one day shape things his way; or would have told himself, if he weren't so reserved, that he'd have fought shy of such a vulgar formulation even in the silence of his own being. Maybe 25% of the useless (I mean 'surplus') graduates decided they were going to write a novel and told their pals about it. Ian would rather have gone to hell, or sat himself down on his own in one of those valleys of Antarctica where it never snows but it's still about -30°C even in summer, and the air is so dry that the bodies of a snow tiger or fox will lie perfectly preserved for thousands of years — he'd rather have done that, than say to anyone he was writing a novel. He'd have had much subtler ambitions than novel writing.

Time passed, he kept quiet: he'd have made no fuss — I know this. He was just a surplus graduate. He had nothing coming. He lived with it. Until, months later, he had a call from a conscientious German named Manuela.

Manuela was a newish tenant in a flat he'd been living in down in Lewisham when he visited Barcelona. By now, he was somewhere like Dalston or Hackney, moving anti-clockwise round the city; but he'd left his number on a folded sheet of narrow-lined A4, and when a girl rang late January asking for Ian, Manuela remembered seeing the paper in a cupboard where mice played, beneath a box of Rentokil pellets, and obliged the girl who'd rung to ask.

Manuela described the piece of paper to Ian (evidently she was also something of an antiquarian): in addition to his number it had blood stains on it, and a shopping list, as well the rings of a coffee mug, unless it was chilli sauce and not blood at all, and the bottom was burnt (from a hot knifing session, fellow antiquarians may deduce). Ian must be more careful in future when girls were trying to phone him — did Ian agree?

Ian said he did. He'd never met Manuela, who was now wondering if Ian ever revisited his old flat. Ian was afraid he did not. Maybe he would have changed this whole story if he had, and had found Manuela on her own on a cold afternoon. But we shall never know what she looked like (and I can't quite imagine a seductive German either, for want of experience probably). The conversation carried on for a while. Towards the end, Ian asked the name of the girl who'd called, but Manuela laughed and said she'd forgotten. Still, this wasn't unsatisfactory to the mage of the burning plaza. Ripples can take a while.

So on a Saturday afternoon in February, Ian was sitting on his settee in Stoke Newington (*that's* where it was) at the age of twenty-seven. Over the last fortnight or so, he'd taken to staying put more than he was used to. What you have to realise is these were the days when scarcely a manjack had a mobile phone. Not easy to form an historical picture of those last years of human silence, but there you are. At the moment, for example, his chums were out enjoying a walk in the fog; presently, they'd be back with a barrel of beer (or some cans, anyway); but Ian had hung around in the house. Earlier, he'd been upstairs at his table thinking of writing in his buff notebook with squared paper.

This notebook, he once told me with a smile that was not warm but considerate, when I caught him drawing a diagram of some sort in it, was where he planned the future. When I asked, 'In what way?', he emitted a crackle of laughter and said it was just telephone numbers, names of bars that were open late, drafts of letters of complaint to Great Western Railways that he never sent anyway and words and phrases from foreign languages that he'd not got round to learning. Then there were notes on people he'd met – I had to press him on this – or overheard, which he had half an idea of turning into character sketches, along with bits of poems and lyrics from folk songs and ballads. Sometimes he used it as a diary or daybook, but never kept this up for long. He wasn't interested enough in himself; and he didn't want to be pushed round by a notebook either. It was quite a miscellany that notebook. I've sometimes wondered whether he writes anything about me, for he has more than one of them. I'd hate to find that he did... Or that he did not.

Anyway he was considering composing a sort of prose poem on the three days in Barcelona, but the time seemed not quite right, so he shut the buff notebook with an elastic band and was coming back downstairs when the front door opened then closed with a heavy click against the fog and the phone in the hall began to ring. One of the returning flatmates handed it to Ian with a smile and cold hand, and said it was Laura asking for him.

★★★

'She'll not necessarily ring you anyway': I set the drinks down. This was another 'hands-off' proposition. Over at the game machine, the Ryder Cup team smacked their main man on the shoulder.

Ian nodded and said yeah. He couldn't be proactive, if I followed him. This was the main thing. Couldn't go tracking her down.

Yeah. I saw what he meant. It was entirely probable she'd just come back within the week anyway – without getting in touch. Was this what he'd be wanting to hear? He nodded in consideration and I was warmed by a ray of sun, as if on a day of ambiguous weather. For a moment or two, we were Holmes and Watson sitting by the fire at the beginning of the story, conversation minimal, each of us with his own thoughts, autumn rain in odd gusts rattling on the window. We were very cosy, or *gemütlich* as the good old Germans called it (= 'cosy with a pint of ale in your hand'). Very *gemütlich*. Then the sun went in: 'D'you think she's safe?' I exclaimed.

'She's gone of her own accord hasn't she?' he replied a bit huffy (or *übelnehmerisch* as the g.o. Germans call it).

All right, he was worried; but he was pissed off too. It made him look a sap. For it was possible – I couldn't imagine it, but it must be possible – that she had taken a week off with a fellow with plenty of money, plenty of sun-filled property, several vehicles for sea and land (and air), and a nice big towelling robe in which to eat his breakfast of fresh figs, one for her too, just her size, a fellow who wouldn't dream of using the word 'shrivelled'. Would that be her sort?... No! Not Laura. Not my Laura. You can't turn Laura's head with wealth, and figs and helicopters. She's far too – she's noble. She has class.

She's a woman though isn't she? Who the hell knows what they'll go for when they hear the words 'already shrivelled' and they but thirty-three? Maybe a colleague from the school with a big dick, an appetite for life and the will to make her feel beautiful. They've run off to a cottage on the coast to screw each other daft over the sound of the gulls. What about us? She'll have forgotten us already, golden legs round him and the gulls screaming. Unless she's weeping for us with a sort of joyful anguish... *Joyful anguish*? Forget it, boyo. What do you know about women? *Nothing*.

Had she left before him this morning?

No. He'd gone first. Always did on Monday.

What had she been like?

Same as usual. They never talked much in the morning anyway.

So she wrote the note when he'd left, then went herself. Which way did she go? North towards Great Portland Street tube, or south to Oxford Circus? Maybe a taxi picked her up. Or a car. Obviously, the manner in which she left counted for everything. What did she pack? What would she have taken with her? How could I ask him? *What knickers did she take, pal?* The answer to this would be the clincher, mystery's end, revealing whether she'd been excited or unhappy… Provided she had taken something.

We had a couple more Stellas and whiskies and it was throwing-out time.

'Will you kindly fuck off, ladies and gentlemen,' begged Rab, looking at us as he cleared glasses. Behind the bar, Mary lit a Regal from her leather case, which resembled a mediaeval Catholic's phylactery, calling, 'Ta ta, boys!'

What was Ian going to do then? Outside The Green Man he looked at me steadily, in the way he has. Was he going to keep working, and so forth? I was hoping he would ask me in for a while, at this time of crisis.

Yeah. He'd act as normal. What was I doing now?

I examined my watch. I was going to fuck off.

I could come in for a bit if I wanted.

At the night, the weather, the time, I screwed my face like an old trawlerman: I really ought to sling my hook.

Well thanks for coming down.

He was to keep me informed, all right? I touched his hand. This was all I wanted. I'd been asked, I had not been pressed.

On the tube back north, I wondered if there'd be a message for him on his landline. There was my face in the black window opposite, whittled from an unskinned onion... Now then, onion face! What the fuck have you been up to? On the piss again?

As long as she wasn't in danger, we shouldn't worry; we had no need to worry – as long as she wasn't in danger... Bollocks to that. At least if she were in danger, she'd be glad to come back. It was if she was enjoying herself, was the main worry... Admittedly (as rogues with no affection for words say) – 'admittedly', love was behind both kinds of worry – granted. But it wasn't the same kind of love. If she were in danger I loved her, with the love of the shepherd for his flock. But if she was getting humped, verily, I loved myself, with the love of the miser for his gold pile, or even as the old fool of Italian comedies who locks his young wife away. And then we had to ask, Who do you love more, her or yourself? What would you rather? Would you rather her in danger, or lying in the bower of bliss? The second preference was selfless, the first selfish clearly. That was clear enough, was it not?... Though on the other hand, we didn't worry about everyone in danger did we? Didn't lose sleep over every disappearance. We only really feared danger when we loved them as our own. Even hostages – even they had to be *our* hostages before we got worked up. Not so selfless after all... But why should she be in danger? She'd left a note. Why should she be in danger, *or* enjoying herself?... Beware of dichotomies!

Outside my station I had a slash in a quiet corner, then walked the mile home. En route, I bought a piece of haddock; the batter was shell hard but the fish was moist. I crammed it in my mouth watchfully, like an infantryman living off the land. Good! Down in three! *Sehr gut.* I make the minimum fuss about food nowadays. Would he have been able to tell which knickers she took? I certainly would if I was him.

I had a whisky when I got in, down on the settee. The TV was showing highlights of the Party Conference, the Chancellor making his speech, the Prime Minister smiling. Lowering the sound, I put on Stockhausen's *Helikopter-Streichquartett.* Turbines began to roar as the faithful stood and clapped. Listen to me for a bit longer, if you fancy, while the rotors fill the air.

★★★

So she rang him that foggy Saturday afternoon nine and a half years ago and she told him who she was. She reminded him he was drunk when they first met. From what he told me, she was dead sweet on this particular point. He wasn't to worry if he'd changed his mind since then. Or if he couldn't really remember her. Just put it down to the booze, and the sun and foreign air. But this just had the effect of getting him going; and her voice had a spoonful of honey in it.

The truth was, he was astonished at how the call was affecting him. He thought he'd been the one to set this in motion, the one producing the ripples, so why should this be? After all, he'd backed himself that hot afternoon, had he not? What manner of magician is it who has trouble talking to the spirit he's called up from the south? What calibre of conjuror finds he can only say 'Yeah', with different intonations, and, a little squeakily, 'Where are you?'

Well, said the spirit, she was here! When he asked her where 'here' was — he was trying to get a handhold — she told him here was Brighton. He took a train to Brighton there and then. Perhaps it was his power itself that was astonishing him, his power over consequences. Perhaps... There was another thing: toward the end of the phone conversation, she said something about 'San Geordie', as if she expected him to know what she was on about. It was dark by the time he arrived.

She met him at the station in a waist-length parka, silvery brown, gold hair filling the hood. She looked sort of cosy and wide awake. Her mouth made him almost tremble. It is the one potentially obscene thing about her. Would he like to walk by the sea? They walked by the black, phosphorescent channel for half an hour or so and he told her what had taken him to Barcelona. She was interested in his squires, she'd noticed them, and remembered. And what was the wedding like? Had Ian enjoyed himself? She knew what to ask.

He wasn't sure when he should first touch her. Her coat was somehow chaperoning her (he himself was wearing a thinnish anorak, in which he could manoeuvre yarely, given the sign). Of course, he in his turn asked her what she was doing in Barcelona. He desisted from asking what had brought her back to England.

In the pub to which she took him, she produced from her handbag the yellow book like a belated identification sign. She asked him which one of the poems he liked best — or if he had a favourite. Ian said that he'd never read Shakespeare's Sonnets. He had read quite a few novels, but next to no poetry. Why did he think that was? Ian said it was because he was a bloke. She laughed at that, then she showed him her favourite sonnet. While he was reading, he noticed her trying to examine his face.

When he told me about this, I wondered if they knew that most of the sonnets are written man to man. They probably didn't – and what does it matter? The great works don't mean anything except what the amorous present wants them to mean; and what does anything I know have to do with the amorous present?

I will say this though, I'll say this to all of you – I'll have a last dram and I'll tell you... he should have had a close fucking look at No. 94 when he was sitting there with her all cosy and romantic. Cos it's about cool-hearted demons like him is Sonnet 94, and fucking suckers like me. Right?... Ah forget it. Didn't mean that.

Anyhow, she'd taken the parka off and was sitting beside him on a high stool beside a shelf for drinks; on the wall were framed newspaper front pages from World War II and big days in twentieth-century history. He hadn't touched her yet, but her arm was slightly resting against his. She was wearing a cream, cashmere cardigan her mum had bought her and smoking one of his cigarettes (a habit he's managed to give up); and now she started – the book was resting in her lap: she didn't want to put it away – she started talking about 'San Geordie' again. Ian asked her what she meant by this. Was it something to do with Paul Gascoigne? (He must have been worrying she was one of these modern girls who go on about football.)

She picked up the book with a brave smile. Had he not known what he was doing when he gave it to her?

Tuesday

Waking from a dream where helicopters pluttered, what was I? A gullet, an overlay of fish notes, a tiny effluvium of burning malt. Waking this was my essence, and well if it had stayed so. But we who live in time are more than gullets; soused haddock was but a passing flavour of the self; the white day was rising.

Like a god of plagues it brought fear and shame: they multiplied and ringed the bed. What was I doing to my glorious future? I'd have wept, but my eyes were quicklime; and this morning infestation was too routine for tears. What in hell was the time? For spasms of inner motion, I could barely move my head. The clock offered the time in red; but I was crawling up my own inside, a slimy-walled well. All the others could handle this kind of waking, handle it as melancholy – or comedy. The hellraisers of olden time, Parkinson's guests, Seventies centre-forwards... *Once woke beside a Pan-Am flight crew and a racehorse... He ordered two whores, a crate of pale ale and a bacon sandwich for breakfast.*

Ah, the 'heroism of modern life' was just a phrase where I was, a phrase without substance, an unmanned concept... As couples have a favourite song, so I turned to thinking of violence, of heroes and glorious deaths, saw and quoted bloody pictures, in my private darkness: Caius

Marcius Coriolanus, Pike Bishop and the Bishop Gang…
At last, this raised me.

On the pillow was a rich brown stain: the area and
colour suggested dribbling, or effluvium from a rotten ear.
The cognoscenti of sleeping alone distinguish such a mess
from the extensive, paler maculation, which points to a
heavy dew of sweat from the head as our solitary sleeper
fights with dreams. And so along to the bathroom.

My dick began to hum like the live rail, as the shower
hissed. Hum and shine. *Enormous.* Phenomenon familiar to
drinking lads, early in the morning. If someone'd walked
in now they'd have copped it. Straight up. No fucking
quarter from the live rail, if they'd walked in now. No
quarter… Oh this private pornographic audacity. What if
the spirits of the dead can see it all? Christ, as their treat,
the whole damn shooting-match… In future, I shower
fully dressed.

Now the rinsing of the gob with chlorhexidine,
recommended by my excellent dentist. *This will do yer
gums a power of good, shipmate.* Listen to me. Take advice
from a sucker. £43 for the polish, £3.75 for the bottle of
rinse. Stained the little bastards bright brown, I swear to
you. White as chopped potato then they fizz and brown
like chips. Back to my excellent pirate, and 43 is 86. Total
£90 for vanity, and has it been worth a penny? Has it fuck!

I could swear I felt different today though. What was this?
Another saving-betraying illusion? I couldn't wait to have
a cigarette and lit one on the way downstairs, nearly
setting fire to the lace curtain which blew in on a draft
from the landing window. The flame on the lighter was

two inches plus, from when I'd lit up in the rain last night. This place used to be a pensioners' house; I sit on the flower-patterned settee at night and watch TV like a widow; as the old fellow did before me till he went into a home. Probably I drink more nips than him however. His son and daughter were glad to let it to me. I pay top dollar and never ever mention refurbishment. Everyone else in my profession's bought somewhere, long since; but I fear it would be tempting fate – as if I expected things to last. This is my home. I live alone, but I imagine listeners. Because without someone to talk to, you go fair mad.

I took the Northern Line down to King's Cross, then changed. Grubby mice frisked on the rails, vanishing into holes as the loaf-shaped carriage of an incoming tube filled the black tunnel and slid alongside. Pardon me, boy! Is this the Chattanooga Choo-Choo? *Nein! Das is der Zug nach Byelorusse, Herr Miller!* Do the gods watch us as we watch the mice? Do they watch us as they looked down on Troy? What you have to realise is that for the gods Troy was virtually TV, an accompaniment to the evening meal. I see Zeus at table, ram flesh and baby goat on silver salver, Hera on the sofa, one breast bared, eyes bright; down below noble Hector and Diomedes, formations surging like fields of corn, bones cracking, helmets splitting, helmets filling with brains. Beginning of violent entertainment? *The Iliad.* Discuss the concept *entertainment.*

Ah, remind me now of a film where an *Einsatzkommando* are shooting at night in fear of White-Russian partisans, red tracer crossing a sloping field and hedges. All they kill is a cow. What's it called? An ambition of mine, to fire a big gun. Dear Jim, can you fix it for me to fire a .20 calibre cannon, preferably at Nazis in a lane? Then for me to die fighting, grey bodies piled like mice around me? Cheers, Jim.

But my profession is the curing one. Russell Square. Here I am.

★★★

What Ian had in fact done was he'd gone and given Laura a book on the Catalans' equivalent of St George's Day – *San Jordi*, they call it. And if you do this, it's a love token. This was what she explained to him that night in Brighton. They're a literate bunch, the Catalans, by the sound of it. Certainly wouldn't do that in this country, would you – buy a woman a book? Get out of it! You'd be blown out for that in England, buying a woman a book to get to know her... Picture it. *War and Peace*, sumptuous box set. 'Oh... you don't *like* war, darling? Or peace? You only like dancing?' Humiliation. It'd suit me over there, I can tell you. I'd be doing a lot better than I currently am; better than I am, and better than I have done as well. But would I be doing better than I will do? Ah, now there's a question; one for the god of split tenses.

It was an utter coincidence. That was all... No! Because as I reminded him when he told me this episode, he'd known what he was doing when he crossed the plaza in the haze, selected the book and found his way back through the thick heat. He'd known what he was doing without thinking about it, he'd known without knowing. He denied that there was any skill in it – indeed it passed his mind that he may have made a mistake; a mistake that merely looked good. Rubbish, I said: this was supreme intuition, his timing was supreme – like Napoleon mounted in the sun at Austerlitz, watching from on high the Russians defile from their key position down into the fog-filled valley: this was *his* moment. He was magical all right.

I can see him beside her in her soft cream cardigan, tight and subtle, her cheeks very slightly flushed from the cold air and her G&T. On the wall just where they were sitting was an old *Daily Mail* front page about the Normandy landings with beach diagrams, and one with Princess Margaret looking brave and sad. He still couldn't get his mind round it. Not with her sitting there beside him, all creamy, soft and gold with that slight flush in her face. It was wonderful; what more could a young man want?

Anyhow, he stayed down there till Sunday evening; and so it started. Laura was renting a flat just along from her mother in Hove. Her father'd died of a heart attack late the previous summer, so she was doing her best for the family. There was no cardiac history with her dad; he bought it after he and the mum had been shopping in Waitrose on a Saturday morning. A good way to go for the one who is going, less so for the relatives. Laura was shattered, gutted, though this was all she ever told me, until a conversation we were having once about my own experiences with the relatives of the dead.

Ian must have been close by; her eyes upon me, virtually the grey of old denim, she said she felt as if her dad had been assassinated, or that something really evil had been abroad in Hove that September morning. This was an unusual description of response to bereavement.

I'd never heard it put quite like that. She mentioned that a particular aunt had been a great support in the months after the death. Anyhow, when she'd finished grieving, she rang Ian on the number he'd written in the book he gave her; it was the New Year by then.

As for how they first – I can't think of a fitting verb or phrase here; and it's not my business anyway is it? I know everyone else can introduce it: well that may be everyone's problem, all right? Everyone's got this perfect facility when it comes down to being frank, and most of all when it comes down to what I can't find the words for. *It's only nature! Human nature… Raises levels of oxytocin.* Buttery professors with their MRI scanners, buttery bishops, counsellors, Tanyas, they all can say it, and I can't. Who's got the problem? Obviously I *have* got a problem, but I'm not the fucking only one. Anyone who tries to understand human desire by means of a plethysmograph has a problem roughly the size of modernity itself… Not that I haven't imagined it now and then. The abiding image is that one of blonde seals ramping, on sand or ice; and her legs. Makes me strange to myself… I've got a thing about nature.

Next weekend, he went down and stayed Saturday night, as he did the weekend following. They went to a fish and chip restaurant where the places were laid with silver; they went to pubs that hadn't been designed in offices, where the locals talked to you properly; quiet, decadent bars with women in black stockings and upholstery of red velvet. Later they walked hazardously on the wet pebbles by the sea in the early spring night. Particularly hazardous for Laura, who was wearing high heels (this fucking gets me going) but never once slipped on her bum.

Soon, Ian was making the trip on a Friday night. He took his bag into the Inkjet Reconditioning plant where he was loading the boxes (Laura loved to feel his arms when he was on top of her) and at 5pm he was out of there and down the line from Tottenham to Victoria. That matter of his arms – it was because he was a slim guy; she didn't expect to find so much tungsten up his sleeve. Tungsten or wolfram (symbol W). Used in tank production.

She was waiting for him at the station. On the train down, he might have had a couple of pills he'd bought off a lad at work; before they arrived at the pub, he'd give her one. It didn't take a lot to get her wasted (prima facie evidence against the charge she had ever been after kicks). Having got her wasted, he'd feel responsible for her. Around 4am on a March morning, they settled themselves in her pink bed, none too wide, for thirty hours or more. She told him about her father, her mother, her eccentric aunt. She enjoyed talking of her family; to listen to her was somehow good. There'd have been no resentment with her. I watch out for resentment in people. I suppose it's been my greatest philosophical lesson, learning the power of resentment: when it's bright over half the world, the other half is dark with resentment. It's a way of being, the way of resentment. Prima facie evidence of resentment? Spiky, bitter tales of the family and your teller's always got some grudge against another member, some remembered offence. Your teller may be as funny as hell, but the humour's metastatic with rancour. I watch out for resentment. I hope to God I'm free of it, but I wouldn't bet on the chances.

Then she got up and made him some toast. He wanted to take her out again, but she brought him toast. I wonder if they could hear the sea. I've not enjoyed such a scene as that; now look at me.

★★★

Nothing left in life. Boo hoo. But I am not blaming anyone!... Thinking of the old newspaper about Normandy in the pub where Ian and Laura first went reminds me of Spielberg's *Saving Private Ryan*, which reminds me the name of that film is *Come and See* (where the *Einsatzkommando* machinegun the cow). And if asked in public about the difference between *Come and See* and *Saving Private Ryan*, I should answer as follows.

Well, *Come and See* has a horrific view of war and human nature; in fact, its view is that in war, humans lose their nature. Meanwhile, *Saving Private Ryan* is ultra-violent; but it is sentimental. *Come and See* is the Eastern Front, *Private Ryan* is the war in the west. The cultured people who write the *Time Out* film guide think *Come and See*'s the truth, while *Private Ryan* is Hollywood. Which is no doubt very true; but what's untrue about sentiment?

I mean, I've spent a lot of today dealing with the admin for a patients' and families' organisation for the disease I specialise in. Now, this is a terrible degenerative disease, which runs in families; a combination of progressive movement disorders – you know, you can't hold a fork, can't open the door, can't walk down the path to the bus

60

stop since your legs are like galvanised rubber – a combination of all that and black depression. Sooner or later, you can't do a thing for yourself. A trip to the crapper's like a royal walkabout. Luckily, your memory's gone with dementia by this time, so you have no recall of your humiliations. Seventeen years or so after it kicks off, it kills you. And you're still only forty-four. How's about that, guys and gals? As diseases go, it's total, like war on the Eastern Front was total; but the care the families show for each individual sufferer – well, are we going to say that there isn't some kind of beautiful sentiment in that? The truth of the disease, the facts of it, aren't the only thing that counts. What about the mothers of the sufferers, who care for them for years without resentment? In this life there's the cruel truth; and there is love. They complement each other, like *Come and See* and *Saving Private Ryan*.

I should be on Radio 3, really, I spend so much time broadcasting like this – though it's on a private channel for the most part. If only there were someone to introduce me, with her legs crossed… Dr Mark C(hopra) MBChB MRCP (BSc Chem, with First Class Hons), trained in the University of Edinburgh, where he was not infrequently totally sauced but managed to win the McEwan Prize for Neurology. Professionally and personally he has no more self-belief than a man carved from an old potato or other menial vegetable, but conceals this with the quality of his suits and occasional verbal flourishes. Lord knows, sometimes he finds it hard to stop; for a passive fellow he does talk rather a lot; but when he's quiet he feels resentful and itchy, like an over-educated servant who's been warned about speaking out of turn and has no proper washing facilities of his own. Besides, talking's hardly an heroic activity, is it? Ha ha! Particularly when it's only to himself. Tonight he will be discussing something he has just thought of. In the second part of the programme, he will recite a poem about sexual disaster in the 'St Swithin's' metre, an old English form widely considered obsolete by specialists...

One more GP letter to dictate, and a couple of phone calls, then I could go home to my books.

Scheiße! Just after half five, I had a call from Ian. Could I come round? He hadn't heard from her. I walked over, past the British Museum, crossing Tottenham Court Road. On Mortimer Street, I said a prayer for her. Time was, I'd have thought praying was pathetic. Nowadays, I pray a lot. Furthermore, I find myself more often than not in a kind of praying mood or frame of mind, as some people are generally full of beans, and others are at ease with things as they are, while others – but there are many many types; and I'm the type that lives in such apprehension that my very breathing is a kind of prayer. Yet today, I have been feeling a little different. Still, I should keep up the prayers for the time being. Aiiiight? Ha ha!

★★★

Sooner or later, Laura was going to want to visit him. This was only fair: he shouldn't be making the journey to her every weekend. She wasn't Cleopatra, was she? And this is how it gets going, is it not? Like a dance – a proper dance, I mean, not the sort you do when you've had a couple of pills. The sort I was made to do as a ten-year-old, with hot-handed girls, under the eyes of a retired tank commander who smelled of warm lavender, our good headmaster Walter Burns. What did I look like then? A leaping, brown-eyed fool. I half enjoyed it, but I was too self-conscious. 'The Dashing White Sergeant', 'Strip the Willow', 'My Lady's Run off with the Blacksmith'. Half enjoyed? I can't have half enjoyed it. If I had, I'd not be remembering it with the sort of shame that makes you shout. Clapped his hands and made us canter, did Walter Burns. Once referred to my father as a 'gentleman', when I was pushing in the dinner queue. 'What is this, Mark! I am surprised to see the son of a gentleman pushing like a thug.' Circa 1972: late autumn. That girl with the hyphenated name, and Joanne Black – when would they have forgotten me? When would they have forgotten the cantering brown-eyed fool? Let them have forgotten me soon, for Christ's sake. My own image of myself is bad enough, without others remembering... Anyway, it's that sort of dance, with reciprocal motions. You both twirl round, then you run down the end and face each other. He visits, she returns the visits.

She'd have wanted to see his mess, and his refinements: his mess was where she could effect some progress, where she could make her presence felt – it'd be evidence he needed a woman like her. His refinements – well, this would be where she'd be trying to discover the traces of other women, wouldn't it? I know this by intuition. I'm not sure about it in much detail, but I know it. I know what they look for.

If she came in my house, she'd be hard put to find any

refinements, I can tell you. Or mess (the pillow excepted). I should do something about this, and will. I'll get a French painting, and some ink-blue cushion covers, and new plates. I'll buy a place that's bright inside and looks modern; or neo-classical, with a rococo fireplace and cornices. But it's another thing I have left too late. She's never been in my house. Not even at the beginning. I should have asked them, but I was ashamed…

Ah how could I have asked them? Not the sort of thing I do at all, *ask* people. I'm not the asking kind. I'll get a painting by Goya. God damn the Impressionists. I'll get a painting by Goya of a grotesque procession. Fuck the visitors.

He had made some preparations for her. Bought her apples for her breakfast, and flowers – he kept moving them back and forth from his room to the kitchen, the flowers; in his bedroom they were somewhat too effeminate, in the kitchen they'd get covered in grease. Christ he must have adored her to remember all this to tell me, mustn't he? And a bottle of cava – he'd put that in the fridge. Furthermore, he'd cleaned the place: I picture him on his knees with a bunched moppet scouring the corners, I see a harvest of beetles and crumbs along the skirting board.

***

I have a Ukrainian in to do my place; they had such a hard century. I don't know what she feels about the past; her English wouldn't be good enough for us to talk about it, even if I had the nerve. 13,000,000 dead between 1931 and

1945. When the Soviets had finished with them, the Nazis moved in. And all people know is that some of them collaborated. *Collaborated*? The Nazis *burned down* 28,000 of their villages, for Christ's sake. Now and then she's still there when I get in, quiet head over the ironing board. Maybe she's just glad to be in Britain in 2004. Maybe she's thinking about Grampa Ivan and the Bug River massacre. How could I begin to ask what she feels? I feel historically inhibited just looking at her. It freezes me. The men who led the men who burned her villages had PhDs in a ratio of 1:3. How can any knowledge now make amends for such educated barbarism? I know other blokes have a Brazilian cleaner with a big arse. A big, happy, lusty-voiced Brazilian, to drink rum and cavort with. Sod the ironing, sod the past. But I have a Ukrainian.

★★★

He met her at Victoria; she had a little case on wheels, blue tartan. He offered to get a taxi back to Stoke Newington. They could drop it off – then go back out. She said it was OK, she'd take it round with her. When he told me of this, I wondered if she might have been hoping to get a taxi to Stoke Newington and not go back out. What would you want to do if you were a woman? Stay in, or go back out?

And what does a case signify, as opposed to a weekend bag? I dunno. I don't believe in semiotics. I don't believe in body language, and I don't believe in semiotics. Nor am I a woman, except in constitutional terms... ha ha! I jest. Pelt me not, good ladies! Pelt not the radio with thy things! I believe in love. I believe in love and I believe in wine; and art. I believe in Goya's procession of loonies dangling sardines. I see the truth in that painting...

Round the West End they went, round and roundabout, Ian and Laura, Ian merrily trailing the tartan case. I see it as a kid with wayward parents who ought to have been home in bed by now. No doubt they had a fine time; but it just went on too long. She was wearing a beret; there was some mishap with it; it fell in a puddle, or somehow it got something unpleasant on it. She'd have kept smiling. Then when they did get home eventually, he played the same record too loud several times. She'd bought him a present. He opened more wine. I think he left the present on the chair. In the end, she went to the bathroom and threw up, Ian having forgotten to take them for anything to eat while they were out. He didn't notice.

He was much better to her the next day though. Apples in bed, and toast and marmalade; then he brought the flowers in and opened his present; it was a shirt. He put it on there and then; he began to do everything properly.

He took her to the National Gallery, where they looked at a painting of a skull, then to a patisserie, where he fed her morsels of millefeuille with a little silver fork. They walked the cake off in Hyde Park at dusk, her leaning against him by the black lake. Then he bought her a scarf, and black stockings with an inset design of flowers, and had them wrapped in silver. All the time he was talking to her sweetly – he heard her tell me all this, and it vexed him, though he said nothing. Next they went for a cocktail, and then for an Italian. In the red darkness of the Montefeltro in Shepherd's Market, he told her he loved her. She hadn't been hungry anyway, this made her angry.

She pushed her plate away. All she'd eaten was the parsley.

I suppose it had been a perfect day till he said that. What did he have to go and say that for? I wonder.

★★★

I pressed the buzzer lightly; with a light click, the green street door gave way to my hand then Ian was at the end of the dark corridor in the doorway to his flat. He muttered something as I approached, lifted a jacket off the hooks behind him, closed and checked his flat door in one movement. No preliminaries this evening. We crossed the road to his local in silence.

'What'll it be, boys?' Mary asked. She couldn't really be bothered to look at us; nonetheless she made the effort.

'Two Stellas please, Mary.' I saw Ian grin in the mirror behind the bar. She comes from East Glasgow. When I was at the Medical School in Edinburgh, I made a trip over there with a drinking pal who knew the area. It was a January night. On the estate where he grew up, ten-year-olds were playing out in T-shirts in the snow, beating sectarian tattoos on the steel shop-shutters. I supposed we were not much more than two such boys to Mary, in for our unvarying tea.

'I don't know what he'll do if anything happens to me.' Tilting the glasses, she nodded at Rab at the bar's end, who was chatting to the hero of the remand wing, arms crossed in his white shirt. 'What'll you do when I'm gone, Rab?'

Like a boulder coming to life, her husband's head rotated our way. 'Aw, I'll manage, hen.'

'I meant when I'm dead, Rab.' She winked at us.

'Mary, I knew what you meant.'

'D'you reckon I will be all right?'

'Give it four weeks and you'll be riding with the Valkyries,' I said. 'Woman of your calibre. You will look ten years younger.'

'Thanks, doll.' She extended her hand across the drip tray as if she were going to pat my head as Ian and I parted in search of a corner with our pints, like children going to bed with a candle.

He'd been to work then? At last we were seated. I meant the question as a way back in to the crisis.

Did I mean today?

Yeah, I meant today.

Yeah. He had.

There was no news then, I took it?

No. He shook his head. No news.

Did he think she had any other reason to have done this – if he looked in his heart?

What did I mean?

I lit a Rothmans and inhaled with vigour.

Now what do I mean by *other reason*? Or what do I mean by his 'heart'? What does *he* mean, asking me for clarification in circumstances like these? My friend here should be ready to answer my question in the form I put it, without watching me from his face of horn and asking what *I* mean. Damn him, he ought to be ready – and willing. It was just the question for the circumstances; I heard it on its way out. But now he puts me in the vanguard of the crisis, like a man who's sprinted to a burning house while his friend strolls down the road behind him; and it's the *friend's* house that's on fire. 'Oh,' says the friend, turning up at last on the lawn, 'I thought I smelled smoke on the way out!' And who knows but that the laid-back fucker didn't start the fire himself? Meanwhile here I am pointing and shouting, with no certain idea what to do next.

Yet this is what I mean about his timing, his way of holding back. He controls the pace, regardless of the circumstances, he decides where we stand.

'I meant reason in addition to what you were saying last night.' I could hear the words in my nostrils' upper reaches. They had that uncool intensity of BBC drama.

What had he been saying last night?

About being shrivelled… I knew he hadn't forgotten; he wanted to hear it from me.

Oh that thing about being shrivelled had just been the tip of the iceberg. He almost grinned, damn him. Did he think it wasn't important? Or was he testing my attitude, sounding out my sincerity?

So it hadn't been the only thing?

No.

What else was there?

He grinned openly now. Last night he was near puking, tonight he's grinning. Was he holding this back last night? Is he holding back the nausea tonight? God damn him, this is his reserve: what he puts up front and what's behind… I dunno – it's like going in a shop where the proprietor's got far more in the back than he ever displays. He rotates certain goods just to satisfy the world he's got a business going; but he doesn't give a stuff whether anyone buys anything or not. He just lounges at the window arms folded, a monster of self-possession.

'There's everything, Mark.' And at the sound of my name, I had to love him again.

'Everything?'

'Yeah.'

'D'you want another of these?'

'Thanks.'

How do you discuss everything? Where do you begin? You have to begin somewhere, but where is the right place to begin? Was telling me about the tears in bed and the ruined lunch the right place? How could it have been, if everything is at stake? Does that mean it was a false start? But you have to begin somewhere. So does that mean it was a reasonable indication of everything that's going wrong between them? Or was it just something he brought out from the back shop to catch my eye and keep me hanging round outside in the dark, the door being locked for business?

I rejoined Ian with the drinks and he began to tell me everything. In a way, it was what I expected to hear. I lack personal experience in this respect, yet what he was saying wasn't unfamiliar to me. In fact, I think it was almost clichéd the way he described their becoming a brother and sister left to their own devices by the departure of the magic that had once attended them like a fantastic uncle. This can happen to anyone; maybe it happens to everyone. I bit my lip. Though I know about it, it's sad when it happens to the friends you love; I'd always hoped they were exempted from the end of magic. I must be no better than a child really. What do I know? What experience do I have? Yet Ian always talks to me as if we're on a level; this is one of his kindnesses: he pretends for my sake. God bless him.

'But Laura,' I said, 'she'll still be looking forward to a long life with you.' I patted his hand. He said nothing; and I knew this couldn't mean to him what it meant to me. He had the experience.

He rose. Whatever it is I love about him is also what I fear.

★★★

He came back from the bar where'd he'd spent a minute or two talking to Mary and Rab's South African helper, Chantal, a brazen creature with blonde ringlets who was going to end up on reality TV if she was careful. Producing a smallish round blue and gold tray, she posed it behind her head like a quattrocento halo, before placing the lagers and whiskies on it, winking for the camera as Ian turned away.

He now told me something that I wasn't expecting. He'd bought large whiskies. I drank mine in two burning slurps for courage, because there was a special fear went with hearing this sort of tale.

Midsummer's Day last year, he is sitting on a bench in Regent's Park reading the paper, having taken a day off work, when he's joined by a couple. The three of them fall into conversation about this and that; they tell him they were on the anti-war march on Valentine's Day, and he says he was too (actually, Laura persuaded him). Next up they announce they are going for a drink on their way home, and invite him to join them. Which he does.

What a life I led. This sort of thing never happened to me, strange couples, conversations, drinks invitations. What a life.

Anyway, they stroll up towards Chalk Farm, the three of them, and they take him to a pub opposite Primrose Hill, where they drink a couple of vodka and tonics. They ask him his favourite film. He says *Where Eagles Dare* actually, which I'd have thought was not the sort of thing to impress new chums with, especially anti-war types from Primrose Hill; but there you are – he'd have been able to say it and get away with it. Just like that. They've never seen it themselves anyway, so Ian explains it to them, the double crossing, and the treble crossing, the cable cars, the castle, the ice. As she lifts her drink, the woman's bracelet clicks. Her shoulders are bare. Believe it or not, she is actually wearing a white bodice like the *Bierkeller* serving maids in the film. Her hair is blonde, she has a rather big nose, dark blue eyes, enhanced breasts. The husband is dark, genial, observant; the shyer of the two.

Drinks and war films... a world close to mine, yet nowhere near. Why couldn't this happen to me? Why couldn't I have any?... Mind you, if they'd asked me, my answer would have been too complicated. I would have had to get the negative in, because I cannot answer simple questions about the things I like. A right-royal fucking palaver I'd have made if they'd asked me my favourite film.

It's the first time he's been in such a situation. It feels a little like sitting with two people at an airport who are asking you to put a bag in at check-in, as a favour to them. He has a sensation of risk; he goes home with them... This was all he had to say.

I'd have been less outraged if he'd said more, if he'd bragged in detail. It was an outrageous haze to me, left like this. As we spoke, I began to imagine the dark husband going down on him while the blonde lady sat on his face still wearing the off-the-shoulder blouse; and on the way home, I saw this distinctly, his fine slim face covered. Yet at first, I did not know where to put myself.

'Does Laura know about this adventure?' I was bulging with hot, negative emotion. Why's he taken so long to tell me? Over a year ago, and I've heard nothing of this. What else is there? What else does he get up to on these sly afternoons in the park? It's sickening. Christ I feel so straight. Where am I when all this is going on? Is the whole world at it? No... I'm in my hospital, and Laura's in her school. It's the rest of the world that's at it.

Of course she didn't, he replied wearily, as if I must know as well as he did.

How did he know she didn't?

Because he hadn't told her.

How did he know she didn't suspect it though?

He shook his head. No reason why she should, man.

Why'd he told me about it then?

To let me know the way things were... He was wearing an ink-blue sweater. He spends less on clothes than me, but always looks just right. He's got *sprezzatura*. That's what he has above all. It's what the old Italians would have called everything I've said so far about him, more or less. It's like total self-possession.

'Was it a one-off?' I saw Laura getting in from school on Midsummer's Day, drinking Ribena and waiting for him. What did she smell on him when he returned? How was he behaving? Could he face her? I'm not sure why, but I hoped he could. Yeah. He could've faced her. He has *sprezzatura*. But how would she have felt if she knew? How much would she mind? As much as I do?… Would she have liked to join in? No. She's no hedonist.

'They invited me back, any time.'

'Did you go?' Must have rated him to invite him back. How would I have done? Fucking hell, doesn't bear thinking about. Where d'you start?

'Thought about it.'

'But you didn't?' I enquired solemnly. The Remand Hero was goggling triumphantly at his men. They'd beat the machine.

He grinned at me. 'No. Never went again.'

'Why not?'

'It was too easy.'

Too *easy*? All right for some, isn't it? 'What were their names?'

'Roland and Carla.'

'Why's it easy?' I seemed to have a quantity of air-dried spit in front of my teeth, a sort of hard foam of resentment.

'Because there's no consequences.'

'They don't contact you?'

'No. It's totally casual, this sort of thing.'

He liked consequences didn't he? He liked them in Barcelona. Liked them well enough to be up to his neck in them now, ten years on, trying to sort things out with me. This was the price of his adventure in a hot square and bookshop in a country whose language he didn't speak – *languages* – and whose customs he did not know. The two of us sitting here drinking on a prohibited night, trying to work out why the hell his woman had vamoosed. He'd have been a damn sight better off without consequences, if he wanted the truth. I'd give the bastard consequences.

If only they weren't very good consequences, at least until whatever it is that's gone wrong began. And who am I to talk of a 'price'? I've had the – the friendship, the affection of them both for the last seven years. I should be willing to pay a price for that. And I should cut out the resentment. Let him have his luck. My life, its peculiar deficits, are nobody's fault but mine.

Had there been similar escapades?

There'd been one or two. It seemed that he'd been staying out pretty late once or twice a month with his work pals, with whom he has sociable, but not affectionate relations. They're a bunch of unmitigated heads (good job I don't work there), who generally have something to celebrate. Anyway, they often ended up at The Infirmary in Chinatown… I didn't listen very closely to what he said next; nostalgia was crying for attention. When I recovered my concentration, he was talking about some Nigerian hookers, who also often ended up at The Infirmary. Anyway, Ian was immune to the hookers qua hookers, but he 'liked talking to them' (and so say all of us). And one night, a hooker called Lady offered him a lift home in a gold Merc and sucked his dick for free; though when (*when?*) my man Ian realised what she was up to, he made an excuse about needing some Rizlas, leaped out and made off.

'Just out of interest', and as a way of sublimating my admiration for this particular action, I went into his confusion with him. He explained that he'd taken so many drugs that night, he thought there was a shadow on Lady's right side who she was going down on, rather than himself. He thought he was feeling her mouth via the shadow's dick – at first.

Ah.

But to come back to the main point, what does it do to the relationship, this sort of escapade? Again it's inconsequential, isn't it? Would any man after nine and a half years' attachment go down the same road? Indeed, would any man not do so? Not easy for me to ask myself this because of how I regard her, but I think it's necessary. What sort of attrition or corrosion does it effect? Or corruption? What does it do to love? Maybe it helps. There's no feeling in it is there, great or small? If she knew would she loathe it? I suspect she may, but I don't know enough. Should she loathe it? I really don't know enough. Wouldn't make her cry though, would it?... Damn it, never made a woman cry.

Laura didn't know about this either?

No.

So why does he tell me? What's he heading towards?

Did she go out with her own friends?... What was I hoping to hear? That she came in stinking of Tequila at 4am with her knickers in her handbag? She'd never be like that, unless he drove her to it.

Of course she did.

Did they go out on the same nights, the two of them?

Yeah. When they met me for example, he said with a sort of brutal fondness.

I pointed out that I'd meant separately, not together.

Oh now and then they did. She always got in earlier than him though.

Always?

Yes. This was where they differed.

I was glad to hear this: it was where I'd differ from her too. Except that I'd overcome the difference. Sit in with her night after night, watch the weather and listen to John Peel. I'd read her bits from books and she'd read to me in French; their authors sound too cold in translation. I'd drink nothing but tea and we'd eat bread and butter. I'd... I'm a foolish old man, aren't I? There are tiny decrepitations in my lungs when I awake, stains on my pillow.

'Can you differ your way home the pair of you?' Rab was standing at an adjoining table clutching a duster. 'The bar is closed.' The Ryder Cup team were enjoying a private extension of drinking facilities as we made our way over to Ian's.

The flat was still empty and the wind was up. We drank a glass of rum. Ian checked his e-mails, tapping softly, gazing at the screen of the PC on the desk at the end of the long living room. He began to ask how things were with me. What about this breakdown that I'd had at the weekend? I said I was only joking and he looked at me over the screen until I said I meant exaggerating. I shouldn't exaggerate about things like that, he murmured. His concern was too much for me. What was up then? I said nothing different; it was the same as usual. The wind rattled in the mews. Was it living alone, was that the problem? I told him I didn't know. After all, I'd chosen my way of living – hadn't I? He came over and poured me more rum, then put a Miles Davis LP on.

'Why don't you do something about it, man?' He looked at me with a sort of cold respect.

'One Day My Prince Will Come' was the track, mournful, inconclusive, agreeable. I noted that I'd missed my last tube. To avoid answering him I swigged the rum. But why didn't I do something about it? Thick caramelised diesel caught my throat. I would have said, 'It isn't as simple as that,' but I suddenly had no clear idea what 'It' was either, or what it might mean to 'Do something'… Do what about what? The rum had no depth of flavour. What was I meant to do about what? *Meant*? What about *want*? What did I want? What did I want to do about it? What did I want to do about *what*?

Ian was now ringing for a taxi. He asked what I thought of what I'd heard so far. I told him I assumed that it wasn't everything, then the street door buzzed, the driver having arrived in no time.

Who did not offer to suck my dick. Would I have wanted it? How the hell do I know? The world is full of sex, it really is compact with sex, as compact with sex as it is with atoms and molecules of gas, and electromagnetic waves; this Ian proves to me. Carla on his face, Roland at his dick, very vivid now. Sex is as present as gravity. Yet when he asks *me* why I don't do something about it, I lose all sense of science. When he invites me to discuss myself, I am as dull as a peasant… *Well oi just cannot see it anywhere, Master. Not for the life of me! Must have flown up the chimney oi reckon.*

I had a house double when I got in; and another, and hummed the tune he played me.

78

Not many people have a memory like me. This is not a brag. It's another reason I am alone. I can remember too much. I'll not say I can remember everything – that'd be asking for it; but it makes me feel old, too old to begin anything now. To begin something, you need to feel fresh. Most people I know can't remember anything, can't tell one year from another. Was it as long ago as *that*? Really! You're kidding! *Seven* years? *Can't* be!

The philosopher says the memory's like the digestive system: when you can't stop remembering, you've got chronic dyspepsia. You're an old man belching after lunch in a green cardigan, burned here and there by cigarettes; you feel solitary, you're seedy. No one wants to know what you remember; you're ashamed of it yourself. People seem to back off like well-trained kids. They want to play, and forget. They don't care about the time that's gone. The resentful care too much about the time that's gone. This too the philosopher tells us. The resentful care too much, because the time that's gone is where they backed off and brooded when they should have got stuck in.

I'd say this is why I drink a lot: in order to remember less – if only drink didn't take mind to the films. Then we begin to leap the months and years, like a horse over hedges.

★★★

It was July 1997 and the weather was heating up after weeks of rain. A colleague of mine was celebrating her birthday with drinks on a roof garden. That colleague was Melania Morgan and I was wearing an orange shirt with short sleeves in which I've since concluded I looked a regular twat, not to put too fine a point on it. There was champagne and Pimm's No. 1 Cup. There was no beer. The guests were in my profession, or its bureaucracy and I was — I was going to say casting a cold eye on them; but that isn't the truth. Somewhat bumptiously, it shames me to recall, and with a sensation of superior incongruity, I was enjoying myself: what was I doing amid these people who couldn't even tell you what the weather was like without checking *TimeOut* first? Did they know how different I was? Blah blah blah. Guests moved on to me, and moved away, as if I were a small dark planet that needed its surface checked out at least.

Leaning on the parapet, his back turned to the solar system, a slim fair-haired young man in white trousers was looking at a green hill. Turning to face me as I stood alone, he asked if that was Parliament Hill. White trousers suited him. How often could you say that? He looked like a character from DH Lawrence, kitted out for a boating party. The neatly clipped fair beard and moustache suited him, like a courtier from another time.

That was Primrose Hill I told him. Parliament Hill was on Hampstead Heath. He nodded. It looked good up there. Reminded him of the Beacons where he came from. In his accent there was a cool green ripple. It was the rain we'd had, I suggested — the rain had kept the grass green. Then he asked if I fancied climbing it. I wondered when he meant. He meant now.

His voice was hesitant, though not from nerves; he

seemed to hesitate for my sake, as if I needed time. I did. His proposition had winded me slightly. Heart vibrating, I said that I'd promised Melania that I would go for the meal that had been arranged in the Artillery Arms. He watched as I explained, reminding me now of a still young man in a Titian portrait. Then he laughed and said that was all right, we could easily go another time.

We introduced ourselves. Ian knew no one. Felicity had asked them. He indicated a figure with an excess of make-up and earrings like small burnished quoits that flashed in the sun who was dangling in the manner of Andy Pandy over a group of women. Felicity Makepeace was PA to Professor Rivington. Meanwhile he was making a sign to Felicity's group and someone was approaching us across the roof.

At first I couldn't see; maybe the sun was setting behind her. I was dumb, my senses darkened. Her bright hair was curled; she wore a blue band in it... Ian introduced us and she said, 'Hi!' Ian smiled and she smiled. I was struck dumb. What was I to say? Of course, I had to speak: speak or die. But does Death ever come when you want Him?

Recollecting the emotion in tranquility, I've produced nothing more than a self-effusion of sweaty orange garlicky shame, as of a peasant in bright-dyed cloth, a wood-chopper, pig-herder, or cook, a sweaty orange pot-stirrer, caught behind the scenes at a great house by a pair of strolling nobles. From my mighty memory, nothing more than this. No wonder I'm no poet. Yet as the great Romantics found, the recollected emotion becomes a new source of inspiration.

So I've discovered analogies from an earlier past for this encounter. I panicked like a schoolboy when a girl smiles in his face. Say he's just come out of the dining room with his belly full of swede and pie and she's sitting on a wall in the sun with her friends in platform shoes like glossy bricks. What does she mean? Or I panicked like a Greek when a god's in the area, clad as a mortal in sky-blue linen, golden skinned. She'll turn him into a frog for looking at her, or she'll shower him with pleasures unsuited to a man. Or like a young man when a woman with pale feet asks for a light, I panicked. It's the bottom of a sloping cobbled road at midsummer, hard by the Hibernian stadium. What to say when the flame drops back in its hole? Lord, what is he to say?

Then someone with champagne on a tray came between me and Laura, and Ian to our left. I lifted a couple of glasses, Laura said 'Thanks!', took a glass from my hand and drank half of it in one go – a fair sign. Ian was now blind side of the man with the drinks around whom a small scrum was forming. I necked mine and seized another glass. By now I had a cigarette burning and was talking to Laura. No longer was death a requirement.

She had the comportment of a child who's just looked out and seen the weather's lovely; then the weather being lovely, so is everything. It was enchanting. I asked her if she and Ian were coming along for the meal. Rhetorically, ethically, on grounds of taste, this was a bloody tricky question. I was hoping very much that they'd be joining us; on the other hand I must convey a critical attitude towards the idea of eating in a pub with Melania's metropolitans. I had to affirm my opposition to a gastronomic trend while reeling in this noble pair. I was a satirist of the state and its cultural apparatus who's suddenly been appointed Head of Tourism by a vicious and whimsical tyrant. My face must have been indicating the conflict within, for at last she touched my arm and said, 'Don't you want us to come?' Then Ian was back alongside her.

Soon we were trooping down Primrose Hill Road to the Artillery Arms – that's funny – a pub by Primrose Hill, where an upper room had been booked for us. Laura talked all the way, inquisitive and charming; there was nothing put on about her, no falsity or calculation. We discussed Felicity Makepeace, who was a cousin of Laura's – not her most eccentric one. She laughed delightfully, honouring me with the scent of a secret. Felicity and Laura had been on holidays in 'The Gower' when they were kids. The two families shared a trailer. I could hear the kid still in her; it was a lovely kid, laughing, clambering. And now Laura had moved to London, Felicity was expected to invite her out. Felicity's mum had told her – here Laura laughed with great enjoyment, and perhaps a little swirl of irony that dispersed as rapidly as a drop of blue-black ink in plain water – Felicity's mum had told her she must keep Laura out of trouble! So Felicity had invited Laura and Ian to Melania's birthday. That was why they were here.

Well thanks to Felicity's mum, I said gallantly, otherwise I shouldn't have had the chance to meet her and Ian. Then Laura was wanting to know where I was going for my holidays this summer, and I said I wasn't going anywhere.

I was aware of the solitary sound of the pronoun and the way she took it in, and knew myself as what I must seem: a gallant, orange fool, a bumptious, lonely little speck.

We were in the pub by now at a long table laid with bread and pots of oil in the neo-biblical manner of England in the early days of New Labour, Laura to my right, Ian across from us. My duty was to stop her eating too much bread; she placed her finger on my arm to tell me. She still had holidays on her mind, wanting to know what I did instead. I said, oh, I did a lot of reading and so on. And what else? I couldn't think of much (except drinking, which it wouldn't be very gallant to mention, and dealing with the emotional consequences of drinking, which would hardly strike the right note in a happy interview such as this). Didn't I go to see films? I said I'd seen all the films I wanted to see. I didn't want to give her the impression I had desires current with the time in which we now sat and talked. I wanted to block myself against the present. OK. What was my favourite? I wouldn't say, I demurred. She laughed as if she'd never heard the like of it and asked why. I said I didn't care for lists, or men who made lists – or for that matter books about men who made lists by Oxbridge grads posing as ordinary lads. This was meant to sound deft, but I sensed a heavy mask clank down and I became a touchy knight in steel-plate armour about to hack the room to firewood in offence at the question of his favourite…

…But how did I know I'd seen all the films I wanted. How could I know? I told her I knew what I wanted. Exactly? Yes. At which she hummed and began chewing a third bit of bread; as instructed, I told her off. I was doing well for negativity. I never went on holiday, I did not have a favourite film, I did not like lists and I wouldn't let anyone eat. I was as much fun as Malvolio, the puritan servant who gets locked in the brig in *Twelfth Night* while everyone else falls in love or has a good time. I had to say something to make her remember me lyrically. I'd never seen eyes that changed colour like the sky before. So I said I'd like to see a film called *La Rochelle*, if I were to see one film more. Ian passed a jug of red wine over and winked at me. He was discussing his travels in India with Professor Rick Rivington, a highflyer of bright and airy intelligence, not much older than myself. I'd been noticing how Ian handled him, timing his utterances with a peculiar authority, holding back on the smile and the nod, by which means, he induced a sort of canine eagerness in the Prof. Laura asked if *La Rochelle* was a new film. I said it hadn't been made yet. She told me she'd been there once when she was in France. It was like a castle by the sea. Then she was being served a brownish piece of fish decorated with a line of green capers, and offered a communal platter of new potatoes and 'roast' broccoli. I shut up about La Rochelle. Her castle-by-the-sea image filled the air.

When my own food came, she asked if I spent all my time in London. I said I was always meaning to go somewhere for a few days, even if only the coast or the countryside, but never succeeded in leaving. I could feel her left knee against my right knee, transmitting to my dick. She was only paying me attention because she reckoned I was queer. With that thought I was accounting for the pleasures of the evening when I uttered suddenly the words, 'God, I wish I could get away!' She looked at me gently and a little puzzled. Like one of those spasms or shouts that attend a shameful memory, it wasn't an exclamation I'd known was coming. Melania waved.

'She's got such beautiful hair!' Laura said. It was as dark as hers was bright. Ian caught my eye, and the time for gallantry was gone. Laura was keen to know how well I knew Melania. I said we'd been junior doctors together. We were now colleagues. She wondered, and I fancied there was a little craft in this, whether we were best friends. Oh, I said, I liked her a hell of a lot. This was manifestly ironic and I didn't care either. I disliked her rather bitterly at the time, though nowadays – nowadays, I do not dislike Melania Morgan at all. I pointed out her husband to Laura, an amiable dermatologist.

I enquired about her own work (I'd been gathering she was a teacher). Well, after she'd known Ian about three months (it took no longer than that), she decided to move up to London from Brighton to be with him. Ah, the world of other people's decisions! And by the autumn of that year, she had it all planned and was enrolled on a postgraduate teaching degree. She was just completing her first year at a school in Mitcham, where she taught English and French. Did she like it? Yes, she loved it: there was something in her tone of the sportswoman who maintains she loves the pain of running long, sickening races. She had mettle. They'd recently moved into a flat near the BT Tower. They were three minutes from Regent's Park. She was so excited. It was the poshest place she'd ever lived.

The food finally ended. I so badly wanted to ask her more of her life that I did the opposite and started messing around (not physically, mind). I didn't want to hear so much from her that there would be nothing left for another time – though I knew damn well there would be no other time. Furthermore, I'd now drunk just enough to mess around, a matter of rather exact calibration in my case. I invented strange circumstances. I asked her to make choices between outlandish alternatives. Sweat was on my throat. I made her tell me who so-and-so was a cross between. She still looked as cool as hell. I wanted to sniff her armpit, I wanted to abrade my tongue on it. From time to time, Ian poured me more wine, Laura covering her own glass with her hand. Between them they seemed to know what I wanted.

We left together and walked south past the dark hill. This phase of the night really lasted, and yet went so quickly. I remember their bright faces either side of me. I remember Laura's dancing, smiling, concerned face up above me when I slipped on my arse. This was in a basement club in Rathbone Place. She was a good dancer. When that shut we went along to a drinking club in Chinatown, which changes its name every so often. It's now called The Infirmary...

...Though this is where remembering comes to an end, since I could never recall a thing we did or said in The Infirmary, though I can still taste the grassy rottenness of Wray and Nephew's rum (64% ABV), of which I drank some glasses with coke. The next memory is standing with them at Tottenham Court Road at dawn, waiting for the tube to open. There were works going on; I was leaning on some temporary railings looking at a hole in the pavement, imagining digging my way home like a mole. Then Laura said something friendly to me and they were gone.

Ashamed of the state I'd been in, I was glad I hardly knew them and should be most unlikely to see them again. To block it all off, I tried to tear my orange shirt in half. The bastard wouldn't give, so I threw it in the bin. But then I kept thinking about them. When I sat on my settee at night, the embroidered figures on the old cushions reminded me.

Wednesday

Wednesday morning I have a clinic. I'd been lying in bed thinking of schoolgirls, manning the guns of a flak battalion at Gumrak, north-west of Stalingrad, as 16th Panzer Division came over the steppe. High yells and low blasts, cordite and fearless hearts. Masha and Natalya, dying at their posts, black as miners, dresses torn. God bless those Russian schoolgirls. They choked me with wonder, and a kind of shame... More than twice their age and I'd done nothing to compare.

And in another twenty years I'd have done nothing to compare with the ageing outlaws of *The Wild Bunch*. Lord when I saw that film as a teenager, it got me as drunk as my first bottle of Bells. They're old men who've stayed wild and they go down fighting in a Mexican town, surrounded by a private army. It was the first Hollywood production to show entry and exit wounds, in gorgeous slow motion. There's a line shouted by a Pike Bishop to his brother Dutch, once at the film's beginning when Dutch's horse has been shot from under him, and again at the end when Dutch has been shot in the lung: 'Get up, you lazy bastard!' Sometimes I quote it to myself, as if I were my own snarling brother.

Ah, what it said about my personality, this kind of morning therapy, God knew. I had a suspicion the politics of it left much to be desired – not to mention the psychology. One day I'd look into it. One day I might sort it. For the time being it served the purpose of getting this miserable bastard up and ready, 7.07 in red on the radio alarm… Jesus but this was unpleasant. This was hard. This was the heroism of modern life. For want of a better word, I was trying to organise a new shoelace.

Why were the bloody ends – why wouldn't they *do*? Why so bloody unductile? Christ this made me dizzy. It was a violent difficulty of no smaller order than many, many past heroisms – no: make that the totality of human glory – to get this fucker *through*… allowing myself a microgram of irony.

I could have puked on my shoe. These late-night remembering sessions, they didn't half impose their cost on the here and now. And I'd not even got as far as the manner in which I hooked up with Ian and Laura again seven years ago. Hadn't had the satisfaction of that. Still, it was all coiled in me like a reel of film… Though it was uncanny – something was uncanny – how things he told me last night were spliced with the reel. If I were a man of leisure, I'd go into this…

Come on, you lazy bastard! Incidentally, Dutch Bishop was the only member of the gang who didn't visit the Mexican bordello, the night before they all died. He just sat outside whittling while the other guys enjoyed themselves. What a pillock… What a strange, strange, holy pillock.

Ha! Do I love my patients? *Love*? In the biblical sense, I suppose I must. The Apostle Paul speaks of universal love, universal brotherhood, the idea being, you have to love everyone, but no one in particular. Particular love – love for *a* person – is vanity; it is pagan, the love of the damned. Better not expect to see your wife in heaven, Jack, or your friends or your kids either. The souls of the blessed loved no one in particular, and this is why they don't grieve to see their wicked children tossed about by devils on reddened pikes down there in the pit. Look over the edge, Jack, and you can see your children tossed. This was the promise of the old Church Fathers. Huzza! Hear them scream! And there's grandma burning like a woolly barrel. Serves her right for concentrating her affection on the grandchildren, feeding them pies till they died of gluttony. And look over there, Jack! Just there! There's a best friend, rolling in a furrow of napalm! Serves him right for loving one woman, one man, instead of loving everyone.

Well now, I certainly felt unparticular love for Chas here, doffing his beige-and-black-check baseball cap and holding it before his groin. Chas was a great big bully of Bermondsey, but now he wanted some treatment he was not sure how this would stand against him in the eternal scheme of things and, like a man who's just stood up in a rowing boat, was wondering whether he ought to be trying to keep his weight to himself. I predicted that Chas would think he had a brain tumour, his GP having referred him to me with headaches that had been recurring for nine or ten weeks.

'Are they occurring daily, Chas?'

'Ah – Mondays and Tuesdays mainly. *Lethal.*'

'How many times on Mondays and Tuesdays?'

'Morning, afternoon, night, doctor. *Lethal* they are – like these little blokes with red-hot razors are hacking bits off inside.'

'Hacking?'

Chas reconsidered his pain. 'Nah. Not *hacking*. Like just pushing the blade through, so to speak.'

'Where does the pain occur?'

'In the eyes; top of the head; jaw.' He indicated with his fingers, thickly forking them at his eyes. 'Nostrils too.'

'Do you sweat?'

'Yeah. Forehead's *dripping*, doctor.'

'Notice anything happening to your eyelids, Chas? During the headache?' He had one of those swarthy, heavy-eyed, black-browed English physiognomies such as you see when our fans are on the news in Euro boulevard or plaza, singing of WWII until the tear gas pops and the windows go *shang* and the Minister of Sport says *tiny minority*.

'Yeah. They're bulging like – like everyone's going, "Fucking hell, geez," – sorry, that's them saying that, ain't me – "you look like a fucking frog nowadays!" That's what they been saying.'

'OK.' I made a note.

'Or toad.' Chas sniffed. 'Call themselves mates. And also, Doc, this is what I been fretting about. I reckon I got a tumour in there. Straight up. GP, fucking P-'... Chas ate air for a while and looked round the room to see if we could spot the guilty party who, before Chas remembered he was talking to me, was just about to say 'fucking Paki'. When he looked back, I was staring at him, into his unbeautiful, coally eyes. It wasn't that they were small, he just had too much face; that was the problem. 'GP, Dr Chauhan, he won't hear it. But *I* know, that's a classical sign of a tumour yeah?'

'What is, Chas?'

'The tumour, right, it grows,' Chas made a cauliflower-size shape with his thick fingers leaving his baseball cap perched on his crotch, 'and it grows, till it comes bulging out your eyes. It literally comes *out your eyes.*'

'How d'you know about this, Chas?'

'My Uncle Albie, he had one. Died of it.'

'And the tumour obtruded through his eyes?'

Chas considered. 'Well I ain't 100% on that, Doctor. But I checked it up on the Web too. They got some images on there – yeah? – like fucking *Elephant Man.*'

'All right. How much do you drink, Chas?'

'Not much. Not during the week.'

Chas was a track engineer. On paper, his employer was one of the companies who maintain the London Underground. In his hands was a slight tremor. I wondered how often he turned up for work; and what other pies he had his fingers in. 'What about the weekends?'

'Dunno really, Doc.' He pulled his ear. 'Don't keep count so to speak.' He attempted a wink in the manner of a pirate. God it was horrible. Behind my eyes, pain went off like one of those drab brown-paper fireworks we had as kids as he loomed at me in three-cornered hat, a green Canarian parrot on his shoulder. They were tied with string those fireworks, tied into tight sinuosities. The big fear was – ha – they'd go up your trouser leg.

'How much do you spend on booze, average weekend?' They sprung and cracked around the floor as each sinuosity of black powder exploded.

'Ton eighty. Round that.' He sniffed.

'One hundred and eighty pounds on drink in an average weekend?'

Jumping-jacks they were called.

'Friday, Saturday, Sunday.' He counted the days on his fingers.

'What d'you drink, Chas? Pomerol?'

'Nah. Stella. That is what I tend to go for.'

'What d'you pay for a pint?'

'Two fifty tops round our way. More in the West End, obviously.'

'You realise you're drinking seventy pints plus of strong lager in an average weekend?'

Chas shook his head and sucked in air as if in revulsion at another man's enormity, contriving to make me feel indelicate and unEnglish for specifying a figure. I could have said, 'And I thought *I* had a problem!' But professionalism aside, this would have shown a lack of appreciation of the function of scale in these matters. What I drink, Chas would scoff at; what Chas drinks, X would regard as a 'sportsman's diet'; what X puts away, Socrates would describe as 'a manly quantity', and what Socrates could hold, Goethe would call elevenses...

'*Can't* be,' Chas was now saying. With a sensation of disagreeable sympathy, I was beginning to feel less unparticular about him. I wondered how he spent his weekends, how like and unlike mine they may be, what he did to other people: I wondered about the men he cracked, the women he forced (*you'll like this, darling!*), remembering nothing. I imagined his horrid crew, saw bright winter afternoons and long foggy nights in Bermondsey and Rotherhithe, London Bridge and the Old Kent Road, Chas and the lads out for kicks. Regimental motto: *Risusne est?* ('It's a laugh, what?').

Emblem: skull in pint glass surmounted by clenched fist. Yes, he'd be a sight less passive than me, Master Chas.

'You are suffering from cluster headaches, Chas. They're precipitated by the amount of alcohol you are drinking.'

'*Cluster* headaches?' He produced a buccal contortion, in the manner of a chimpanzee or the Chancellor of the Exchequer; I found I was doing it too. It was the smile of the week.

As he continued to pout, I said, 'Yes.'

'I ain't got a brain tumour then?... Ah!'

'No tumour. What you have to do now is reduce your drinking by 75%.' This still left him plenty of bad units, by official guidelines.

'No probs, Doctor. I can do that.' He straightened his back, stuck his chest out, braced his shoulders for the task ahead.

'OK, Chas.' I smiled at him, not warmly, but not just for form's sake; not falsely.

'I'm well relieved, I am.'

'I'll do you a prescription for oxygen and ergotamine, OK?'

'That's cool, Doc.'

'The pharmacy's the other side of the gardens. Red-brick building – sixth floor.' I handed him the paper. 'Were you scared, Chas?'

As he stood he expelled some air from the left corner of his mouth, reminding me of my dad in his pipe-smoking days. 'Not scared. Not as such... Thought I'd never get everything done though. Six months left and that.'

'What d'you want to get done?... Tell me if it's not my business.'

He watched me, in case I was taking the piss, then said

reasonably, 'Ah – travel and that.' He pulled his cap over his right fist, as if trying to produce a puppet. 'Go back to college. That's another aim, Doc. Blew it first time.'

'Be lucky, Chas!' I said.

He lifted his chin, then stooped a little towards me: 'Let me know if I can ever return it, Doc.'

'How d'you mean, Chas?'

'You was ever in trouble, I can make it cushty for you. Know what I'm saying?'

'Thanks.' He turned and walked out still carrying his cap. While I was waiting for the next patient, I had a flash fantasy of sitting down for a drink with him and discussing life. He was a louring, barbaric slag (to go easy with the noun), and didn't care either; but I imagined talking to him would be as bracing as talking to a soldier, for whom all the things that worry us are strictly civilian and molehill. He'd not necessarily be able to explain anything, but he'd toughen me out of my fear, sitting over a dark mess table with our drinks in our fists. We'd get onto Laura and he'd say, 'Basically, you have got two choices here…'

I saw a couple more headaches, then a woman called Margaret with mood swings and depression, and family history. I referred her to my special clinic. This was a damn sight more serious than Chas's affliction; this was total war, whereas the affliction of Chas was a mere mess-around or skirmish. Finally I saw a middle-aged civil servant with the sort of moustache that went out in the Seventies, who was showing signs of what I reckoned was an FTD; this is an inherited dementia which I have to take care not to mistake for my own specialism, though it interests me for philosophical reasons.

On my way to lunch with Melania Morgan, two smokers in wheelchairs and an old man on a stick began to look at me; I found I was humming in the street. I'd be a hypocrite if I said it was to cheer myself up; I hum when I *am* cheerful. It's a sign of living alone.

Arrived, I asked Melania if she could name the tune I'd been humming on my way to meet her, and performed the opening chords. Of course she couldn't. She wasn't into trivia – and good on her. Well it was 'We're All in It Together' by The Pirates. I told her I'd seen a young man with cluster headaches who looked like the guitarist, which had triggered a bout of humming. Strange how the mind works, strange what makes it drag its own depths. Full of holiday invitations from what we're meant to be thinking of, is our old friend the mind.

★★★

At least we were in a pub of the old style, furnished with English oak; the stools, the three-sided bar, the broad window ledges and the tables were polished, dented and humped with use; on two sides of the bar were Victorian vanity hatches of frosted glass. Our table was an up-ended barrel, with a raised brass rim round the circumference that might have been useful to stop dancing sprites or homuncular sailors intent on performing the hornpipe from tumbling into the abyss, but impeded the wrists of the common punter, la!

Yes, Melania said, but I wouldn't be making such a fuss about the furniture if I hadn't felt guilty about drinking at lunchtime. I was just using the furniture as a distraction.

I was only having a pint, and didn't have to defend it either.

But I already was, with my tone.

Listen. What she was doing now was interpreting disagreement as denial: this being one of the traps set by the culture of therapy for everyone who believed they were actually all right. The culture of therapy said with a smile, 'You are *not* all right, whatever you believe. So get in here, pal, lie down, confess, cry your eyes out! We know you better than you know yourself.' This was the imperialism of therapy. This was therapy's violence... We'd had this sort of conversation a number of times, in the seven years since we'd passed from competitive hostility to the status quo.

She laughed this off. Therapists didn't say 'pal', for a start. I'd obviously had a few last night. And hadn't slept much either. She could see it in my eyes.

Wondering if I should have tried a double dose of mouthwash this morning, I suggested we order.

Wasn't I meant to have stopped drinking in the week?

I'd have the liver. Yes. Liver and bacon. That would do nicely.

God knew what state my own liver was in. When was I going to have a function test?

'Don't make me think of my innards, Mel!' I told her merrily. I was going to quote the speech of white-bearded Jack Falstaff when he's sitting with his tart on his knee. She's just begged him to stop fucking and fighting, and patch up his old body for heaven, and he says, 'Peace, good babe, don't be speaking to me like a death's head!'... But it would hardly have been apt, would it? Never mind.

I observed a little tic of self-restraint in her throat. She has a kid of her own now, so knows how to resist provocation. She thought she'd like liver and bacon too. It was a treat for her when she had lunch with me; as a rule, she was thoroughly metropolitan in her diet. I was meant to be educating her about neurology and culture: as a physician and scientist, she was way beyond me; but on the artistic and philosophic side of things, she did feel herself to be lacking. I told her I could do her a reading list, but she was having none of that: I would have to teach her; it was up to me.

Well, I said, couldn't we just talk about culture on its own? But it had to be neurology and culture. She sees everything under the aspect of neurology. And so we had these lunches. She'd been trying to get this going for a long while now, since the last World Cup in fact, though this was only the third or fourth meeting... I suppose I'd been dragging my feet a bit, a habit of mine in the face of initiative.

I thought I'd seen an FTD this morning, I told her. I'd sent him on to the Hun. This was Professor Rivington, who'd lost hair over the years since he sat talking to Ian in the Artillery Arms, preserving a sort of spike in the middle of his head, as on a World War I Pickelhaube.

We weren't meant to be discussing business, Melania advised me. The plates of liver and bacon arrived with mash, gravy steaming to the rim. Little did she know I'd be imagining the chewed mass of offal and pink bacon sliding down her throat. Disgusting. But I did get off on her throat, which was the colour of high-quality sand, such as I'd seen around the outdoor pool in a five-star conference hotel. This was not adoration. I adore only one woman. Melania was more like, ah – I know: more like my student. I wished I could have another pint.

Oh this wasn't business. I wished I could learn to sip. Did she remember what I'd been on about last time we met? Our topic then was Friedrich Nietzsche's final and protracted illness, or in unenlightened terminology, his 'madness'. It began with childlike behaviour in Italian drawing rooms: the philosopher would open the lid and belt the piano with his knuckles; he'd sing a silly song and do the hornpipe, hopping and grinning; he'd have his dick out to play with while middle-class matrons looked on gagging; he'd shit himself and play with it, uninhibited. Poor bastard. When the period of his antics was over, he lay down quietly, very quietly; for ten years he spoke to no one. At last, he died.

I'd propounded the theory that this was a case of GPI (General Paralysis of the Insane), which appears in the late, or tertiary, stage of infection with syphilis, my intention being to present to my colleague an instance of cultural as opposed to medical diagnosis. To put it in other words, *the* subject in psychiatry around the time Nietzsche died was GPI; this being the case, we may have inherited an historically mistaken idea of what it was that actually killed him and a lot of other people, since they've been drawn erroneously into a once-fashionable diagnostic category... I mean, we all deserve to have our deaths recorded straight, don't we? How would you feel if everyone thought you'd died of pox? Particularly if you'd never fucked anyone in all the days of your life.

'You said Nietzsche didn't necessarily die of advanced

syphilis,' Melania replied with her mouth full. 'You said he did "scurrilous leaps and dances".' She'd enjoyed this phrase. It wasn't my own, but from a letter written by an onlooking friend of the philosopher.

I finished what I was eating before I spoke. That was right.

Go on then, Mr Manners.

More likely he'd died of a Frontal Temporal Dementia or FTD.

Really? When had this come out?

It hadn't been published yet.

So it was just a theory?

I'd been talking it over with Ulrich Uhlmann. Ulrich wanted to do a little essay for *The Lancet* – me and him.

Melania considered this, sucking a rasher of streaky bacon from her fork intact like a large bird on the lawn. Doubtless she was wondering about its institutional research value, balancing this with its worth as a constructive pastime for me, Ulrich being a dementia scientist with certain interests in common with my own, but more energy.

Opening her dark eyes wide, she said, 'Wow! That's fantastic!'

Oh I didn't know. It might be amusing... But the main thing was, right, a lot of the big names who'd written about Nietzsche, they'd had to make up a brothel visit.

Why?

Well they'd had to convince themselves that Nietzsche once visited a brothel – just once. And it was on that visit he'd contracted syphilis.

Why had he only had to go once?

Ah – well the point was, he never had a sexual relationship in his life. In his letters, and the accounts of his contemporaries, no sexual relationship was ever mentioned. But there was no record of his visiting brothels either. However, the GPI diagnosis meant he had to have had sexual intercourse on one occasion. Therefore, he must have visited a brothel once. She was watching my mouth… Next time I could tell her how Thomas Mann traced the Third Reich back to that brothel visit.

'Oh they went all the time in those days!' she scoffed. She'd finished eating – believe it or not, she had actually raised her plate to her mouth with two hands and licked the rim for gravy – so I lit up. She wanted a cigarette too, could hardly wait to be asked. Then Melania must have one, bless her. I made a secret sign to the barman to pass over another pint for me. She couldn't scold me with any sincerity now she was smoking… Lord we drinkers are manipulative.

'Nietzsche didn't,' I said religiously. 'He was different.'

'Do you identify with him?'

'Now you're being pert.' But pert was hardly the word for her with her tremendous brown-black hair of woolly curls which made me think of the words 'Assyrian', 'Phoenician', 'barbaric'. She dressed expensively, but there was something barbaric about her. Mid-winter she wore a Shearling coat and these heels that went clink-clak like little stonehammers. What had she done to men in her time? What could she do to me? Smoking and checking her lips in her mirror for gravy. Fucking hell. What do I know?

'Am I making you blush, Mark?'

I drank deeply. 'I never blush!'

'D'you have no shame, Mark?'

'Yes. I've got plenty of shame. But I don't blush about it.'

'Why didn't he have sex?'

'He was in love with someone but she didn't return it… She didn't return it that way.'

'Who was she?'

'Her name was Lou Salomé.'

'Who did she love?'

'She loved his friend.'

'As ever,' Melania said.

'He honestly didn't know if he wanted to anyway.'

'Didn't know if he wanted to fuck little Lou? What sort of man was he for God's sake?'

'He was a philosopher,' I said and I felt ashamed; and I knew my knowledge was useless.

On the way back up Lamb's Conduit Street, I asked Melania's advice about Ian and Laura (disguising their names) and Melania took my arm. Had she been in touch with him? Had she left a note? How long had they been together? Nine years? Then she must have gone off for a fling. Had he been neglecting her? He had? Then that was what it was. Melania'd do the same thing herself. Why was I so worried about it? Melania clung harder to my arm. (I wanted to shriek Germanically, 'You are hurting me!', like Peter Lorre in *The Beast with Five Fingers*.) What state was my friend in? Worried? Had he contacted her mother? No? Why not? Didn't want to worry *her*? Well was *he* worried or wasn't he? What about her friends? Didn't want to worry *them* either? And her work, what did she do? She was a teacher? So had he contacted the school? Not *yet*? Why not? Didn't want to cause trouble?

'Maybe he's pleased,' Melania said. We were now back at work.

'He isn't.'

'You probably like her more than he does.'

This worried me. 'Of course I don't!'

'So stop worrying. She'll be back.'

'Are you sure?' I sounded like a little lad.

'Positive.'

'Why, Mel?'

'To get her things, stupid!'

'Oh yeah.' I was about to say, 'They once came to your birthday party.' For certain reasons I desisted.

Late afternoon, she texted me to say I could come to her for advice whenever I needed.

★★★

It would have been the best part of two months after the celebration of Melania Morgan's thirty-third birthday in the fashion we were watching last night, that I was woken early by a broadcaster calling upstairs one Sunday morning that the nation was mourning. Being a lonely bastard, I sometimes leave the TV on at night for company. You can fall into these habits. I resented being told I was mourning. I'd decide. Once I'd established what the fuck was going on here. On the stairs I slipped on my arse and banged my coccyx, which put me in just the mood.

This was nothing more than state control! State control

of mind and heart. I gave them a fucking hard time, the presenters, the reporters, the Prime Minister of London. Irony, mimicry, vituperation – I blasted away with three barrels at these simpering punks. After a while, I became self-conscious about sneering bollock naked, went up for a shower, dressed, returned for seconds. By lunchtime, I was fed up with being ironic on my own: lots of my best lines were going unheard. I left the house. Where I was bound, and to what end, I did not know as I ascended the hill past the graveyard and the library.

Families and groups of families were walking to the tube with bears and flowers. All the other ironists must have stayed at home. I whistled 'McNamara's Band' as I passed one group and the mother murmured, 'He's got no respect.' I turned and glanced at their hot, solemn faces; they were ready to hate. A grandfather said, 'They never have any respect.' Bitterly I hurried on. If grandpa'd been my age, I'd have dropped him. Beneath my breath I cursed his eyes. His eyes were jellied piss. His eyes were eel-coating. The whole world was a bladder, pissing through its eyes. I was as bitter as the railers of the Jacobean stage, I had a chip on my shoulder, it was made of flint, I was Daniel de Bosola, I was a 'deformed and scurrilous Greek'.

On the tube it was no better. Half a million of them were on their way to Kensington Gardens; each of them wanted to feel like one in half a million; each of them wanted to feel half a million strong. I reminded myself of the average attendance at the Nuremberg all-German Party rallies (1926–38): half a million. An unjust thought there and then, but it made me feel better. And indeed certain mob acts in the days following against bear-tamperers, against flower pilferers and shopkeepers who refused to shut, bore out in traces my sociology.

At Camden, the carriage crowds were giving me the horrors, so I got off and took a Northern Line tube on the other side of the V, away from the city centre. I didn't want to be alone, I couldn't stand crowds. What was it with me? At Chalk Farm I alighted and wandering south 'found' myself beside Melania's flat.

Curiously, I retraced the route to the Artillery Arms, along which the three of them... us, had passed, and she'd asked me of holidays. Identifying roughly the spot where we'd taken the taxi into the West End later that night, I almost shouted for shame. The words, hanging in my throat, were beyond my control, as in the case of the Tourette's sufferer. The sensation was mixed with longing. Where did the past go? Who could say? Well in the theory of the 'block universe', it didn't go anywhere: we walked through time like the land we inhabited; the past vanished no more than East Finchley vanished when I come down to Chalk Farm. It did not go; it was just behind me. I suppose I hoped that theory was true, and a couple and a man were still walking down the road beside the green hill, would always be walking; for I would not see them again. My occiput was larding in the heat. What the hell I was doing there, I did not know.

Crossing Regent's Park Road, I backtracked a little and began climbing Primrose Hill. I had a gravelly thirst. I smoked a cigarette, which aggravated it. I should have bought a can of Fanta. Better still, I should have conceded the failure of yet another Sunday, another outing, and fucked off home. Two men who looked like brothers, Italian or Anglo-Indian, and a little boy who was distinctly Indian, were flying a kite. Further up on a ridge, a pale man was peering through a large telescope on a tripod; beside him, a skinny red-faced loon in a Millwall shirt looked at me, put his finger to his lips: 'Don't disturb him, son! He's calibrating.' Could they see a bedroom, a couple mounted, a man with his dick in his hand? Heart twanging I carried on. Near the top, I was wondering if the world changed its appearance on a sunny day when you were in the first phase of a myocardial infarction, taking on the visual texture of felt, when I heard my name called. I supposed this was Death, or my heart's valediction. My name was called again: to my left, almost concealed by parallax now I was passing a bush, was a golden head. I came back and took the bush on the left this time: there was Laura. She was sitting on a bench, Ian beside her.

Part of the magic of the old romances is that characters can bump into each other anywhere: this is the law of time-space in romance – it is never improbable that significant characters meet each other exactly here, just now, in this meadow, or strand or mountain pass. It's still true in *Don Quixote*, which is meant to be teasing romances. In *The Faerie Queene* it is very true. Even true in modern Westerns, such as *Blood Meridian*. That I had to be so damn hot each time I encountered them was a personal genre difficulty.

I went forward with my head bowed in the manner of a peasant at last approaching the shrine, not wanting to look them in the face too soon, delving with the left hand in my occiput, which by now felt like a bundle of wet rushes. Planning my opening line, I managed to light a cigarette as they smiled up at me: Had they come here to avoid the hysteria?

It didn't articulate so well: I'd have done better to choose a line with fewer aitches, after climbing Primrose Hill on my lungs.

They came every Sunday, Ian told me with a smile.

'We come every Sunday to wait for you!' Laura cried. 'We thought you didn't like us!' There was a fineness to her voice that hadn't been paid for at a posh school. I'd promised to meet them. She wagged her finger at me, reasonable, natural, pert. I'd promised to meet them the day after the roof party.

I was dumbfounded. Did she mean up here? She certainly did! I attempted to apologise. I felt disgraced – almost dishonoured.

'It's all right!' Laura laughed benevolently. 'You were drunk. You both were,' she added for my sake. 'Ian couldn't remember either.'

'That's right, man!' Ian laughed. 'Come and join us.' I settled between them like a plump bird. Ian patted my shoulder and rose to sit on the grass. *Sprezzatura*. From the beginning. We had a talk about the death of the Princess of Wales; it had upset Laura, which made me ashamed of howling at the TV in solitude this morning. During which irony exhibition, moreover, they'd been getting ready to come and wait for me for the seventh Sunday running. Were they telling the truth? Could they mean it? I have never stopped wondering.

There and then, however, I just felt fabulously lucky. They could have trooped along to Kensington Gardens but instead they'd come to wait for me. In a state of serene cheer, disgrace overcome, not far perhaps from joy, I was sitting with my arm on the back of the bench several inches clear of Laura's bare shoulders, which were making me think of my father's old trick of pouring cream into coffee over a spoon reversed, when she poked me and said, 'You didn't ring us either!'

Cheerfully, I replied that I hadn't had their number. On this I was corrected. She now told me that I'd made them give me it. *Made* produced a qualm, as if someone were at my intestines with a heavy-duty stapler. How insistent had I been?

'You wouldn't give us yours but you made us give you ours,' she continued, and I was well again, as if we were infants in the yard, or teenagers sparring in flirtation. Her pertness had some range. I'd have liked to study it. I'd thought a woman who played the little girl was a transparent thing, and maybe a trashy one; yet this attitude in her was as strong, even athletic, as her shoulders.

What could have happened to their number though? As I forgot nothing, so I lost nothing. This was a mystery.

From where he was sitting on the grass, hands stretched behind him like slender buttresses, Ian asked if I had any plans. Did I fancy a drink?

We descended the hill and walked away from Chalk Farm towards Regent's Park, taking our time. It was a great moment of my life. We had a talk about the media working everyone up, we wondered whether the media could ever be sincere. Laura thought so, I didn't. Outside the Black Star in Camden, we stood and drank on the hot yellow-spotted pavement. They would not go till I wanted to. There had to be more than pity to this, hadn't there? I'd had people liking me before, of course, but this was almost preposterous; or would have been if it weren't so natural. We talked and talked, the three of us. This was the time I heard about Señor Norbert and her flight from France. When Ian went inside, she told me that stuff about *Eramos amigos nada más*. They had some sort of private joke about a woman Laura called her aunt; I let them keep it private.

A few days later, it came to me that I must have put their number in the pocket of the shirt I threw away. They'd given it me again, however, and this time I'd given them mine. That was August 31st 1997.

***

I was down with Ian again tonight. During the afternoon I'd been brooding about what Melania Morgan had said at lunchtime. I wasn't pleased. How could a woman with table manners such as hers presume to talk to me with an appearance of shrewdness? She was well out of order. I had a good mind to cancel our lunch arrangements *tout à fait*. Yet as I sat facing my friend, who still had the best part of everything to tell me, her opinions formed nothing more than an occasional back-rattle, like the carton lids or leaves on the street that distract the night-time reader.

These days, Ian works as a recruitment consultant. It's better paid than what he was doing years ago, and has the similar benefit of offering him no sense of fulfilment. It's not an especially worthwhile job; he treats it without much respect, but also without contempt. He has a peculiarly light way of going about it from what he tells me, which I admire. On the whole, he seems to regard it as a branch of his social life, since his colleagues are very social animals, as we know; while his clients – well they're apparently in no rush to get recruited, and some of them turn up the other side of the desk so often that he takes them for coffee in the cafes of Clerkenwell. He likes listening to their life stories, and excuses. This much I was aware of.

I wasn't aware he had been fucking them too, which is what he told me now; he spoke with a cool hesitancy that didn't come from shame, but from regard for me. Was it the right time for Mark to be hearing this? Such would have been his calculation.

I felt I concealed well enough my first reaction. The blackboard caught my eye, where the Remand Hero's second was carefully chalking a dish of steaming peas the size of alleys of jade beside the steaming sausage. Rab and the Hero looked on from the far side of the bar, arms folded. The golf machine must be *kaputt*.

He'd actually used the word 'them': this seemed to be the first challenge, the potentially multitudinous nature of his confession – or rather, his confidence, since I was not his priest. *Them*. I needed to meet his regard for me. I needed *not* to ask, 'How many?', since I was unlikely to be able to raise the right tone of enthusiasm, or admiration. I said just a minute and went up to the bar for a strong round of drinks, in order to regroup.

As Rab proceeded eagerly my way, I had time to analyse my concern. In the mirror behind the bar, Ian was checking his phone with that expression of a Cardinal's secretary that I'd witnessed two nights ago for the first time. Perhaps he knew I was watching him. How much self-control would it require for him not to text her or leave messages? 'Maybe he's pleased,' Melania said. How glib can you get? *Them*. Potentially, this sounded infamous – it certainly would if I said it: 'My patients – I fuck em!' Can't be done these days. A similar law inhibits most professions. We cannot enjoy ourselves with people in dependent relationships with us: *He did the whole platoon over two nights, him and the Colour Sergeant… He kept a black book in which he marked every student he'd had on a range from First to Fail.* Infamous.

Yet the enjoyment of clients wasn't really a violation of professional ethics where Ian was concerned, for the reason that he didn't regard himself as having a profession. It wasn't this that was appalling me. Rather, it was unethical in the classical sense, since it was intemperate… Was this it? Was this why my hands were shaking? But surely my reaction was intemperate too. Everyone fucked everyone else in the modern world. It was no big deal, was it? So why did I suddenly find him evil? That was the word. His neglect (to adapt a word used glibly by Melania) – his massive neglect of the woman he owed his affection and his time was evil. Damn him. He'd been neglecting me too. All this alternative recreation showed massive contempt for our friendship. Wasn't this evil as well? But I needed to beware of resentment here; resentment was my own potential evil – or rather my dirty little failing; for resentment was many times less grand than evil. And I wondered now if it was his grand and

112

destructive audacity that was appalling me. I was witness to his smashing the temple he'd put such style into building. Yes – this appalled me, as a lover of the past… But I needed to hear more. As I set down the large nips and the lagers, he began to go through the list.

Fucking hell. Here was intemperance. Lisa, Magda, Fatima, Irene, Koo, Jo, Bran… 'I've mentioned them to you before,' he said. He meant as acquaintances.

'Some of them. Not Irene. Or Bran.'

'It's short for Branislav.'

'Ah.'

'You thought it was just having a cup of coffee though?' Here again was his trick of asking me for clarification, when the obligation to come clean was his.

'That's what you said,' I replied, with less force than I'd have liked. 'I didn't look into it any further than that.'

'You thought it was just friendship?'

'If that. I thought it was just coffee. Coffee with an acquaintance. Whatever the fuck that is.'

'You don't believe in coffee do you?'

'Not as something to have with people.'

'What's the prerequisite? With you?'

'To have with people?' I could see where this was going.

'Yeah.'

I hated his face with its frosty composure, not because it was corrupt but because it was at this moment in possession of truth. 'As much as I can drink,' I said. 'That's where I'm at. As you know full well.' There was one word for him here. I'd not use it to his face.

He nodded because he'd got what he wanted, but he was struggling a bit when he said, 'And with me it's fucking whatever's got blood and soul. I can't just sit and have coffee with someone either.'

'Well that's a classy bit of logic,' I observed, 'but it's far from a conclusion.' Funny how at home he was also making me feel.

'Why's that?'

It was the texture of frost his face was reminding me of, as much as its temperature. 'Because the two things that you're making out are similar are also different.'

'Well done,' he said with inconsiderable irony. 'Knew I could rely on your intellect.'

'Oh that's an old principle that is,' I said modestly. 'You've got to see the difference in like things, as well as the similarity in unlike things.'

He smiled in such a way as to suggest that I should be smiling too. I blinked peaceably instead. Something seemed to have been discharged, for the time being. Having bought more drinks, he began to recount his escapades with his clients.

What a tale he had to tell. What a tale of deep, perfunctory lust. The standard message was 'D.Y.W.T.F.T?' Then he'd turn up at the client's flat early evening, or lunchtime if it was close; there was also a church in Bleeding Heart Yard, just west of Farringdon, where he went among the graves; and if it was with guys, he tended to use the toilets of the National Postal Museum. Joe (it was that spelling) and Bran were the guys, though there wasn't any actual penetration with Bran, who looked like a wolf. I was profoundly jealous, profoundly envious; and I use the word carefully – 'profoundly' I mean – because I felt as if I were watching his liaisons from a cliff top, while

114

he scurried about on the valley floor with his cock in his hand looking out for anything that moved. I wasn't getting any myself, but I was in a position conducive to some form of greatness; he was in the depths.

I don't know that I wasn't on the verge of finding it all hilarious, on the principle of 'the more the merrier'. I found my eyes on the steaming porker and the dish of steaming peas and barked. Trust him as I did, my friend was putting me in mind of the strange scene in *Macbeth* where good Lord Macduff turns up at the English court. In conversation with Malcolm, a son of the murdered king, he begs that young man to come and relieve Scotland's woes. Let them replace the tyrant Macbeth by force of arms. Malcolm replies, you would not want me as king, because if you think Macbeth is black with wickedness, wait till you catch me with the ladies: I cannot keep my dick in my trousers you see. I combine all the evils of Macbeth with voluptuousness that has no bottom. I am a veritable sink of lust.

As it turns out, Master Malcolm is making this up (so he claims), defaming himself as a stratagem, since he needs to test Macduff; though the reason for the test isn't 100% clear, and Macduff doesn't appear to be passing it either; because instead of walking away in lonely outrage, he says, Come anyway. You can fuck all our maids and daughters, no problem. We will lay it on for you... Unless he's now doing some testing of his own. For this is how people talk to each other in totalitarian states, in a coded, testing manner. And Shakespeare knew it by 1605. It's a sinister scene all right, *Macbeth* 4.3, profoundly sinister – and these are meant to be the good guys of the play. That's what they tell you at school. Jesus Christ.

And then I began to wonder again how Laura taught this ominous, sinister play to her multicultural kids. 'Malcolm's just making this up!' Is that what she'd say, and pass on? 'He's just making it up to test noble Macduff!' Would she say that, without pausing to look further into what he was saying about himself? Without pausing to consider whether he wanted it to be true? And would she have the generosity to overlook the fact that noble Macduff is also a yellow-bellied louse who left his wife and kids to the slaughter when he ran off to England?

'And Laura doesn't know about any of this either?' I put it to Ian.

'I don't tell her. Don't tell her what I've been up to.'

'But women suspect.'

He could reasonably have said *How do you know?* To which I'd have had no better answer than, *It's well known.* Instead he asked me, 'Do you think she can tell?'

'She must be able to. Surely?' This seemed obvious. Obvious. But what did I know? People are cheated on all their lives. You read about this in the obituaries, and the lives of artists. He kept a mistress in Kensal Rise and a whore in Betterton Street and his wife did not bat an eyelid. He'd fly to a resort on the Gulf of Cádiz with wife and kids; his mistress would be on the following flight.

Maybe she suspected, but deceived herself he was faithful. Maybe she managed to avoid suspecting. But she still walked out one day, and did not say where she had gone. 'She must have gone for a fling,' Melania said. Which is the sort of thing you would say if you didn't know Laura. Shallow. Meaningless.

'It's not everything,' was all he said, with an air of dismissal.

'What?'

'It's no big deal.'

'How do you mean?'

'Cos it's got nothing to do with spirit.'

'You think they're separate?'

'Don't you?'

Did I think my dick and matters of the spirit were separate? I couldn't answer this, for several reasons. Instead I asked a practical question:

'Where did you tell Laura you'd been on the evenings – the *early* evenings I mean – when you were fucking your clients?'

'I told her I'd been with you,' he said brightly.

A lie admitted without shame – how often do you come across such a thing really? It's a shock. In psychiatry and psychology, the reckless liar is sometimes identified with what's now called, in value-free terminology, the 'anti-social personality'. As for the big thinkers, well Montaigne wrote that there was nothing worse than the liar, because he tears the frail bond that joins us one to another as human beings, the bond that depends on speaking true. Dante placed frauds and false speakers at the bottom of hell because theirs was the deepest wickedness. But although it's a shock, a lie admitted without shame is almost invigorating, like a cold shower or a blast of air from the north. I barked with laughter again, not merrily, nor hysterically, but in a sort of convulsion against the cold.

'You've got some brass neck haven't you?' I cried.

'I wanted to involve you, man,' he said, a little hesitantly.

'*Involve* me?'

'Yes.'

'Well that was most sporting of you.' I lit a Rothmans and inhaled it like a hoover. 'Could I ask why?' The tip glowed and crackled as if the pub air were pure oxygen. It was the time for outrage; I should have – ah, should have cursed him for eternity, knocked the pus out of him, broken his dirty back and walked away from there for good. Anyone would have told me that: anyone was just living in theory. As was his way, he'd timed telling me with a sort of perfection. He'd brought out what he had stashed away in the back-shop with the finest appreciation of the occasion. So that being involved felt as if it were no bad thing; felt quite different from being used for an excuse. For *involving* can be a benevolent as well as harmful activity, as usage demonstrates: *He does his best to involve everyone. She was only trying to make me feel involved, bless her. Don't hang about by the wall! Come over here and get involved, bub! We need to do more to make minorities feel involved in the civic process.* See? I felt involved with a thrill of ambivalence; I knew it was bad, and I knew that I was going to be revolted by his lie and by my ambivalence when I returned home on my own; but in the here and now, I was on top of the world because no one had shown me such thought before. I felt like Nietzsche on one of those high walks in Sils-Maria among the trees and snow when he'd cracked the problem of fate and time, and felt as fit as an ancient Greek athlete. At the far end of the bar, the Remand Hero made some sort of sign to me.

Then I saw what appeared to be the slick of a tear in Ian's eyes. I was gutted. Just when I hit the top, my friend falls and drags me with him on the rope by which we are joined. Never before had I seen my friend close to crying. We began to drink fast to drown our sorrows. He told me about Irene. Irene was the best; she was fifty-two (he knew from her file), but she fucking loved it.

Late on, I put it to him whether Irene wasn't shrivelled. He told me that just wasn't the issue. That wasn't it at all.

Thursday

Waking I stiffened, a beast exposed to strong current. He'd told Laura he was with me when he was with them. I could have barked with shame. She would now think I'd agreed to this and was party to his rotten secrets. He'd turned her against me as much as against himself, maybe more. My friend was a liar, but I was something worse. The Remand Hero began to make friends with us last night. The Remand Hero is a convicted fraud. That's who I was down with. Liars and frauds. Creeping like a dog with the liars and the frauds. She'd have gone away to kill herself with disappointment, because between us we'd contrived to break her heart. She'd walk into the sea, drop herself from a bridge. I'd not see her again. Not alive again. He was meant to take her out the Friday before Christmas last year, but he told her I needed to see him urgently... Ah, tonight I should put out his life, if I had any honour. I should break his neck. Was there anything worse than these lies? With a curse against my friend and myself, I heaved myself up, lungs decrepitating. The pillow was a disgrace.

I smelled of drink I did, Melania advised me. Pooh! I stunk of it. She could smell it from there. My friend took Joe round to Irene's flat that night when I needed to see him urgently. Three of them. Two clients, one consultant. I had seventy-seven electronic mails to attend to, along with some cock adverts. What a miracle if there'd been one from Laura Blake. Just for me.

'I'm sorry about that.' It's a small office.

Melania entered, hands on hips. She must have been here betimes this morning, since she was without her lady-assassin's handbag and the little leather rucksack in which she keeps *Annals of Neurology* and *Cell* to read on the train from Barnes Bridge.

'Do you have a clinic?' She was wearing a red wool mini-skirt, black jumper, black suede boots. Lethal.

'No actually.'

'Good thing too. Do you have an alcohol problem?'

'Not in a new way.'

'I enjoyed our topic yesterday.'

'Thanks.'

'You don't have to drink to be interesting.'

'I don't drink to be interesting.'

'Why do you then?'

'To whip my thoughts.' I was blasé because I was desperate. That was all. If there'd been any hope, I'd have crawled to her and hugged her knees and said *Help me!* But it wasn't like that. There was no hope.

'Don't be ridiculous. You haven't slept either. Your eyes are red, Mark, and they're all creased underneath. So unprofessional.'

'We live in different normalities, Mel.' Her normality was a Clinical Research Fellowship, a house by the river, a delightful dark-eyed daughter, an excellent, patient husband, a future.

She hummed, thinking she knew my view of her normality, aware that the word 'bourgeois' might be levelled at her and her life and her kind, who hankered to do something *edgy* once in a while, on the advice of the papers and mags they read, and the friends they had round to dinner.

'Before the Battle of Jena, Napoleon went seven nights without sleep. Or changing his underwear.'

'D'you think you're like him?'

'Not in many respects.'

She left with her nose in the air, considering this. He was Goethe's hero, Nietzsche's hero. Why? 'Napoleon was the man! Always illuminated.' He always knew what the hell he was doing. That's why. Always. The spirit was always with him. Of course, they never had to stand downwind of him. He wasn't as clean as me; but the spirit was with him, the little stinker, and I have none.

Among Melania's clinical interests is AIDS-related dementia. Presently she returned online to tell me about an ADC patient who'd reported having sex with a prodigious number of men, in the UK and South America. What did I think? I thought he might be exaggerating the number given by a factor of ten. Not that he was lying; his memory was demented... He must have had a dick of whale-flesh this one, mustn't he? By Jove. A dick of whale-flesh and the spirit to go with it.

She replied to ask what was the latest on my friend and his woman. I said there hadn't been any development really. Would I keep her informed though? OK. I would. Minutes later, she reappeared in person – she really was a fucking jack-in-the-box this morning. Now she stood gravely in the door frame with her hands behind her back like a Harrow schoolboy, to make an announcement that this couple were affecting my health and well-being. I'd better be careful. I really must be careful. Beneath her black jumper, there were her breasts. I told her this was garbage. I told her not to be bourgeois. She bit her lip and shook her head with an air of knowing better that annoyed me like a child. She turned to leave and said something like, 'Be careful for me.'

What the hell was it to her? I sucked my teeth… But narked as I was by Melania's solicitude, I rather badly wanted to ask my colleague a thing or two about Laura. Specifically, would she think that I was in with Ian on his rotten hobby (supposing this was why she'd gone)? Or would she suspect that he was lying twice over, and I had nothing to do with it? And if so, why hadn't she been in touch with *me* to talk about it? Why hadn't she been in touch with *me* for comfort? If I wasn't an old tramp who leaks on his pillow, I could have sobbed. A woeful dichotomy! If she didn't think I was complicit with him, hugger mugger in his infamy, it was no better than if she did, since it meant I meant extra-nothing to her. Evidently I did not count at all. But had I ever?

***

The time she told me of her first visit to him in London, we were having champagne in a bar I'd selected as tasteful (if a champagne bar can ever be anything but 245% vulgar) on the street where cholera was identified as water-borne by the good Doctor Snow, during one of the 1830s' epidemics. She was scandalised. He'd taken her for a night out and all they'd done was drink. What was more, her new beret'd got wax all over it and the wheel had come off her weekend case with his tugging. When they went back to his flat – at long long last – she'd been sick because they'd had nothing to eat all night and he'd made her drink more wine. Did I think he'd looked after her when she was being sick? Oh no! All he'd done was play 'Send in the Clowns' about fifteen times. It wasn't the song as everyone was used to it either – that had been a favourite of her mum and dad's; it was much faster. The singer sounded as if she'd bite you. Scandalised Laura was sweet, so sweet I was nearly speechless before her big marine eyes, incredulous lips, her pressing forefinger and tiny frown.

Perhaps if I'd been less dumb-enchanted that time, she'd have come to me when he scandalised her nine years later by saying they were shrivelled already. If I'd responded the first time, maybe she'd have met me this week to press her finger on my arm in a tête-à-tête with champagne, just the two of us; because part of the difficulty of responding the other time was that Ian was present, gazing tactfully elsewhere as he heard himself slagged off. Not that I wasn't grateful for his presence. Indeed, he'd endured Laura's reproaches with such calm, such lack of defensiveness, that there and then, I don't know if I myself wasn't more scandalised by her indiscretion than by anything my friend had done or neglected to do. And of course she left first that night as always, whereupon Ian said with a smile, 'Well what d'you think of all that, man? She was the one who insisted on coming to London!'

Later I interpreted his behaviour according to the doctrine of success. Careless, unchivalrous as he'd been with her, she was still with him and manifestly in his power. I'd not have treated her in such a way if she'd come to visit *me* – this was what she'd been implying in front of the two of us. Very likely she was implying as well that this was exactly why women like her visited Ian's type, not mine.

Which has been agitating me for a long time. I'm too good for women? Bollocks. I'd gladly make her drink herself sick if she came to visit me. I'd mess up her beret good and proper. I'd put on a CD of brass bands. I'd lick her arse like a hellhound... wouldn't I?

***

My unhappy meditations had by now left a long way behind the question I'd been wanting to put to Melania, who was still hovering electronically about me like that creature with the Welsh accent called 'Raggedy' who appeared on the American version of the *Rupert* show in my childhood. I have noticed that for a woman at the top of her profession, she does spend a lot of time in pursuit of gossip, though I suppose it's just a sign of her efficiency. Anyway, she was now wondering if I wanted to bring my friends round to 'supper'. In the course of remonstrating about the vanity of this and her ethical kitchen table – a twenty footer these days – in the course of remonstrating, I gave their names away: Laura and Ian. 'You put her name first,' Melania replied pointedly. I replied that I couldn't bring them round because no one knew where the hell

Laura was, for the time being... Anyway, no more time for this: I had letters to dictate to Alison.

Alison Dale has a zest for life; this is why she's about thirty pounds overweight, at a generous underestimate. Once or twice, I've been the beneficiary of this goodly corpulence, Alison allowing one breast or the other to rub my shoulder as we stare at the computer waiting for something to come up. She has two daughters has Alison Dale and a bearded, dapper husband. I fancy they always have dessert in her house. And roasts and barbecues and curry evenings. She can sink a bottle of Irish whisky without making a fuss. She just gets jollier.

★★★

We had a gas at our Christmas lunch last year, held at the whim of the department's social cabal on a retired-from-service battle cruiser. The food from the galleys being cadet standard, my metropolitan colleagues were provoked into a great demonstration of sniffing, poking and grumbling. Whose dumb idea might this have been? The soup was bright red Heinz, the gravy was from the sachet, the turkey was from the freezer, the roast potatoes were from Iceland, the sprouts were overboiled, the stuffing balls looked like teratomas. By Christ they make a fuss about food, these modern middle-class metro-professionals. It's actually become their vulgarity, this consistent gastro-prattle. And what it betrays again and again is a fundamental lack of taste. Give them a plate of fish and chips, they're calling out for balsamic vinegar. Stomach hedonism's their version of the good life, a witless munching discussion. *Excuse me! Where's this haddock sourced from?* It's sourced from the fucking sea, Christabel. Meanwhile, and not without a nice sense of contrast on my part, Alison Dale and I tucked in with gusto; my gastritis was well at bay that day. We'd had a couple in Southwark before the off (we'd also brought our own bottle of Bushmills in case of stingy allowances). I told her yarns of the convoys to Murmansk, to keep the Russians equipped against the Nazis. I had her imagine how cold it was on the dog watch. Did she know how many British sailors died in the icy waters of the Barents Sea? In those days, no one moaned about their food. My own mother made sure I was wise to this as a kid. She'd lived through nearly eleven years of rationing. Alison Dale liked to hear about my mother. She slapped me on the back and gave me a sly rub (or allowed the latter to occur, to be ethically accurate about it).

Around us glances were cursing the seating plan. I'd begun to notice, but I didn't let on. Everyone wanted to be where we were. Mark the envy that lurks in the modern soul, mark the nostalgia. Mistress Dale and I must have seemed like two merry peasants from another time, or two A-list celebs, lost in enjoyment. At length, Melania came over with Bernie Henderson, the Clinical Director. These two we admitted. They took a drop from our bottle, gawped at Alison's peaks. Then the managers started dancing and we laughed for an hour. Hell that was a spectacle. The night ended too early.

Luckily I found something else to do. I rang Ian, who was at a loose end that Friday night, picked up a cab from the river on Tooley Street and went in fading triumph to see him. I should have gone home while I was still standing, like Alison did.

★★★

Today Alison was wearing a white blouse and a sailorish blue cardigan with brass buttons, which reminded me of that Christmas. Her husband, his photo framed on her desk, looked like the sailor on the Navy Cut packet. How often did he put it to her? Maybe they just sat together and laughed at TV. I didn't know the ways of couples. Maybe she carried him by direct attack. I dictated a letter to Chas's GP.

'Why've you left this till today?' Alison asked. I could see boiled sweets in her drawer. 'You saw him yesterday. Don't hum like that, Mark. You're not meant to leave it.'

'Never mind. I was busy.'

'No you weren't.'

'Was.'

'No you weren't particularly.'

'How do you know?'

'I've been keeping an eye on you that's how.'

Nosy cow. 'Why have you, Alison, been doing that?'

'You know why, Mark.' Her buttons gleamed like a commodore's.

'I think I don't!'

'Oh I think you do, Mark.'

Damn her. '"*Wen nennst du schlecht? Den, der immer beschämen will.*"'

'Very clever. What does that mean please?'

'"Who do you call bad? The one who always makes you feel ashamed." Good quote what!'

'So why not say it in English in the first place? You're not in a state to be quoting, sunshine.'

'Bollocks!'

'There you are see! Feeling guilty so he uses language like that.' She rotated anti-clockwise to her computer as I left for lunch hating her.

Something drew me to the Bramah Centre. I had a hot wholefood item which gave me gastritis, so I bought a can of diet coke and left my food to go outside and smoke. In the corridor of the Bramah Centre I passed adverts for Spanish Classes and Confidence Classes, Resipiscence Training and Bridge-Building with Narratives. I was wondering what the fuck Bridge-Building with Narratives might be when I had a little reflux of the uncanny. This time it came with a sensation of being double-booked. It was something – its clarity was going already, like dreams or drunken hours – something to do with Irene and Joe. Something said about them by my very good friend, a specification of time or date that… then I lost it.

In the afternoon, Alison invited me to confide in her. She invited me to come and stay at her place, if I was ever down on my luck. She asked if she could bring me food in, just in case I wasn't eating properly. She said all this without spelling out the problem as she saw it, for which I loved her. Loved her for her great, English 46DD tact.

As a reward, I told her that it was my pal who had the problems, not me. She shook her head in sympathy. His missus had left? I didn't need to tell her. It was the oldest story.

That was right. She'd gone. Had she run off with one of his pals – his *other* pals – or was it an unknown party?

Well this was what we didn't know.

Now would she be the one who phoned me now and then?

Oh no. Certainly not.

Alison patted me. It must be a patient she was thinking of.

It certainly wasn't her. I was adamant.

Oh Alison was just pulling my leg! Very sexy voice for a patient though.

Really?

Oh yes. Hadn't I noticed?

Noticed what?

The patient with the sexy voice?

Couldn't say I had.

Now I wasn't doing what I shouldn't be with my patients was I?

What? What was that?

Avoiding them when they phoned to speak to me.

★★★

There was a Sunday newspaper supplement on the squat coffee table.

'Someone lent me it,' Ian murmured on his way to fetch cans. It was open at an article about bio-immortality. Laura liked the weekend papers. Now and then I've been round on a Saturday or Sunday and she's been lightly absorbed in them on the settee; or she was on the floor in a yoga position, legs crossed, her papers spread around her like the charts of Sun Tzu. Beside her was a bowl of pips and stones smeared white from some fruit and yoghurt she'd been eating, a heavy tinted glass for juice and a large, half-pint pink and white hand-painted coffee cup with some sort of blue or green fruit on the side. She had everything she needed down there, classical in her relaxation. Sol would have shone upon her in that long living room, had he been able to find his way in through the narrow high-walled mews. Was it Ian's doing, that bowl of fruit and the pleasant beverages? How much did he tend to her in privacy? Was he still bringing her apples in bed? I hoped so, though in accordance with the law that all systems tend to run down, I supposed he may not be.

Another time I beheld her with the papers over her legs like a traveller's rug on a sleigh ride, or journey by coach through winter. On that occasion I deduced she was wearing next to nothing below the waist beneath the *Sunday Times*, having covered herself with it suddenly when I appeared. Deduced? Ha! – deduction's a rational process. The sensation affecting me was none too rational when she sneezed and raising her hand I witnessed a golden expanse and small patch of pale blue, a sight that produced a sort of jolting momentum so that I carried on to the end of the long room as if I'd been bound there from the second I entered, in order to examine the view across the mews. Lord I'd have jumped from that window to my death rather than have it falsely thought that I'd been lurking by her wishing I were a snake, or other creature that hung out close to the ground and was accustomed by nature to look up. Across the mews there was nothing to examine; it being the weekend, all the creative people had flown. The drop from the window would not have been fatal; you'd hardly have sprained your ankle, unless you dived head first with the zeal of a saint. At last that Sunday, Ian returned with some dry-cleaning.

I looked down now at the paper he'd been lent. The paper's clever man was digesting an interview with a Cambridge gerontologist who sounded like the sort of loop-de-loop who was educated at home and never played at football with the other boys. Touching six foot six with a beard an owl could hide in and a rapid squeaking voice, Alekhine de Munt was unattached to any named college, being a kind of independent researcher, in the tradition of Charles Darwin (or certain gurus of our own time whose books appeal to those who don't care for footnotes, indexes, and other dull evidence of scholarship). Why anyone now under 30 years of age could not live to be 900, there was no reason, in principle. With lifestyle vigilance and advanced cellular repair techniques, the human span could be increased by a multiple of ten, in principle. Upon this our Alekhine insisted. A couple of American scientists were now adduced. Hal Berg and Bob Thallion had published a book on bio-immortality. It was selling well. Regarding lifestyle vigilance, Hal and Bob had a hard rule for anyone who might wish to live into their eighth or ninth century: smoking – don't even think about it. Alcohol and animal fats – ditto.

I supposed Laura would get points from the Yanks, being a non-smoker, a positively moderate drinker (two glasses max – except when Ian was making her drink herself sick, a practice which had surely gone out of fashion almost before it began), and a great avoider of pork pies, steaks, cheese melts. There was a necessary accompaniment to lifestyle vigilance which may, however, have been beyond her – beyond many people's – means. This was a total health investigation every five years to keep an eye on our friends the cells.

What were the economics of this? Who was going to be paying for all these total health investigations? If you paid privately, it would likely cost you in excess of £500. On the NHS there was no such facility. Perhaps it was lifestyle vigilance for those well off enough to have a lifestyle and a perma-tan, as opposed to those with a damp house and a perma-cough, such as I used to visit on the estates orbiting Edinburgh during my clinical practice years. But they didn't want to be 900 as a rule. It wasn't a priority.

There was, however, a justification on the largest scale. Utopia! Acceptance of death would at long last be revealed as a sign of human backwardness, like the belief that God created the universe in a week. We could now stop devising ways of explaining death to ourselves, and producing compensations for the pale rider and his works.

Utopia? Certainly – for those who could afford lifestyle vigilance, and hated the culture of the past. But what was going to happen to all the philosophy, the religion, the art that's accommodated us to death and trained us for it? What about the cathedrals and *Hamlet*, Tennyson and Mahler, Heidegger and Socrates and Old King David? Were they all to go the way of the 116 lost plays of Sophocles? Where would culture go when people themselves were living to cathedral age? This Utopia was culture's deep grave.

I'd have been more contemptuous of what I was reading – no: I'd have been totally contemptuous – if I hadn't had a notion that it might have appealed to Laura if she'd been there to read it herself, since I knew from talks the three of us had enjoyed that she wanted to live to be 90 at least. Very enchanting she could be about this, particularly to a type like myself who tended to keep mortality well in mind. (400 years ago, I wouldn't have had my picture taken without a skull to hold.) You see, Laura thought that at 90, she'd merely be a smaller, wrinkled version of herself with exactly the same pleasures, the same loves and friends. It was naïve enough to break your heart, I swear, yet it was grand as well, a grand and simple notion. And of course, there was the little dream of living abroad with Ian, and him 90 or 91 as well. I read on.

Unlike some big thinkers, Thallion and Berg knew how to reel in the common punter. For sure, Bob wanted to be having sex when he was 230. Would that be with his wife of 201 years, to whom he was still bringing uxorious apples? His research assistant (Mona, hitting 185)? Or an 18-year-old waitress from Chihuahua? What did he mean? What did he *think* he meant? What did he think he *wanted*? In God's name, but this was infantile. Like kids with pink cake, they wanted an eternity of pleasure. I saw the world filling up with the undying. Saw them in the trees humping like baboons, saw fields and lay-bys swarming with copulators...

'Thought you didn't like newspapers,' Ian said, placing six cold cans on the table. He'd heard me rant enough about the media. In fact, he knew my grouses so well I'd resolved never to repeat them, one of the grouses itself being that the media were forever saying the same thing for the first time. Instead, I had a swig of papery Holsten and asked him if he'd read the article.

He hadn't. Hadn't had time yet. What was it about?

Living forever.

Was it a pile of shit?

I didn't say yes, out of loyalty to Laura. I just drank my cans quick and smoked three or four Rothmans. If there'd been any animal fats lying around on a saucer, I'd have licked em up like a cat.

Mary asked him something at the bar. Maybe about Laura. *How's your young lady? Nae proposed to her yet?* That time she had the newspapers over her, she was wearing a blue gingham top up front. Made her tits look rustic. I'd come over against my conscience tonight, Ian having phoned me at work around five. My justification was that the outrage of being involved in his lies called for a degree of confrontation. To stay away – ah that would have been like not coming back to school in the afternoon after you've been hit in the morning. I was going to give him some tonight, like my ma used to try and tell me.

I picked on him about the word 'shrivelled'. I picked him up on it anyway. Rab was watching us, like a guard in a tower. I suggested this was the tipping point, never mind the other escapades, never mind 'everything'. When he used that word, he told her something about time. His face had a cornet texture this evening, a dry fragility. He wanted to quell me, but with sarcasm it might have cracked. I advised him you weren't meant to say love seemed longer than it had been. That was like saying a short novel felt like a nine-hundred pager, a real yawn-maker. He knew. You were meant to say the opposite weren't you? Yes you were. Rab was signalling from the bar.

You were meant to say it only felt like yesterday darling, only felt like yesterday you first set eyes on each other. That was right. But you of all people, he told me, you of all people had to know time wasn't like that. For a man with a memory like mine, time must stack up like mountains. Cunning. I was meant to be giving him some stick but he brought it round to me. Rab appeared to be tutting now as he watched us.

How many pages did my life feel like? Well considering how little had happened to me, considering how fucking little I'd done, quite a lot. Seven or eight hundred probably. Right. Standing above us, Rab set two pints of Stella on our table. Had we nae see him waving? I was afraid we hadn't. Well these were from Jerry. He indicated the Remand Hero who was casting sharp goggling looks here and there at the bar and now made a complex sign in our direction. The gift was evidently another sign of our growing acceptance after five years of pretty solid attendance, a welcome to corruption. With heavy tread, Rab set off on the long march back to the bar from which he'd set out when the snows began to thaw, around the spring of 1947. Ian gave a sort of two-fingered salute to the Remand Hero. What would have made it quicker then? My life? Yeah.

I did not know what would have made my life quicker.

Later at the bar, the Remand Hero's second was just along from me, a handsome middle-aged scumbag with old-style tats on his forearms and eyes as shiny as a dog's. He asked if we'd enjoyed our pints. Sincerely I thanked him. With lowered voice, he advised me that Jerry'd had a bet on the hostage.

'How d'you mean?' I asked him.

'The one they clipped tonight!' he laughed.

I could say nothing. How many centuries of bio-immortality would it take this spaniel to acquire a conscience?

Smiling Ian came up and asked if I was OK. He put his arm around me. Did I want to go?

God so I did. We took our drinks out on the pavement. I told him I couldn't handle it in there anymore. He knew what I meant. I couldn't breathe. He knew very well. Above us was the head of the BT Tower with its red anti-aircraft lights. We drank in silence then took a walk, southwards past the Middlesex Hospital, right along Mortimer Street. 'Noble Mortimer', 'revolted Mortimer'. Odd role in Shakespeare, Lord Mortimer, Earl of March. Was he or was he not a traitor? A civil war was fought for him. First Part of *Henry IV*. No one notices him because everyone's waiting for Falstaff to reappear with a pint of sack in his fat hand. We went along Nassau Street, Candover Street. The question of Mortimer's treachery just gathers dust. Ian was telling me that with one other person in your life, the thought of growing old never left you alone. With one other person, it was worst of all. The houses of Hanson Street stood high above us, crimson, broad, established. When I asked why, he explained that it was because with one other person, you never knew for certain whether you'd chosen wisely, or were just taking it easy. And any time you decided you were wise, you felt carsick with complacency. I could have asked him how he thought it was for me, but he didn't deserve my resentment.

'How come you can do it all on your own?' he asked suddenly. 'That's what I admire about you.' We'd stopped on Great Titchfield Street by the Homeric aroma of Efe's, where the skewered meat broils on coals. This was a marvellous compliment. He stopped and patted me just over the heart, on the lapel of my jacket.

★★★

A marvellous compliment, but did I deserve any of it? In the first place, I felt I failed on both sides of his formula regarding love for another and truth to yourself. Manifestly, I hadn't chosen wisely in life; but I certainly wasn't taking it easy. As for 'doing it all on my own', did I have any integrity at all? This morning I was creeping like a dog. There'd been further to fall: drinking with punters who bet on the lives of hostages being the latest descent. Was this the true bottom, or were there lower depths? Say I had hardly started...

I was pouring myself a house double of Wood's Navy Rum, with a china thimble's worth of water. The thimble was painted with the head of the old Queen Mother, a leftover from the previous residents of the house, who collected these little pieces in a wooden rack. I needed a grog. It was a dumb idea, but good sense wasn't going to save me in my present state.

Ah, the bells of self-corruption have a nauseating chime. When I told Ian that Laura hadn't confided in me recently, I spoke with an excellent conscience. But is an excellent conscience any more honest than a boat that doesn't sink on dry land? At no time recently had Laura spoken to me privately – this was a literal truth. Though not necessarily for want of trying; since as Alison Dale had been glad to remind me this afternoon, someone had been phoning for me. Say I'd been dodging the calls, in case it was her. (Imagine the disappointment if I'd answered and it was just a man with growing numbness in his left arm and shoulder.) She'd not have given her name in case I took fright, or some manly form of evasive action. (Strange that Alison had not extracted it secretarially; but perhaps Alison was playing along in a woman's intuitive manner, as a mother might with her teenage son, not wanting to frighten the girl off – there having been quite enough trouble with the lad and his solitary practices as it is.) She'd have tried me only at work, for anonymity's sake. I'd never offered her my other numbers anyway; she'd never asked either. She was too subtle for that, unless she wasn't bothered – no: say she was too subtle.

She was used to being dodged… Grog fills the skull with tarry fire, la. The fantastic sport known as interviewing me about my love life might take the following form…

So why did I never invite Ian and her round to my place? Oh, there wasn't much nightlife where I was. Wasn't like the West End, or Fitzrovia, or the Borough of Soho. She didn't *mean* for the nightlife. What she meant was my house, where I lived, as I knew very well. Why did I never ask them? The truth was, I was ashamed of it – never had it decorated. Still looked the way it did when pensioners lived there. How sweet! She'd love to see it. She could imagine me there drinking cocoa, and feeding birds. Here I'd laugh, with the air of an ancient man who's found peace at last in simple things. This wouldn't satisfy her at all. I'd accepted the caricature much too willingly. It wasn't an OAP's house at all. Her eyes began to show blue, like a sky in a poor August.

No. She bet it was a fantastic house, exquisite: I had my own designer. I was wise to what she was up to here: implying certain things about the sort of people who have their own designers, in order to provoke certain disclosures. *We got Clive Jackson in to do the whole lot. He's actually a friend!* 'We' being the critical term. The truth would still do here. My house was by no means fantastic. Oh yes it was. With a painting by Renoir − a peculiar fancy of hers this − a painting by Renoir my aunt had got me for my twenty-first birthday. She touched me on the arm. She was implying now something about the kind of men who have rich aunts. What might this be? I played along for a while, exploiting the implication; then said with a laugh that seriously, I had no paintings, or aunts for that matter. I had nothing but books, a calendar of showdogs for 1982 on the wall of the boxroom, a barometer and some thimbles. Since she couldn't be sure whether this were a camp profession of domesticity, a strange index of genuine asceticism or merely a pitiable fact, here was a truth she elected to ignore (and hence a successful dodge). Instead she bet outrageously that I kept my poor friends at arm's length (and regularly had housefuls of public schoolboys and glamour chums taking drugs and having a right royal knees-up). I continued in the way of truth: no one ever came to see me; my house was a shell, a place of drought, a museum to old age.

She pounced. Let her and Ian come up one weekend and help me decorate! It would turn my life around. I explained that I couldn't. Not without permission. Whose permission? My landlord's. She had difficulty accepting this. Still renting accommodation at my age, in my position? Her eyes broke into full blue. The truth was dawning! These excuses I made about my house – what it all boiled down to was that I did not live on my own. She'd suddenly realised! That was the reason. How silly of her, to take so long. Now she understood! That was why I never asked them round. Wasn't that so? She nudged me in what she took to be a man-to-man fashion. I had here a tactical dodge that took the form of charging straight at my opponent. Actually she was right! That was it exactly. She'd got me! This tactic induced her to scatter temporarily. She went home on her own soon after, leaving me and Ian drinking.

Another time we were all out together, she'd made up her mind to interpret that tactic just described as an admission. But why had I been so secretive? I said I'd been secretive in order to create an atmosphere of mystery around nothing, my domestic void. It was a pathetic dodge, that was all. I lived with no one but my own shadow. Her eyes greyed over; she was sad for me, so sad… ah she saw through it! I was down on myself way too easily here. 'Pathetic dodge' her foot! That was very crafty. Not only was there someone else: they must be very special indeed for me to be so secretive – very special, or extremely ugly. Ha ha ha: the second alternative seemed to amuse her greatly. Perhaps she'd gone too far though. She lowered her eyes. What if it was true? Say I'd married a woman with a false leg out of charity. Now she'd been extremely hurtful. Ta-ran-ta-ra. My signal to charge. I had a most repulsive lover. I confessed. Looked like a sumo wrestler crossed with Liaqat Bromley, the prize-winning magic realist. Weighed in at 287lb. She didn't laugh. She was tantalised: why would I say a thing like that unless I were really covering up a much better truth? Genuine modesty, or some such – that was what we had here. She was greedy for the truth about me, but for some reason, it had to be splendid in the love department. Ian evidently told her nothing. Or told her everything... It didn't matter. It was only a game we used to play.

She could be shrewder. What had I been doing since I last saw them? Had I spent all the time on my own? It made her sad to think that, my being all on my own in the pensioners' house, night after night. Now I couldn't admit to drinking, reading, howling at the TV, beating up the newspaper, talking to myself, talking about myself, imagining audiences, praying, writing down prayers and burning them quick in the sink in case I died without warning of an MI or sub-arachnoid haemorrhage and they were found on the table then scrutinised at the inquest, and scrutinised after the inquest in a quiet tea shop by those who loved me. (*We just had no idea he was so religious.*) I couldn't admit to any of these practices, the truth having no game value when it wasn't also a dodge. There was no sport in just telling the truth, as we probably knew.

Thus I had to suggest that I got up to things that she'd not care to know about; I did this in such a way as to put a bar on her imagination. I was subtle; I named no one, mentioned no places. Now she was caught, she was in a dilemma: would she prefer the pathetic truth about me, or the sordid, nay disgusting, truth? This was an effective dodge.

'Twas on the good ship Venus!' I helped myself to another strongish grog with a pipkin of water. I was adept when it came to dodging Laura. Lord save me, maybe I was even wondering if I got her hot, when down came fear like a sparrowhawk on a garden pigeon. She'd been phoning because she was frightened. She'd received warnings, hints. Now it was too late.

In a small room meant for bar staff to lodge in like that brazen angel Chantal, Laura was being roasted by the fiends from Ian's local, taking turns with her while they went back and forth to the golf game. Tiny room above the bar, no window but for a skylight, stinking of feet, cock, stale biscuit. Day after day they've watched her passing, scratching their groins. She's felt it coming, felt their eyes on her. The note she left written under duress. That was easy. Just wait for Ian to leave Monday morning then buzz the door: they're from Camden Council about a mouse infestation. She'd open up like a shot. Poor Laura. Knife at her kidneys while they dictate, long thin blade, a scaling knife. Just put what we say, sweetheart. *You've gone away for a while. You want to have a think about things.* Rab wouldn't bat an eyelid when they took her up. No more humanity than an *Einsatzkommando*, on a Ukraine killing spree. Mary can't climb the stairs on account of her heart. No idea what's happening in that little room. No wonder they've been buying us pints. They are laughing themselves silly. *She's gone of her own accord hasn't she?* Own accord? She's been taken... God gimme one more. Small house double and a pipkin. Thank you Ma'am. There was a thought too terrible came next: my friend was in on it.

Then I saw her down a drain or ventilation shaft. Torch shone in her face to check her, morning and night. No facilities; Christ, no facilities. Like an heiress taken when I was a boy, by a hooded man who left a peculiar note... Except this wasn't ransom, but revenge.

Why had we never reckoned with Señor Norbert? Because he was just a solid Spanish lad in a check shirt that Ian had run rings around when he was feeling like Napoleon? Yeah, feeling like Napoleon and desirous of consequences? Well this was one consequence he never reckoned with, wasn't it? That Norbert would come back for her a decade later. *Revenge is a dish best served cold.* An old Spanish proverb. And by Christ it was true. Those cruel tales from the days when the English were first starting to go abroad, what did they say? Beware the pride of the Spaniard! The Spaniard would tear his own heart out and put it on a barbecue next to yours like a 'rasher' if you challenged him. If it happened you gave his mistress a present in a hot plaza, be sure that you kept her well locked up once she crossed the sea to your bed, because the day would come when he returned for her. But he'd wait until you'd forgotten the offence you'd caused him. This was the special pleasure that he took in his revenge, the long wait.

Unless – I had to have a last one, this time with an aliquot of water – unless she had gone to him, of her own accord. Once I thought Señor Norbert might have looked like me; there the similarity ended. Must have been some kind of man. Must have seen something in him in the first place, which she never let on about. That's a woman's tact. Ten years she keeps it quiet while Ian dries up on her, and hey presto! – she's out of there. That's a woman's Napoleonics, knows exactly when to make the decisive move. She's gone out to him. Gone back to the sun. My friend can sit and shrivel on his own now. I'll show the silly fucker how it is done.

If only I'd answered the phone. Maybe she wanted me to help her to the airport.

I took 200mg of Tramadol, against the pain of thinking about her. What was left of the night I spent dreaming without sleep of the time she asked me swimming. She went every Monday. Would I like to join her, a smoker like me, for heart health? I said no, out of shame – and also propriety. Ian didn't go along for heart health; it was quite out of order for me to. What next! (He'd given up smoking by this time, but that was distinctly beside the point.) I found her question so vulgar, so forward, so naïve, it knocked the wind out of me. My excuse was I couldn't swim. It was genuine. Oh, she'd show me! Fucking hell. What would this involve? What kind of grips, or hands-on? No no. I really couldn't. Thanks for the invitation though, Laura. With good conscience I denied her.

Carpe diem! Soon after I bought a swimming book.

Standing up, then lying on the carpet, I practised the breaststroke. I hoped she'd do the breaststroke. I'd go behind her and have a good look with the use of some Olympic-standard non-mist goggles I'd seen in John Lewis's. Four weeks I practised, down on the carpet; I gave it a week to focus myself, then on the sixth week went along to the pool she'd nominated, six o'clock on a Monday evening. By 6.25, I'd been offered advice, looked after, and examined sternly by an Australian lifeguard and his Serbian sidekick who'd evidently been putting in some time at grinning classes. Like this with the legs, mate! Did mate need any help? What the fuck was mate actually trying to do? At the poolside, swimmers had climbed out to point at my dark thrashings. The Serb went over to concede them justice. Others were clustered at the shallow end, arms folded. Of Laura there was no sign, though my Olympic goggles weren't up to much. Somebody seemed to have been frying bacon on the lenses. I gave up, I left the pool, hating those swimmers like a terrorist. But there are some things you just can't learn from books.

That, however, was not the end of it. For some reason, she'd selected a leisure centre popular with gay men. A horrid old fruit whose obituary would probably mention he'd been to Winchester, followed by service in the Guards and a career as a planter grinned at me in the shower and tugged his piece like the bell-rope for ordering tea. As I was dressing, he sauntered up to me with his towel over his shoulder and murmured, 'So sorry if I embarrassed you in there, but I was delighted to see your cock!'

Surely it wasn't in Laura to play a trick on me? I never asked. Of course I didn't. I never disclosed a thing about this pitiable night. Nothing.

Friday

'You haven't just done a ward round smelling like that have you?'

I found myself replying to Melania in the manner of an owl. Listen. This was the noise Dr Johnson made – let her look at me gone out – this was the noise of Johnson absorbed in an aesthetic object, let us say a book upon a table in the corner of the room or a painting, oblivious of those around him. *Tu tu tu tu.* Whereas your *Owlspiegel* was a mischievous clowning hero of German folklore in the sixteenth century or earlier. Let her look at me gone out. But he was still around, your *Owlspiegel*, different in his outer form but underneath the same. Perhaps we all knew one! Let her shake her head, goddamn it. In a tight purple dress with a low neck and mysterious pattern of black web-like circles, she resembled a Sixties heroine (cult); yet her head was modern-savaaage. The Sixties head was a sleek head.

'What the hell are you talking about?'

Ha ha. We hadn't touched on Dr Johnson yet had we?… I'd been reading Boswell's *Life of Samuel Johnson* in the khazi this morning to cheer myself up. Everything he wrote Boswell wrote with a hangover; but he couldn't half cut it.

'When haven't we touched on Dr Johnson?'

We hadn't touched on Dr Johnson in our lunchtime conversations on neurology and Western culture.

'Did you get my e-mail?'

I felt sure I hadn't received her electronic mail, I was afraid to say.

She shook her head and came to straighten my tie; while she was at it she brushed lint off my shoulder – a sign a woman's hot on you. I'd read about it in a magazine while I was waiting to get my hair cut. What if I stuck my tongue in her mouth? She was a mother and wife. My dick stirred, a deep-sea vegetable in a beam of passing light. She fancied me, didn't she?

'You're disinhibited too!' she cried, recoiling. 'God what's happening to you? Listen,' she gave me a BBC-drama kind of look: 'I've arranged for us to have lunch.'

Excellent.

As it happened, the arrangement wasn't altogether excellent since we were to have lunch in the Brahma Centre (unlicensed) along with Ulrich Uhlmann. I'd been hoping to get some more opinions on Laura from Melania. Melania, however, was dedicated to making me talk to Ulrich about our paper on Friedrich Nietzsche and FTDs. Her efforts to set me on the straight and narrow were so obvious, so contaminated with the spirit of daytime TV and talk-show 'intervention', that they provoked me to new excesses. Extending my right leg to the limit, bringing the left up to follow, I called to her to watch me. I was in carnival spirits, hardly knew myself. When I turned she was yards away, shaking her head and murmuring something about what they were doing to you.

But this was how Dr Johnson had walked! As witnessed

by James Boswell when they visited the West Country. All the way down the A354 Johnson walked in precisely this manner. Let her watch me again. Here was another: a move which called to mind a Seventies impressionist taking off Ted Heath doing the twist during the Three-Day Week. By now she was gaping, somewhat nauseously. Or was this extravaganza turning her on? Hogarth – she'd heard of Hogarth: he painted lives and marriages going to ruin – Hogarth had seen Johnson rolling himself like this in Samuel Richardson's house. They were all chums in those days. Richardson wrote books about chronic virgins. Anyway, Hogarth thought, listen, it must be the village idiot rolling himself in the corner. Johnson's face was in shadow at the time. Hogarth did not realise he was in the presence of the great Doctor, *Dictionary* Johnson!

'You're still drunk!' she called across to me. We might have been standing either side of a marsh.

No no no no! I was asking her to make an historical diagnosis. What was up with Dr Johnson?

'You're avoiding the issue.' Firmly she closed her eyes. 'They're destroying you!'

Let her not be blaming them. I'd always been like this.

'You have not!'

She didn't know what was wrong with Dr Johnson, but she thought she knew what was up with me... Why didn't she open her eyes? She looked like she was waiting for a present.

At this point, Ulrich Uhlmann came along the corridor with his watchful saunter and a cry of, 'On your way to reception? Wonderful!' He had with him a big-breasted geneticist, Ella Charalambous. Ella was a full foot shorter than Ulrich even in heeled boots. Melania, who'd been planning to lose her temper with me, now had to throb in irritable peace.

'Hello, you two! I was just asking Dr Morgan for a diagnosis of Dr Johnson,' I announced heartily.

'Ah – this is interesting – yes!' Ulrich nodded, arms folded. 'Sunday I am visiting the Johnson House in Gough Court.'

'Really, Ul? Next Sunday?'

'No! Many Sundays.'

'Ah – I see. I misunderstood the German use of the progressive tense!' Ulrich laughed and I nodded at Melania to show who was the boss where grammar was concerned.

'Next Sunday,' Ulrich inclined his head in naughty benevolence, 'I will take Ella. To see the gout chair of Dr Johnson.'

'Ella hasn't been yet?' I winked at Ella Charalambous who blinked gladly, hands crammed in her coat pockets; their secret was out. 'Watch this everyone!' I performed the walk of the stretched leg. 'This is how Dr Johnson used to walk.'

'Really!' Ella called. 'Did he wear a bowler hat?'

'No. He was wearing a wig,' Ulrich informed her accurately.

'And Dr Morgan here is unable to make a diagnosis from the evidence of Dr Johnson's gait.' They were now standing apart from me in a little group; Melania'd swept her barbaric hair from her forehead in chagrin. Behind them a cleaner and a receptionist appeared to be filming the performance covertly on a mobile phone.

'Oh I am surprised to hear this!' Ulrich raised his head like a cock. 'Surely we are seeing a Tourette's case – hm?'

'Of course,' Melania said. '*Obviously.*'

'We should add him to our club,' Ulrich said lankily at ease. 'Yes? Dr Johnson and Professor Nietzsche.'

'Yes!' Melania saw her opportunity to encourage the possibility of more sober work for me. 'Definitely.'

'Why don't we all go to lunch and talk it over?'

'To the Brahma Centre?' Ulrich wondered.

'Oh I think we'll go to The Lamb shan't we?' Melania shook her head at me significantly. 'Yes. Dr Morgan is shy about being seen there. It'll be all right though. Come on everybody!'

'TGIF!' Ella Charalambous glimmered as they fell into step behind me.

As we passed the garden, Melania set up a hard murmuring to my left. I was to tell Ulrich she'd spoken to Dick Cleveland. She'd known him at Cambridge. Dick was editing a book on neuroscience and philosophy. He had space for an essay by me and Ulrich. The deadline was 28th November. Dick was expecting to hear from me this afternoon. I said Dick most certainly would, but now I wanted to ask Ella and Ulrich, who were gladly holding hands to my right, a scientific question about degrees of kidnapping and the normative range.

'Don't answer him for God's sake!' Melania snapped. 'He's just fixating on his friend's wife again.'

Hm hm hm. We were all squashed round one of those brass-rimmed barrels in The Lamb, the four of us. Willy-nilly, I was consuming a pie while Ella Charalambous shared Ulrich's high-stacked burger. Temporarily I was somewhat fuzzy. Melania had a glass of tap water with lime, and appeared to be in a kind of fury. I couldn't see why the hell she didn't just go, instead of sitting there and trying to give me a dead leg. I tried to advise her that I had to see this thing through, which made her hiss while Ella and Ulrich kissed each other frankly. Softly, precisely, the kisses clicked, Cupid having magicked away the burger debris. He tickled her, she tickled him back, Melania tutting beneath her hisses, a moralistic Medusa. As I slid my first pint down, however, she became solicitous, watching, I had little doubt, for signs of reactivation of the overproof rum I'd been drinking in the small hours. She cared too much. Like the mother of a baby with manifest gripe, she half-tried to feed me a forkful of my lunch, which gastritis was making it hard to get down the hatch. Her mood having become gentler, I seized the opportunity to return to the topic I'd brought up on the way.

'So you were asking,' Ulrich hummed, 'how was it? – about non-traditional types of kidnapping?'

'That's right, Ul!' I lit up. Melania wasn't having a cig today.

'Hm. This is a kind of paradox?'

'Oh it is no paradox!' Ella said gravely. We were as tight around the barrel as if we'd gathered for a session of table turning, or ouija board. My smoke twisted and rose above our heads in thickening streams of white-blue. For example there was Scientology. Her cousin had been taken by the Scientologists, but they did not imprison her. What they did – Ella turned her hot-coffee eyes around the three of us – was persuade her. Lucky Ulrich thought I to myself. She gave them £6000 in de-radiation fees. What on earth for? Because she'd been persuaded she was infected with alien radiation. It was her monitor who told her this. She was quite free not to give the money, but she believed her monitor.

'What's the matter?' Melania asked me. I hadn't thought of cults. That was the matter. A barmaid removed my plate. The smashed pie crust looked like a farm outbuilding which had been demolished by a Tiger Tank with an 88mm gun, rolling up behind the broccoli. War on my plate. Cults. This might explain a great deal.

'Was your cousin abroad?' Ulrich enquired of his coffee-eyed lady.

'No. She was here. In Enfield.'

'Enfield?'

'Yes.' Ella watched me curiously. 'All the Greeks live there.'

'What's the matter now?' Melania demanded, moving back on her stool to examine me, arms folded in front of her diaphragm as a sort of plant-box for her tits, which were being suppressed by her mysterious dress. Enfield was the matter, being of course where Laura taught.

Say she'd been kidnapped voluntarily. It was what happened. Some of us have our books for help, others have their selves or the parish church; but a lot of people have nowhere to go when they run out of meaning except a foundation called 'I-Kala' or 'Helion' or some such. You see the adverts in respectable places, the tube, the classified pages of the *London Review of Books*. What they offer is a sort of three-card trick: mind-science, life-philosophy and spiritualism are the cards – except it's not a trick in the mind of anyone involved. Serious rubbish. Easy to laugh about, too easy... Maybe you'll go along yourself, when you run out of love.

'Was your cousin married at the time?' I asked Ella solemnly.

'Yes,' Ella nodded. 'But she was very unhappy.'

'I am not wanting you abducted, darling,' Ulrich stroked Ella's arm. 'Please phone me every hour. To let me know where you are. Yes?'

'I think I've got to go,' Melania said with a sort of tender misery. I'd been expecting an outburst after my question. 'Promise me you won't go down there again tonight.'

'Where?'

'You know where.'

'Ah, I may have to,' I said. 'You don't understand.'

'You think her cousin was a sucker?' Melania hissed and rose. On her way out, she murmured something to Ulrich, who promptly offered me another pint. By hook or by crook, she was going to get me doing this bloody essay on the philosopher and his madness.

Ha ha. What it did not take me very long to gather was this: she'd said something to Ulrich like, 'For God's sake keep him here! Don't let him back in this state.' Yeah all right. I saw it all. But I did not make Ulrich uncomfortable by letting him know. I let on I was unaware of the plot, as innocent as a baby or a lamb. It wasn't the first time I'd adopted that dodge. Let them practise on me. One of the high forms of cunning.

When Ella'd returned to her lab, we had some general talk about the neuroscience-literature question, skirting as if by agreement our special topic. Ulrich was a tough insister on data, methods, experiments – and refutations. 'Proust was wrong about memory!' he said, pointing at me with his tickling finger. He'd assumed a hard-arguing smile.

'Only if,' I replied, 'you try and say that Proust's descriptions of memory – and on either side of the argument hardly anyone goes beyond the fucking cake on page 49 out of 2,400 anyway – only if you try and say the descriptions actually intuit organic theorems about brain sites.'

'About the hippocampus, wrong!' Ulrich karate-chopped slowly the air, arresting the slice of his right hand half a foot above the barrel top, as if time were stopping.

'Yes,' I said, 'but Proust doesn't theorise *about* long-term memory sites. He just provides wonderfully rich descriptions of memory as *the* world-producing activity.'

'Meaning?'

'Memory paints the scenery, it gives everyone their lines. It's like Michelangelo crossed with Shakespeare. It says "This is how it was" and you open the box and there it is. There's no first time, until memory gives you a present.'

'All very well for *inactive* persons,' Ulrich grinned. 'Some of us like to *get in amongst it* as you say' (here attempting a Cockney accent) 'from the beginning.'

'It's not just memory,' I said, wondering if he was having a go. Of course, he'd be looking forward to getting in amongst it with Ella and her coffee eyes this evening – not just remembering it. 'With Proust you get these descriptions of consciousness – I mean if he was writing about you and me here now, he'd have this brass rim round the top of the barrel, he'd have one of us noticing a movement of light or reflection in the brass that coincided with an emotional shift; that darkening of beer on the wood where I knocked my pint when you brought me it – he'd have some focus on the way that's gone from shiny to matt even at the same time as we'd be disputing the difference between noticing spills and their meniscus in a scientific way as opposed to an artist's way or a housewife's way; he would have some sort of vibration from a word or sign that meant something to one of us and led to a new topic that drew out something that had been lying in wait to – to *be* drawn out... like,' I looked around for a likely example of a word, or sign, 'like the board there.' I indicated the wide, shallow blackboard above the lintel to the No Smoking area, with its bill of fare in script of Gothic chalk. 'The name of the pie I had.'

'The "1649 Pie"?' Ulrich said. He was digging me now. He knew I wasn't as pissed as rumour'd been having it.

Yeah.

By the way, what did it mean – *1649*?

I didn't know. The Lamb had an excellent policy against the overdescription of food... Maybe it was a Republican pie.

Of course. Ulrich gave me a drollish look. We had held a king-killing that year. What a great year for Great Britain!

What a disaster for Germany! What a stinker! How they had envied us.

Why?

Because at the same time we had taken control of ourselves and our politics, they had gone under. Total passivity. Two hundred years of it. No – *more* than two hundred years. We had said, Listen, no king, prince, foreign power, is telling us what to do OK? For Germany, the total opposite... I knew the Thirty Years War, yes?

Yeah.

He watched me with a belligerent doubtful movement of his head, a cockerel seeing the farm dog coming its way. 'Thirty years of massacres.' He took a firm sip of his beer. Many foreign powers kicking ass. Swedes, Spanish, French, Austrians, mercenaries, Scotch. On top of a civil war. Where did that remind you of in the present day? Imperial Germans fighting Lutherans. Where did that remind you of?... So, Ulrich came from a village thirty kilometres west of the Elbe, OK? Other side of the Elbe, Magdeburg. Lutheran population. They were waiting for the Swedes to arrive. Johann von Tilly, Catholic, meant to be a spiritual guy – he let his men loose on Magdeburg, April 1631. Burned the children, raped the women, slaughtered the males: population of 30,000; 5,000 survived. The survivors they kept as sex slaves. All over Germany this was happening. Three *decades*... What did people know the Swedes for nowadays?

Abba. High taxes. Social justice. Nobel Prize.

He nodded. Check this. The Swedes burned out 18,000 Catholic villages in Bohemian Germany. In eighteen *years*.

Which averaged twenty villages per week, the women

raped and abducted, the men mutilated and hacked: the table overturned where the woman was forced, the pot spilled, thatch crackling. You thought it was the *Wehrmacht*, the SS, the *Einsatzgruppen* and the *Feld Polizei* who were the atrocity specialists. Belarus, Ukraine...

Population of Germany had been reduced by 30% by the war's end, Ulrich went on. And when it was over, the victors had kept control of all ports and trade routes. Also, they had dispermitted Germany to become a unified political nation.

And so, I thought, they took it out on the twentieth century.

'This is why we had for so long our peculiar attitude,' Ulrich explained. By now his chin was in his hand, our glasses empty. He got me another drink.

Which attitude did he mean?

The same attitude I had.

And what was that?

Oh, the attitude that it was much better, much *truer*, to suffer as yourself than be happy in the way everyone else was.

I was offended by this Kraut; I was also somewhat impressed.

Ulrich laughed: 'You are too German, ja! Long past, short future! Terribly short!'

'What about you?' Even as I asked, I was thinking of Thomas Mann's identification of that bestial opera the Third Reich with the composer Leverkühn, modelled on Nietzsche, who made sure he contracted syphilis at a brothel visit. Leverkühn didn't want too much future. Wanted just enough to achieve an unloving perfection in his art. The devil guaranteed him the time. Exactly the span between Hitler's becoming party leader, and his death. Exactly the span allowed Doctor Faustus, in every version. Uncanny… But was this anything like my problem? Of course not. I was no artist.

'I, my friend, am a neuroscientist. I am European. I am just a bloke.'

I patted his arm. Strange how many opinions of myself I was hearing these days. Maybe things were coming to a head. We talked a while longer but Ulrich didn't want any more beer. He was a reasonable man.

Anyway, the upshot of all this was that having lined my stomach at lunch, I arrived at Ian's early, a kid who's been told he doesn't have to sit down to tea tonight.

★★★

I had a feeling I might have surprised him. Indeed I'd said last night I'd try and come over from work around seven, but it wasn't yet five o'clock when I pressed the buzzer. The green door had not been secured so I walked down the passage to the black door of the flat, which he opened as if he'd been waiting for me anyway, conducting me along the short hallway and into the living room. On the coffee table, a buff notebook was lying closed on some sheets of lined A4 paper.

'I've been writing,' he said behind me. He'd also been drinking coffee.

'Ah.' Turning I touched him on the shoulder significantly. In such a book he'd been writing when

Laura came into his life that foggy afternoon. Now she'd gone, he was expressing himself, copiously. Tactfully, I kept my eyes from the writing on the paper; it was a script of pale blue biro with scimitar-shaped strokes at the ends of words that curved back to cover the letters as if a breeze were blowing against them. There was a charged feeling about the flat, as if a record one had long been waiting to hear had been taken from its sleeve.

'Let's get a drink, man,' he said, watching me.

I ought to moralise with him about the ethics of the clientele in his local – this I knew; on the way over, I'd almost resolved to do it, the atrocity pictures I'd received in my talk with Ulrich Uhlmann about the Thirty Years War having filled me with the necessary severity. But now I was here, in his fair and vigilant presence, I felt bound to acknowledge there might be at least as much evil in my imagination as anywhere else in this particular neighbourhood. The images of Laura I'd beheld last night in that small room were more evidence against me, as was an unmentionable thought I'd entertained about him. I would not moralise with him today.

'Don't you want to sit down for a bit?' The charged feeling of the place late this afternoon, the sensation of presence in the dark narrow flat, was attractive; perhaps Ian had been conjuring with a benevolent spirit. I went to the window. Across the cobbled mews in the first-floor office, the creative types were knocking off, laughing, inspecting their mobile phones. I thought one of them, a Slavic looker with a black symmetrical bob, waved at me and smiled, but inevitably her eyeline was to my left, as if connected to another window. 'Don't burn your brains too much tonight, darling,' I said to myself. 'Have some regard for your liver.' If anything, it was a prayer for her.

I asked Ian what time he'd got in as he led me down the hall past the bedroom and the doorless kitchen. He'd taken the afternoon off. I was inclined to enquire if there'd been any particular reason, but felt this wouldn't have been playing the game; besides, something was distracting me. He lifted a sailor's jacket with silver buttons that he wears now and then from the mass of the coat-rack. What had made him choose this tonight, with its connotations of a 'spree'?

A wide, labile mood in which fuzziness alternated with ripples of intensity was carrying me, a mood as shallow as an old river, with snaky, shining movements at its surface. I'd been going a while now, I could deal with anything. Either it sank into darkness, or twisted on the surface and was gone. Thus I absorbed the lapses of the day, the freaks and unwrapped conversations.

'How's the sausage trade?' I asked Rab as he filled our glasses.

'All right.'

'What flavour d'you get asked for most?'

'Pork mainly.'

'Punters somewhat unadventurous?'

'You taking a rise out of me, son?'

'Certainly not.'

'It's nae my fucking idea anyway.'

'One of these fools in marketing is it?'

'I would think so. Five fifty.'

'Here you are!'

If I'd been a young British artist, I'd have carved Rab's

head on a wall, removed the wall from the building of which it formed a part, and entered it for the Turner Prize as a parody of Mount Rushmore, I told Ian as I sat down with the drinks. He'd been watching the window behind me with the look of the Cardinal's secretary; he laughed in appreciation. His laugh was a breeze on water. If we could get through this weekend, there would at least be no more to get through; she had taken only a week off. In a fit of bravado I cried, 'It's Friday, it's five to five… and it's—'

'Crackerjack!'

Behind me, a middle-aged blonde with fine bones and D&G spectacles was looking up from a book. She had the appearance of a girlfriend of the Rolling Stones, or some other legendary minstrels; until her eyes met yours. 'You're old-school, dear!' she laughed. Her smile had warmth, but the eyes remained steadily on me. There was an ocular fixity something like this in early supra-nuclear palsy; but here I detected no pathology. The gaze was an effect of will. It had a sort of 'I-can-stare-longer-than-you' power to it, which it might be silly to compete with if you weren't particularly bothered about such things, or dangerous if you were.

'Yeah,' I said. 'I reckon I must be!' She laughed again. Since I was more or less looking over my shoulder, the option now was to return to face Ian, or shift my chair backwards to include her within my world. Which was what I did, since it would have been tight-souled to leave it at that; I moved so I could see her too, and her book. I was old-school and shallow and labile (as well as being too German). I wanted her in.

What was she reading?

She lifted the book from the table to show me, in another gesture that I half-remembered from the TV of the past. Ah, I said, that was OK that book – not wanting to get too heavy on details of literature with a stranger with a steady gaze. Was she enjoying it? Yes she was, as a matter of fact. She was reading it for her A-level course. Her voice was husky, low, rather taut. She smoked B&H, and she exhaled precious little.

Now regarding this encounter my man Ian, sitting there in his sailor's jacket, was comporting himself in something like the manner we have noted of old, which is to say he was attending to it in a reserved, though not neutral, way; and it did occur to me that he might have invited Irene along this evening as a sort of surprise – this here being Irene (52) who loved it. The surprise being that she and I were going to hit it off very pleasantly before introductions were made, when I'd not be in a position to disapprove with proper vehemence. She'd been in the flat when I arrived of course, this being why the bedroom door was shut. He was compromising me viciously. Unless he was doing me the honour of making me first *confidant* of his new life; and Laura was never coming back. Beyond the window that looked onto the side street, the Remand Hero's second was tearing into a kebab.

'Your friend's quiet!' the woman laughed. *Call My Bluff!* was the programme she'd reminded me of when she held her book up to show the title. The BBC's finest moment.

'Oh,' I said expansively, 'he's soberer than me.'

'Is he all right?'

Evidently this was *not* Irene. On the whole I was glad.

'It's been a difficult week,' I informed her. I was now so placed in my chair that, like a pub bore, I had command over the attention of the pair of them.

'Now why would that be?' the woman asked. She was drinking a half of Guinness and blackcurrant. I felt disinclined to give a flip answer, because of the impression she gave of driving the question straight at me. It was the spectacles that did this, supercharging her gaze. Nor did I want to set forth the truth, since it was hardly my business. The second balled his wrapper, tossed it onto the road and rushed in through the side door to the golf game.

'Ah it's a bit complicated,' I said.

'Well don't say more than you want to, dear,' she replied. It wasn't easy for her to return to her book, now I'd assumed this commanding position. 'It's obviously been a hard week for the both of you.' She smiled sweetly; she wanted us to be OK with her. She must know what her eyes could do. 'I suppose she's run off to the gypsies – not yours, dear. His.' She nodded Ian's way.

'That's right,' Ian said. He wasn't fazed. He was going to be up to this.

'More bothered than you look aren't you?'

Ian laughed: 'That's easy!'

'What wouldn't be easy?' the woman said.

'If you could tell us something that wasn't just a fair guess.'

'Oho!' The woman stubbed out her cigarette with a crushing motion of her forefinger. 'Now you're putting it on me! What's your name, my friend?'

He told her his name, and I told her mine then she told us hers. It was Joan Hunter. 'You won't have heard of me,' she advised us. 'That's no matter.' A modest enough introduction, though of course it had the effect of setting the memory to work, just in case you had. And her gaze disinclined you to say, 'You're quite right, sweetheart, I have never heard of you!' Maybe she'd been one of the schoolkids who climbed on stage in *Crackerjack!* circa 1967. Maybe she'd been married to Keith Moon for an afternoon, or she'd done a thing that was news in the times before celebrities were as numerous as they are nowadays. You could have heard of her, that was what she meant.

'And I will tell you something, if you fancy,' Joan Hunter said. 'That's up to you, my friend.'

'What d'you think, man?' Ian asked me. 'Do we want to know something?'

We did, of course. But did we want to know it here and now? I felt that to say yes would mark me out as a superstitious mutt, a mere hoping boy; while to say no would indicate a lack of faith, a lack of care about Laura. Our glasses were empty, which did not help.

'I'll get us all a drink,' Ian said, 'while you're deciding.' As he rose, I noticed that the buttons on his sailor's jacket were embossed with a lion's head.

'I haven't seen one like that since the 1970s,' Joan observed to me.

'What's that?'

'His jacket. I wonder where he had that from?'

'You used to be able to get ones like that from Wakefields,' I said with a pleasant feeling. 'When I was a kid. Army and navy surplus.'

'I'll bet you couldn't!' Joan Hunter laughed. 'Not

exactly like that – with lion buttons. I knew one fella had such a jacket, but he never bought it from any army surplus.'

'Where did he get it?'

'He had it off a French sailor that was dying... Nice in here isn't it?' She looked round.

'Yeah. Quite nice,' I said obediently. 'Haven't seen you here before, Joan.'

'Oh this isn't my backyard, Mark.'

'Ah.'

Ian returned with the drinks and Joan Hunter said, 'Can I ask you to do something for me, Ian?' He stood over her in his jacket, a Nordic sailor, fair-bearded. 'Can you go and get me something of hers?'

'What like, Joan?' Ian said evenly.

'Oh anything will do. Providing she's been near to it lately. Will it take you long?'

'No,' Ian told her. 'I only live over the road.'

'Off you go then.' And he was out of there, as if this had all been ordained by some regional god of Fridays. 'Now you know who you remind me of?' Joan said, cruising her eyes at me.

'No I don't.'

'Anthony Hopkins!' She laughed. 'In a film called *When Eight Bells Toll*. Remember that one, Mark?'

'Funnily enough,' I said, 'I think I do. Wasn't he a sort of secret service diver?' In fact, I remembered it pretty well. Remembered the book too, because it opened with a line about the difference between being shot by a .45 revolver and an automatic weapon. The revolver bullet tore a hole the size of a grapefruit in you, whereas the automatic –

well all you did was say 'Damn', light a cigarette, pull out your own piece and blow your assailant to kingdom come.

'He was gorgeous in that,' Joan said. The gaze that better not be responded to had changed into a tone of voice that wasn't to be disputed with, unless you really fancied yourself as an opinionated sonofabitch.

'It was a long time ago,' I said. 'Thirty years or more.'

'I would think you're right. Early Seventies. He had this blue-black hair. About your height.' I laughed and looked out into the street. 'He was from South Wales though, Anthony Hopkins,' Joan continued.

'Yeah.' I was hoping Ian wouldn't take too long. Her smiles and comparisons were making me uncomfortable. She had a ring of white metal with a red stone that had a sort of dull hot glow like a tiny coal.

'Trying to work out where you are from,' she said with a strange affectionate girly oscillation of her head, and hummed to herself. 'Where you are from, and why you are in this state.'

Ian came back with something in his hand and dropping it in front of her asked if this would do.

Joan Hunter looked up at him to see what sort of wiseguy my friend Ian was being. I wished to God he'd brought something else. A pen or something, or a necklace. 'There'll be more trace on those – than anything else,' Ian pointed out.

'I daresay.' She was still staring at him. I was as hot as the stone in her white ring. Hot with shame. *She's been in there* – I was hot with that thought too. I lit a cigarette. It tasted of malt. I could hear my heart beat now and then like a lewd but bashful reptile, down among the original slime. I wanted them. Wanted to kill my senses with them, slay and cram my senses. Then I'd happily dissolve into the air.

'Cunts come in different forms don't they, Ian?' Joan Hunter was saying, with a hint of the Noel Cowards. 'Natural, and self-made.' Making a quiet horsey sound through his nose, Ian took his seat, while Joan placed her right hand upon the pale blue lace. She'd taken off her jacket to reveal a blouse by Anne Fontaine. She had some class, did our psychic.

Her breast heaved once under the white silk as she sat with eyes closed. It was horrible, daft and horrible. What the hell was going on behind the lids? Were the irises as red as suns? My own body was trembling. Behind the bar Mary was watching us curiously. Only Ian seemed himself. Sweat was on Joan's hairline. The fingers of the right hand were pressing down on the skyey lace in her cigarette-stubbing gesture. She could have been trying to dislodge an eyeball. At last she emitted a grunt.

'What do you reckon then?' Ian said.

'Give me a chance!' She took a good slurp of her stout and black. Her eyes for a moment had lost focus. 'Light my cigarette,' she said to me. 'Thank you, dear... The pictures I get, they're all melted up with smells and what have you. Like dreams. Or sometimes it's a vibration in me, then it turns into words, or a message.' She waved her smoke away in annoyance. 'She's gone from the city. OK?'

'Where to?' Ian asked, his face composed, horn white.

'My feeling is she's gone to Whitby,' Joan said huskily.

Ian said 'Whitby' to himself... Was this the knowledge he wanted?

'Will she come back?' I enquired thickly.

'Now that is properly your friend's question, dear!' Joan warned me.

'Yeah,' Ian said. 'How does it stand?'

'Ask what he asked!' Joan told him with a hard crack in her voice. 'Ask exactly!'

'Will she come back?'

'That depends. Depends who fetches her!' Joan laughed, not for joy. 'That's all I'm telling you. Frankly I don't know any more. There you are. Take it or leave it.' She finished her drink and stood up, and alongside her on her right, our good old friend the Remand Hero was coming along like a truck.

★★★

Carrying all pints at once, he was eager to get back to the game. Under his eyeline Joan stood on the hard-shoulder.

'Excuse me, my friend!' she called amiably enough. 'You're spilling beer.' The Remand Hero goggled down at her, at the piss-yellow lager on her sleeve. 'My best blouse this is,' she added patiently. And no doubt because he had every right in the world in this particular situation, in this pub of all pubs, like total usufruct, not the tiniest chink in his armour, and Joan was not above five three in height, the hero of one week in Wandsworth for VAT fraud told her to fuck herself and drove on his way.

Whereupon our Joan, who couldn't have weighed more than 125lbs, picked up two-handed the stool she'd recently been sitting on and swung it with a motion in which blonde athleticism and femininity were uncannily fused, such that it whacked with the deep thud of axe on wood the upper spinal column of the Remand Hero and down he went with a crack and pop of glasses from the table he took with him.

I didn't see a thing, but with a tautening of the guts I remembered it instantly. I was thrilled for our team and star striker. I wanted some of that myself, wanted to crack an enemy with furniture; until the counter-thrill ran through me. He wasn't moving well. If that blow had dislodged a vertebra into the spinal cord, she'd have paralysed him. Joan was standing with her hands on her hips, steady as you please. 'Went down like a Soap Sam!' she said in a strange music-hall tone of banter and connoisseurship. Ian laughed as if he'd heard that one before and hoped some time to hear it repeated.

Rolled to his side, the Remand Hero was being tended to. There was blood on his face and his shirt and upper legs were darkly sodden which I thought with horror meant he'd incised his own femoral artery with the glasses he was carrying. Joan was now regarding me, Ian too, with a kind of concern, as if I were a kid failing to enjoy a boisterous treat on a family outing to the seaside, and quite likely to puke any minute or burst into tears.

'He'll be all right, dear,' Joan told me. The recovery and accusation operation was proceeding before us, Rab crouching with two women drinkers and the Remand Hero's second, who was saying, 'Jerry, speak to me mate!' Jerry wallowed a bit longer then got himself up like a baby learning to sit and looked our way.

'Thought them lot was my mates,' he mumbled; and though he bet on the deaths of hostages, and regarded women with contempt, I pitied him. Maybe it was the way his trainers were sticking up like rabbit's ears from the ends of his cheapo jeans that made me so sad. Maybe it was because he had a name. Was there ever a softer-hearted sucker? By God, what was wrong with me?

Relentlessly now, Rab rose from his crouching position to tell us we were all barred for life.

'Come on then, lads,' Joan said to us and we filed out behind her from the silent pub. But at the door she turned and said huskily, 'I predict there'll be a death in this house within the week!' At the bar, Mary fingered the leather cigarette case on the chain around her neck and mouthed to me 'Goodbye'.

We followed Joan Hunter over to Ian's place. If we could get through this weekend, there'd be no more to get through. In a cold spasm the thought returned to mock me, as I reckoned how much weekend was still left and what else I may be up against. I was a talent-show Napoleon who had now to review his imaginary troops. Tee hee hee scream the judges before awarding the first ever *minus* score to this emperor of delusion. Joan was saying she'd be off, she'd caused us quite enough trouble; sorry and all that, but sometimes you had to show you weren't going to take that sort of disrespect from a geezer, specially one that was not much better than a Soap Sam. But Ian was pressing her in for a glass of rum in his sailor's jacket, and saying she'd done a big favour trying to tell us where Laura was. It seemed to me that it was the first time he had used her name all week, almost as if it should mean more to Joan than to me or himself. And Joan said, ah well, one for the road and that was kind of him.

As Ian removed the sheets of paper with the scimitar script of pale blue to make room for the rum bottle on the coffee table and set about pouring out the tots, I asked Joan Hunter when she'd first discovered she had this psychic knack. We were sitting beside each other on the leather settee. She'd had it as a kid. It wasn't that uncommon. There'd be rooms you knew someone had died in: you could feel it like a stuffiness or lack of oxygen, even if the windows were open. As if the dying had sucked all the air into them in their last breath. Her knee was almost resting on mine. Death created a sort of pressure drop in the room, a mustiness that stayed there. Her knee was now against mine. She had a way of finding lost things. It wasn't a matter of looking for them. They just turned up when she was doing something else. Something her mother had lost, her purse, the Green-Shield Stamps book, or what have you. Joan'd find it. One day in 1970, she was coming home from school and saw her mother at the bus stop on the Harrow Road. She shouted and waved but her mum was getting on the 52 that went west up to Kensal Rise. When she got home, her mum was in the kitchen with her hand on her side.

'That was her fetch I saw, you see,' Joan told us. 'When you see a fetch, it means the person's going to die. Well she was gone by Christmas. She'd had the pain for a year almost, but she'd told nobody. By the time she saw the consultant, it was too late. Much too late for her.'

'I'm sorry,' I said.

Joan laughed: 'It wasn't last week, dear!'

'But what happened to you?' Though I hardly knew her, I wanted there to have been someone to look after her.

'I ran wild, dear.'

'What did you do?' Over the way, Ian was skinning up some P-52, which I could foresee wasn't going to do me any good.

'I did everything, honey!' Joan laughed. 'Absolutely everything you could think of, I did it. Right along the range, good, bad, middling. I have been there.' Her knee and hard lower thigh touched mine. I hoped to God she wasn't coming on to me. 'I've sat on Copacabana Beach reading fortunes, dear. I've poured boiling water on a geezer's feet.'

'What was that for?'

'Because he was getting iffy. Pal of my dad's. He had acrylic socks on – waited till he took his shoes off. You scald someone in acrylic, they get the message in no uncertain terms. Cotton's different.'

'Bloody hell!' As Ian passed over the spliff, the smell melted in my mind with the hiss of boiling water on man-made fibre.

'Don't worry, dear. I'm not a maniac. Nowadays, a pizza and a good book'll do me nicely. That's all I ask for. That and a bit of respect.' She had a go on the spliff and passed it to me. 'One thing you've got to do in life, Mark – hear me?' I nodded. 'Got to back yourself.'

'I know,' I said thickly.

'Do you back yourself, dear?'

'Not exactly.'

'It's not a matter of right or wrong, honey. Nothing to do with good or bad. Either you back yourself, or you don't... Jesus Christ our Lord backed himself, yeah?'

'Sure.'

'So did Adolf Hitler. As do bank robbers; and the Prime Minister… Savvy?'

'Yeah.'

'You see, I personally am done with the active life. That's why when you came across me tonight, I was sitting quietly with a book. But I do know about backing myself.' I had another long hot rank draw. My lungs were cathedral capacity. 'And I fancy that is what you need to start doing, babe,' Joan went on. My chest cavity as wide, as black as the gallery in the Blue John mines we visited on a school trip. Peak District, June '78. Prime Minister Callaghan. A girl called Angie Alexander following me round. Pale, black hair, she looked about an eighth part African, something about her mouth, the tight curls in her hair, but she was paper pale. Why didn't I give her what she wanted in the dark caverns? Why?

'Where should I start?' I heard my voice in reverb. Over the way Ian sat on indifferently.

'I told you where she is!'

'Laura?' I looked at Ian in comradeship. With something not far from hostility, he looked back.

'Yes!' Joan said, with not much concern for Ian's look. 'Go get her, dear!'

'How?'

'Don't tell me you don't know how, honey!' Joan seemed to call from behind a cupped hand as if at some distance, and laughed. I was tripping, for it was now my sense that she was speaking from the sheets of paper that were no longer on the table with the pale blue writing, fine and hard as lace. Over there Ian was crouched in the armchair, a dark seal. I could feel my dick-end conjoined with my knee-cap in a hot pebbly protruberance. I thought *it ought to be now* but the thought spread out through the time of my life like ripples blown on a pond or pale waves of fine biro ink, until I'd lost knowledge of what *it* was.

'I – I'm not sure.' I turned to her and Laura was looking at me with her golden head.

'Oh don't be silly!' Laura said pertly.

'Here she is!' I called to Ian like an old Christian desperate for signs and miracles, but knowing it with my science to be a mere phenomenon that has yet to be untangled, this effect of skunk on the neurotransmitters that changes the world of appearances. Then Joan was re-emerging as if from behind a sunflower mask, and saying, 'What is it, dear?' There was a tear on my chin.

'I thought I saw her fetch,' I said.

'Of course you didn't,' Joan said kindly.

'I'd been thinking she might die,' I said in Joan's ear like a little lad. 'I'd been thinking it all week since she went.'

'Now how was she going to do that, silly?' Joan murmured to me, ultra-kindly.

'Down a drain.'

'Now who was going to put her down a drain, hey?'

'Lad called Norbert.'

'And who's Norbert?' One inch from my face, Joan was oscillating her head in that girly affectionate way. I drank more rum, with which Ian appeared to be keeping us supplied. It made me gag, like the cherry linctus I was given as a kid, February 1970, lying in bed with fever, a comic of heroes on the blanket. My spit thickened nauseously; then I was well again.

'He's a Spaniard. He's from the past. He wears a hood – no: he wears a black mask – like the Black Panther. He kidnaps women, you see... They don't want to go with him... Then he takes them upstairs in The Green Man.'

'Norbert hasn't taken her. She's gone of her own accord!' Joan stroked my cheek with a cold finger. She must have had probs with her circulation.

'How d'you know though, Joan?'

'Because I can see, darling... Remember how I did it in the boozer?'

'Yeah.'

'Remember what I had in my hand for the contact?' I nodded. She stroked my cheek with two fingers, as if she were trying to warm them on me, like a visitor to a corpse. 'Remember where I said she'd gone, darling?' As a junior doctor, I witnessed kisses, sometimes furtive, on the lips of the dead. I gave tea and a diazepam to a woman who'd tried to mount a corpse. 'Remember?' Joan's lips insisted.

'Whitby!' That was the name.

Huskily Joan said 'Uh-huh,' and asked me again.

'Whitby!'

'There's a good lad. And she wants you to go and get her!'

'What about Ian? Why doesn't he go?'

'Don't be silly. That isn't the right way to get her back at all is it? When the king and queen have fallen out, the knight gallant has to go and get the queen back. That's the tradition, dear. You know that from all your books.' Joan had a deep draw and passed me the duchy on the right-hand side. I'd have liked me and Ian to go and get her

177

together – we were pals after all. Then the three of us come back here and sit exactly like this, and everything be as it used to be – though with the supplementary benefit of being like this, Laura exactly beside me, touching my face and Ian yonder like a seal of obsidian or black marble. Sit here exactly like this forever.

'What are you, honey,' Joan was putting it to me, 'a knight gallant, or a Soap Sam?' She moved back from me a little and began to drive her eyes, which said I had to be the knight gallant.

'What's a Soap Sam?' I asked her. I heard the seal laugh through a hole in his black glassy covering, then the hole was stopped up as if by a hovering priestess.

'It's a porcelain sailor, dear. They were popular austerity knick-knacks.'

'Why, Joan?' I asked with a kid's absorption. She was wearing an expensive grapefruit cologne. She had class for a lady who boiled people's feet.

'Because you could put all your scraps of soap in this little tray that he held and make a new bar of soap... I used to work in antiques.'

'Ah.'

'Trouble was, they were top-heavy, Soap Sams. They'd fall over and crack on the bathroom basin. Chip badly. Sometimes the whole bleeding head would come off... Are you all right, dear?'

I was having hysterics. It was the funniest thing I'd heard, it was the saddest. Over my own noise, I heard Joan say, 'It's just a silly five minutes. Not to worry!' When I'd finally recovered myself, I stood up. I was going to Whitby.

'There's a train to York at ten. I can get that... I'll have a slash first.' It was not much past nine in the evening. Time was sporting, swagging in its own channel. I was as astonished as a sleeper rising with full bladder from the carnival of the dark: so much has happened in his dream and yet the clock shows he retired only lately.

'What are you doing, man?' Ian was behind me.

'What do you mean?' I examined what I had in my hand. Joan seemed to have had an effect, Joan, the skunk and attendant hallucinations. I pissed out the evening's drinks, thickly at first.

'Where are you off to?'

'Whitby – if I can get the last train tonight.'

'This isn't like you, Mark. Why are you listening to her?'

'Because it's time I did something like this.'

'Like what?'

'Something active. If Tony Blair can go haring off to Mesopotamia on a supernatural tip, what's to stop me?... It's only England.'

'Are you taking this seriously?'

'Hoy!' I turned to face him. 'Look at the fucking state of me. Of course I am taking it seriously. I've had wive of the first – I mean *worst* – I've had five of the worst days of my life since you told me about all this.'

Over in front of the sink, he smiled at everything I was getting wrong. 'I meant are you taking Joan Hunter seriously?' He'd shut the bathroom door. 'Are you taking what she told us seriously? That's what I meant, Mark!'

'Is she still here?'

'Yeah she's in there on the settee. She's waiting for you.'

'Of course she isn't. Do you mind if I wash my hands?' We manoeuvred round each other in the narrow space by the bath like the infantry of Pippin Fort.

'She's fucking coming on to you.' He raised his voice above the sound of the taps.

'No she isn't. No one ever comes on to me.'

'Really?'

'Not as far as I know,' I declared with some élan.

'Well it's time you started knowing. What if she's working on you, "Knight Gallant"? What are you going to do in Whitby at 4:30am in the morning, when you alight from the milk train? What are you going to do exactly?'

'Why would she be working on me?'

'To take your mind off the issue we've got. To distract you… Obviously.'

'She's doing the fucking opposite!' I turned round to him. 'This is the first bit of help we've had, for Christ's sake!'

'What if she wants you away from here?' Patiently he stood, hands in pockets.

'Well you're making sure I don't make it!' I examined my watch… I'd never do it in twenty minutes. 'Why would she want me away from here?'

With an air of frank apology, Ian said, 'I don't know.' There was a buzz in the hall. 'I don't know what she's up to. I don't know where she's from.' There was another buzz. I wondered if this might be Laura. I was utterly unprepared. 'I don't know who she's from,' Ian went on. There was a knock on the bathroom door. 'Don't know who's sent her,' he murmured.

'Shall I get the door, lads?' Joan shouted.

'Yeah,' Ian said. 'If you would.' He dropped his voice further: '*Laura* may have sent her.'

'Why?'

'To find out how we're doing. To report back. To bamboozle us — it's called *spying*. It's called *counter-*intelligence. C'mon, man! We're in a war here. This is meant to be your field.' There were voices at the flat door. Joan was laughing with mild triumph. 'I told you Laura'd gone of her own accord. D'you think she's not up to this kind of trick? She's a fucking woman, Mark!'

'Laura wouldn't do this.' I was straining to hear if it were her voice out there.

'Not in your book she wouldn't,' Ian said softly. 'You've shown a side of yourself I wasn't familiar with tonight by the way. All that crying about drains.'

I, or we, were saved here by a shove on the door and Joan saying, 'They're in there the pair of them!', whereupon Mary began to enter the bathroom, a phenomenon as arresting in its way as the passing of someone recognised from TV on the public highway. Never before had she been encountered outside her bar. Close up there was something moleish about her. Much of her life had been out of the light; her cardy was the hue of venous blood, her eyes were soft and dark.

She hoped she wasn't disturbing anything, but Rab wanted to unbar us. He'd not meant for life. He'd meant for an hour, this was God's truth. It was just he was terrible upset to see his pal Jerry down on the floor and feared he may be reduced to a vegetable state. Anyway Jerry'd insisted we were invited back, we all of us being his friends and let's bury the hatchet for goodness' sake. There was enough killing and mayhem going on in the world without us in The Green Man adding to it.

'I'm for it,' Joan said, behind the door. 'There's nothing worse than bad blood.'

'What d'you say, boys?' Mary looked from one to the other of us.

'I've got a train to get,' I said.

'You're better off going in the morning,' Ian advised me with a stare. 'First thing. It's too late now. There'll be one at six or seven... Yeah OK, Mary!' As we manoeuvred from the narrow room, he murmured that we should stick together. This was evidence Joan was connected. I remembered her saying that we wouldn't have heard of her. Others evidently had. What were we up against, if it wasn't prudent to bar Joan Hunter from your premises?

We were greeted back like a yacht that's been in hard waters, Rab, Jerry (as we were now begged to call him) and his second forming a row mid-pub to wave us in. Like a Premiership coach whose relationship with the media has flayed the skin off his charm so that it can be displayed now only esoterically, Rab, inclined after his own fashion to do us proud, told some inoffensive punters the bar was now closing, their table being reserved for a private party. Meanwhile Jerry and Joan were shaking hands, Joan expostulating against herself huskily while the fallen hero would have it no other way but that he'd been well out of order.

Chantal came with free drinks for us on her quattrocento halo, Mary bringing up the rear to empty the ashtray of the former tenants. Joan and my friend I noticed had little to say to each other. Mary had something to discuss with me. They were opening her up next Tuesday. Along at the Middlesex. Between the two of them there was an atmosphere of reasonable unlove. I told Mary they'd take good care of her there. She'd be fine at the Middlesex. Such unlove as you get between ice-skating partners with separate lives, or comics who only write together, otherwise maintaining a mutual distance. They'd take really good care of her there. I was a doctor wasn't I? That was right. I smiled miserably. She was reminding me of the profession I ought to have honoured. Couldn't have long left now. She smiled back. Feared they'd be carrying her out horizontal. I told her not to be daft, touching her on the arm through her dark-blood cardy. Had Rab ever been nice to her? Had he once said a loving thing? She'd have to say goodbye to the cigs though. I stubbed my own out in the clean ashtray as an example. The bypass grafts wouldn't work otherwise. She'd need to start walking too.

'Oh where will I walk?' she cried standing back. 'I hate to walk so I do!'

'Regent's Park!' I ordered. 'Once round the park every morning.'

'Oh my God!' she placed her left hand on her heart. 'What about they hoodies?'

'No harm will come to you, Mary.'

'And I'll see you boys again?'

She'd see us again. God bless her. As she made her way back to the bar with her ice-cream tub of butts, my eyes were hot. Joan was watching me with approval.

Maybe Mary'd been the real prime mover in getting us re-instated, in order to obtain a reassuring consultation with me. As I recalled Joan's prediction when we were expelled, this idea drew me on, until I saw that it was still her power that was the effective force, my reputation being merely incidental. It was as well we had her on our side, this sibylline hardcase – if on our side she was. It was essentially unclear.

Chantal appeared with a silver salver, which she carried with the aid of a clean white tea towel. Rab had sent us a dozen sausages, parsley-decorated mash and a little rack that held three pots of mustard like tiny yellow cooling towers. Joan and Ian were watching me. I was in a labyrinth; they seemed to have grandstand seats like spectators above some ancient form of entertainment, or pantomime of horror.

I wished Joan'd kindly – kindly not be here any more, so I could address one or two issues with Ian; but now she was tucking in to a banger, daintily biting off its slightly blackened end. On the other hand, I could do with Ian going away for a spell. It seemed impossible to get anything straight with both present. In the horror pantomimes of Ancient Rome, the actor playing Hercules really burned to death in a shirt of fire; the pornographic acts were unsimulated, and fatal. More than anything, the watchers wanted reality.

'Now it might take you some time to persuade her to come back,' Joan mused. 'These things aren't straightened out in five minutes.' The question of where exactly I was going to find her in a Yorkshire seaside town hadn't yet been raised. When I could think straight, I felt it would become clear of its own accord. 'You'll need to find a bed and breakfast,' Joan continued.

'Yeah.' I tried a sausage. It tasted of kipper.

'One day,' Joan murmured, Ian being distracted by a diplomatic representation on the part of Rab, 'you will take her to La Rochelle. That's my prediction, dear... Does that make you happy?'

'La Rochelle?'

She nodded: 'Provided you back yourself.'

When I hear that name, it's like a song to me.

The night went on and on as it had to. Ian was wanting to talk to me in private, so, I finally twigged, was Joan. At certain points (if that be not too precise a phrase) I thought I was with Ian and Laura again that summer night seven years ago when I met them. For some reason, we attended the drinking club we'd been that night, The Infirmary, after dawdling in the street to smoke more P-52. Nostalgia induced me to take a couple of Wray & Nephew's overproof rum and cokes. Analysing its bouquet of rotten grass and laundry that has taken too long to dry, I lost my footing. As when a little lad is pushed head first into the public baths, the water churns with its own lights, sound misses the ears, panic winds him round; so I fell into the rank, pissy sweetness of my drink. Then they could say what the hell they liked to me, Joan Hunter and my friend. I could no longer hear them.

I was on the verge of knowing for the first time in my life since what was said late that night in '97, on the verge of a full recollective flashback... I'm telling Laura something (about myself?); she (punching my thigh?) is telling me something about Ian, something like *He has such cold hands*... when on a floor through an arch where a sound system was, I thought I saw a golden-haired girl in a pink raincoat and a white-faced Slav with bobbed hair dance themselves dizzy... Thought I saw. But we cannot see around our own corner. I can say that in German you know – listen: *Wir können nicht um – um – um*...

Then there was less and less; until there was nothing.

Saturday

The trousers were the first problem. Where in Christ's name were they? I was still in my shirt, still in my tie for that matter, and underwear. Darkness was above me, pale light behind. Everyone had gone and left me without trousers, in the midst of unfamiliar blocky structures. My occiput was tearing, as if another self exactly my size but facing rear were trying to break out.

After the exams in the summer term of 1986, some of my pals from the Medical School said let's check out the hookers in Leith. I went along with apprehension, making sure I got well pissed first. By the Hibs football ground on Easter Road I was accosted. Her name was Baby. She had these green suede sandals, three-inch heels. Her feet were white as paper, her hair red. She asked for a light, my pals seemed to fade... I came to on my own beneath the Forth Bridge. How I got there I don't know, four miles west of Leith. It was mid-June and the light never really disappeared from the night sky; around me were unfamiliar squat structures. Had I run away, or been abandoned? I never enquired, never learned the truth. Sometimes when I wake I think I'm there again.

Presently I began to apprehend that I was actually on the settee in Ian's long living room. If I'd been a woman, I'd have wondered if I'd been sexually assaulted; my concern – my first concern – was to try and listen to the noise from the blackout phase, since I was convinced there was a message somewhere in there that I needed to record. I lay without moving to encourage it to come, until I heard Joan Hunter in a crackling wave: 'Can't you see it, dear?... Can't you see it?' That was enough. Noise may masquerade as message.

I got up fast and down the hall into the bathroom where I retched a bit for form's sake then pissed at length into the toilet, which, I noticed, Ian kept thoroughly spick and span for a man whose woman's gone. Noise may masquerade as message. We may think we heard what we expected to hear, as monitors of radio transmissions used to find at wartime listening posts. The live rail hummed in my hand. The bedroom door'd been shut. It wouldn't have been difficult – under the aspect of eternity, it would not have been difficult to go in there and... but we don't live under the aspect of eternity. As the philosopher says, we just live in our own corners. None of us can see around them. '*Wir können nicht um unsere Ecke sehen.*' And I didn't know who'd be in there either.

My trousers were hanging up on a rack in the bath, almost entirely dry – I was bloody glad to ascertain this – but damp at the bottoms. I put them on, for what is a knight without his armour? Ian cared to hang my trousers up for me, he cared to look after my trousers. He'd make a good wife for someone, that young man. I could have cried for gratitude. 'Truth is a trouser word,' said JL Austin. What do you think he meant by that? In the mirror where Laura would do her hair of a morning, I noted I'd regurgitated rum on my pink shirt, though it must have been the coke staining it, Wray & Nephew's being clear spirit. Fuck knows what JL Austin meant. What did Ian's cock look like of a morning? It's the time for anthropologists the morning, the time for zoologists. *So sorry if I embarrassed you in there, but I was delighted to see your cock.* Take so little to go in and check. It would be an 'experience'. Discover him lying, St Andrew's Cross. Yeah, and Joan Hunter sliding up and down on it in her D&G spectacles, eyes shooting through space like musket balls. You'd be walking into a massacre, son, in the manner of the Imperial Guard, up the ridge at Waterloo. Pow-pow-ping.

I went to sit on the settee and drank a half-tot of dark rum that'd been left on the table for my headache. What I really needed to do was think; this was as obvious to me as it would have been to anyone who'd been observing me since Monday night, supposing I were the subject of an experiment in simultaneous overload and deprivation. Not that I mightn't have been suggested as a suitable subject some time before last Monday, considering the terms of the experiment. Come to think of it, I could well have been suggested any time in the last twenty years or so; but no matter, it was the past five days that were experimentally critical. What I really needed to do was think, about everything that had been going on, about everything that had been said – said and suggested; but I was in no state to think. My mind was full of noise, drek, fancies. It was a theatre with a capacity audience who have not been allowed to exit for close to six days because a ransom hasn't been met. The conditions in there were desperate, insanitary.

Listen. If you want to think a problem through, you need out of the hurly burly. What you don't need is to be part of the structure where the problem is seething and milling, worrying yourself sick about the recent fate of your trousers with a rabies of a headache. This is fundamental. No philosopher would dream of starting off in conditions like mine.

The first thing a philosopher would do would be sit somewhere warm, dry and bloody quiet on his own like Descartes. They say it was an oven, but in truth it was a kind of oast house. He sat in there with his pipe and thought; he got rid of every notion, every buzz and whim and flitting phantasy until he had one rock solid thought left to his name. That rock was his foundation, and he rebuilt the rest upon it; he founded all meaning on that one thought, and then was Descartes sure. Or take Immanuel Kant. Another who wouldn't abide by other people's flim-flam explanations of all things and their paste and tinsel metaphysics. He took a wrecking ball to all that and called it 'Critical Philosophy'. But all the time the ball was smashing down the trashy palaces man promised himself he'd be invited to one day, Kant was sitting quiet in his house; at 3pm he took a walk (at his own pace) around the square. They knew how to clear the ground before they could work things out for themselves. They knew how long it took to clear the ground too, those old philosophers. They knew the preparation required. What chance have I got? I disgust myself. I do the opposite of withdraw. I am stupidly involved. Like a dog in a pond. There he goes chasing the swans again! And now the swans have run away across the top of the water; and the swans have flown; and the dog is drenched and alone; and when he gets out he's gonna be in big trouble from his owner. He'll get a kick in the guts from his owner, and the swans are all gone to the air. Here I am, a dog in a pond. Clever!

I do not know how to withdraw. Ask Edmund Husserl how. He knew how to de-involve, did Husserl; ultimate perfection of method: like a train reversing into a tunnel, he slid back into the purity of consciousness from what everyone else had professed as truth, so as to judge what he really knew, then... then the flat door opened from outside and Ian entered. I could have gone into his room, because he wouldn't have been there anyway; could have gone in to have a look at him in the morning, but I'd only have found nothing.

Apparently we'd walked home from The Infirmary, which would be about a mile and a half from Ian's place. Apparently, I'd refused to get in a taxi. I'd also picked a fight on the way, with a group of youths who said something to Joan (in my interpretation) on the corner of Wardour Street and Oxford Street. This news subjected me to an astonishingly transient sensation of worry which ran through me like an express train.

'Ah come on!' I said to Ian, as the express exited my little station, its roar suddenly dropping to a kind of surfing click. 'Did no such thing.'

'You did, man,' Ian grinned. 'You were putting on that northern accent.'

'I've got one anyway.'

'No. The strong one – when you say "cunt" without a *t*.'

191

'Oh dear!... Why didn't Joan fight them herself though? Fully capable I should have thought.'

'She was letting you be her knight gallant!' Ian laughed. 'She was well impressed with you, my man!'

Odd. How many of them had there been? Why didn't they twat me?... Maybe they were overcome by pity.

'You're a hero, Mark,' Ian was now saying softly.

'As to my trousers,' I suddenly felt bold enough to ask, 'what went on there exactly?'

'One of the youths on Wardour Street – he was eating a pie and sauce.'

'Ah.' This would have been from Dionysos, a renowned seller of food to revellers and fools.

'When you kicked him, it stained your trousers.'

'Badly? They looked as good as new this morning.' I gestured confidently with my foot.

'Oh not at all really. I just rinsed them for you – just the bottom. You were making a hell of a fuss, man.'

'About taking them off?'

'Yeah. I know how much care you take over your threads. I was only trying to help.'

I didn't want Joan to have been here when this act of charitable laundry work was going on. Not daring to ask him straight, I thought I'd better work round gradually to ascertaining who was present. Retreat in order to advance! *Reculer pour mieux sauter!* (Napoleon Bonaparte.) 'I actually *kicked* him?'

'You did, man.'

'As high as his pie?' I hoped not.

'No.' Ian tried to recall. 'Not that high – wasn't like kick-boxing.'

'Not surface to air?'

'Oh no. I mean you were getting stuck in, man, but it was old school. Wasn't like kick to kill.'

This was exactly what I wanted to hear. Ethically perfect. 'And how did the pie – how did it get where it got? I'm finding it hard to trace the vectors here.' You could see I wasn't used to fighting. Does any self-respecting hardcase worry about *pastry vectors*?... But I was losing focus. I had to find out whether Joan had been present when he was washing my trousers. Not that I wasn't also concerned about hurting someone badly.

'It just sort of tumbled from his hand.'

'Ah – then we came home I suppose?'

'Yeah.' He sat down in the armchair by the door. He was still in his sailor's jacket. What the hell he'd been up to, I did not know; but he looked pretty fresh. I apprehended that unless I asked, I wasn't going to find out whether Joan had seen me without trousers, or whether it had been him alone. A better man than me would have been able not to bother.

'You know why we went down to The Infirmary don't you?' he asked considerately. 'You remember?'

'I will remember. It'll come back to me.' I lit a cigarette. Nothing shamed me more than this, this drunken forgetting. Of all my faults, the most pathetic; vicious, beastly.

'Joan wanted to get you some sniff. To sharpen you up for your journey. She knew someone down there... And I – d'you remember I was trying to tell you this? – I was wanting to ask Adi Chalice something.'

'Who's he again?'

'Guy I know from work. He goes in there all the time. He knows a lot of people. Wanted to ask him if he knew of Joan Hunter.'

'What did he say?'

'Actually he wasn't there. Joan's girl with the drugs wasn't there either.'

'Oh yeah. That's right.' It was all coming back to me. We'd wanted to get some sulphate from Joan's girl (it occurred to me that Joan Hunter was almost a model feminist); and we'd wanted to have a word with Ian's guy, whose name is Adi Chalice.

'The thing was – I was probably being a bit paranoid about this last night (I know you thought so) – I had this idea that Laura's with someone who's fairly dodgy. And he sent Joan to suss us out, you and me.'

'Why would he do that, Ian?'

'I dunno, Mark. It was just a feeling I had.'

'I can understand that – it is understandable.'

'Because she was lying in wait for us. In The Green Man. That was my sense. D'you reckon so?'

'Well I see how you're seeing it.' He watched me with his hands clasped behind his head, a sailor sitting against the mast in a novel of Conrad, or Stevenson. He knew when to be idle, but his idleness was watchful; he was reserving himself for the time when he should need to act. Fair-bearded northern sailor. 'I mean, I didn't think of it that way. But now you've said it…' Now he'd said it, and he was saying it in the bathroom last night too, as I now recalled – now he'd said it, it seemed, well, not improbable. Because why was she there at all? What was a lady like her doing in our local, well out of her own jurisdiction – as she'd implied? Yet known enough to get herself unbarred after assaulting the local hero. Why did she leap in when I was doing my *Crackerjack* impersonation? Why did she – yeah, why say, 'I suppose she's run off with the gypsies'? She couldn't have *known* that – unless someone'd told her. Ian's paranoia had probability on its side. And as Aristotle says, probability is the cornerstone when it comes to good plots.

Yes. Now he'd said it, I began to feel that Joan had been well briefed. And of course she'd have been happy to hang around with us for half the night so as to gather information for her report to Laura's vicious new boyfriend, would she not? Wasn't this probable?

'But why would someone have sent her? I mean, what's he going to do with what she tells him?'

'Maybe he wants a laugh. I dunno, man... I just don't know. Maybe he's a psychopath. He's fucking Laura, that's not enough for him. He wants to fuck up you and me too. He wants to get you going to Whitby on the night train when you're already in a rotten state; he wants me isolated. All that stuff she was saying about backing yourself, that was to separate us... I mean without you, I don't know what I'd have done this week. He's taken away my woman; he wants to take away my friend. I don't even know if he's forced Laura away...'

'You don't,' I said with ardour, 'mean he's sort of semi-kidnapped her?'

'To tell the truth, I hadn't thought about it that way – until you said that thing about a guy in a hood last night.'

'Was I saying that?'

'Yeah yeah – in here; you started crying.'

'Sorry.'

'That's all right, Mark' he said, hands still behind his head. 'Don't be sorry.' He had the generosity not to go into my emotions, the generosity, and the subtlety. My friend had a subtle heart. I had no inclination to agree with Joan Hunter's observations on his character. She was as violent in word as she was in deed. He and I were in the labyrinth together. I would not go to Whitby this day.

***

Not long after, we went down to Tony's in Wells Street to get something to eat. Where he'd been this morning I did not enquire. No doubt he'd answer frankly if I were to, but I wished to learn nothing more for the time being. Already I had so much to think about that fresh disclosures were just going to get lodged in the tailback at the head of which we were motoring slowly across the weekend, in each other's company. Indeed, I had so much to think about that, as I'd been noticing, I was falling now into the habit of forming metaphors relating to the difficulty of thinking, instead of applying myself to myself with the instruments of reason. Was this a left or right hemisphere habit? Rational, or intuitive-creative, which of the two? Ah, that was one for the neuroscientists of cognition; if only the neuroscientists of cognition had a full understanding of metaphor, which I'm afraid to say they don't. No real *feel* for metaphor, your neuropsychologists, your cognitive biologists, your heterophenomenologists and consciousness explainers with their peanut-butter optimism. They think metaphor is a 'tool of thought'. Wrong. Metaphor is no tool; metaphor is a toy. There is a difference.

The breakfasts were coming. Across the street, early-autumn sunlight lacquered the walls and windows. In my early days, a loud and curious boy, I'd been a hog, ventripotent. Then eating became part of my anxiety. What was I sustaining myself for? Did I actually assume my life had a purpose for which it needed to be sustained? Very well, I tended the sick, but it brought me no sense of magnificence. The complacency of conserving myself, that's what it was that troubled me. Why conserve? Why polish my shoes, take Vitamin B, and feed and feed? What for? Dissolution was the truth. It was *my* truth anyway. Dissolution, and recurrent, burning gastritis.

Yet today, I fell to my chips, and my egg, my bacon and sauce with better appetite. Maybe it was because at last I was enduring something that meant something to me personally, and with my friend at my side it felt as though we'd gone to the wars. So what if we didn't know exactly what was going down in this conflict? When were the infantry ever in possession of full intelligence? There was black pudding too, beneath a black and field-grey mushroom. Perhaps heroism is impossible without ignorance.

'How many youths did I pick a fight with?'

'Eight.'

I picked a fight against the odds. I had no doubt but that it was a low-farcical encounter, with more gravy spilled than blood; nevertheless, the spirit must have been there. 'I look forward to another,' I said with bold irony. 'Could have been our last stand, but here we are as right as rain.'

Last stands have always hooked me. This must go back to when my old man took me to *Custer of the West* as a little lad, around 1968. Custer in his buckskin jacket and long yellow hair, the dark blue men of the 7th, fighting and falling on the hill slope above the Big Horn River, Crazy Horse's men circling, Custer waving his sword, the last but one to die. 'Ah Dad,' I lamented, 'why did they have to die?' I was a boy and this image filled me. With pencil and wax crayons in which the blues, the yellows and browns, were too shiny-intense, I drew and coloured it; I searched the kids' library for a book on General Custer; when this turned up nothing, I had my mother borrow me assorted histories of the West from the adult section. In one of these I came across a reference to gonorrhoea.

As a six-year-old I did not see that the 7th Cavalry were getting what they deserved, though my old man quietly tried to explain. Later I read about US Army extermination policy (covert), and Government apartheid policy (official), for the native Indians in the 1870s. I read about these policies with outrage, but the death-image of the 7th still affected me. The year of the Mexico World Cup, my old man took me to see *Butch Cassidy and the Sundance Kid*. They got blown away at the end too, by the Bolivian army; but they were wisecracking till the last volley. I wished they hadn't had to die either, but they were cool. In fact, the film froze in sepia their final moment, so they didn't die *exactly*. It was the Sundance Kid who'd had gonorrhoea in the book my mother borrowed for me. I remembered, of course.

My other images came from a book full of grand, northern mythic pictures, which I borrowed from a kid on our estate and never returned. It showed Siegfried clad in furs, and the last stand of the Niebelungs. Their shields were hacked, and embedded with spears, their biceps bled with thin cuts from blade wounds: there was a great, aged warrior with a walrus white moustache, he was Hildebrand; a shifty and alarming red-headed Saxon called Hagen; two fierce queens, Brünnhilde and – I forget the other. It inspired me. I didn't then know what was wrong with myths.

Later, I found that when Adolf Hitler was picking his own lice in a Viennese dosshouse and designing advertising posters for foot powder and bed-feathers, he inspired himself with the same images.

One afternoon as a schoolboy, when my pals were lying at the field's far side with Angie Alexander and her mates, I read in a history book of La Rochelle, its garrison holding out ten days or more *after* the death of Hitler and the fall of Berlin. Were they ultra-fanatics at La Rochelle? Or were they just fighting for themselves, for the love of a scrap, in honour and deep ignorance?

Maybe La Rochelle was the dodgiest last stand of all, maybe it was the purest. Whatever, I couldn't help seeing an unshaven sergeant and his unshaven men steadying their last Panzerfaust in a street of broken, sooty white houses, gulls circling and crying from the harbour. So many tanks they'd shot up, but US XX Corps had a thousand more. Nor could I help seeing the high-fronted Sherman through their sight. Last night they played chess and drank the last of the Calvados. Maybe they visited a brothel. Maybe one of them sat outside alone like Dutch Bishop before the last stand of the Wild Bunch, thinking of his parents and his sins. Today they've come into the street to die. On the hedges round the town are white blossom and pink.

Another year, I found out the truth about La Rochelle. But I went on preferring my image.

'Do you know,' I said to Ian, 'that Adolf Hitler once designed an advert for "Teddy Powder"?'

Ian shook his head. 'Who was that aimed at?'

'Postmen with stinking feet.'

History was very strange, said Ian and paid for the food and back we went into the autumn sunlight. Last night's rum was repeating on me. Rum for courage. At Waterloo, they were off their faces in the British squares, the Inniskillings, the 71st, the 79th. The piper of the 79th, he was that gone he came outside the square to play, under heavy fire. Often wondered what he played. How would I have fared at Waterloo? Would I have fared OK if I'd been pissed? Or ended up like Lord Portarlington, officer in command of the 23rd, who arrived late because he'd been on a bender in Brussels. Ian and I discussed the British squares at Waterloo as we walked along. We thought the piper'd have played 'Over the Sea to Skye', and an anti-French medley. Twenty-five yards down the street, The Champion was just opening.

I'd get these. The walls were decorated with tiled pictures of inventors. Portarlington accompanied the 18th Hussars on a death charge because his own regiment had already joined battle. His horse was shot from under him and he tumbled on his arse. Couldn't die with honour if he wanted to, poor bastard. Excuses were made for him: notably, that he'd been stuck on the khazi with violent diarrhoea when the 23rd advanced; but nought availed his reputation. He died in shame in a slum, 1845. Unmarried. No wife for Portarlington; no glory. Maybe his name doomed him to ignominy. Kind of hybrid of Portsmouth and Darlington... Ian asked what I was laughing about, as I set the drinks down. I told him I'd been thinking of the biggest loser at Waterloo.

My phone emitted 'Where the Bee Sucks'. There were several missed messages from Melania Morgan asking me to call her, the first from 8.03am. I saw Napoleon in his tent with his charts and information and his orders of the day, Portarlington on his arse in the mud. Which sort was I, and which my friend?

Ian was now staring at his phone as well. There was to be no calling out. That was the game. That little blue-black-silver rectangle was his Imperial Guard, not to be employed until the game was up. At last he rubbed his eyes laterally with the palm of his hand: 'On Monday, it'll have to change. Game ends.'

When the game ends, things get serious. When the game ends everything ends... Which was it to be? Which of the two? And what would happen to collaborators? The noonday sun burnished the dark blues and blacks, the crimsons and saffrons of the inventors on the tiles. Eddison was there, and Mike Faraday in a frock coat; but not Daedalus who built the labyrinth, Inventor A No. 1.

She was going to be somewhere.

***

Around two we took a walk into Soho. We inspected the architecture and the noodle shops. We checked out the spot where Marx got turned on for interfering in a domestic, around 2nd October 1854. The crowd didn't want no foreign bleeder coming between an Englishman and his missus. We were the lads, in our sailor coat and suit. We haggled for a gram of amphetamine sulphate in an alley that smelled of onions with an urchin who seemed to have tiny crosses carved in his teeth like decorations on ivory. He wanted a deposit while he went off on his bike. When I said we wouldn't see head nor tail of him again, he spat near my feet so I kicked his bike (hard – on the wheel spokes so I shouldn't hurt my foot). It was a 'stand-off', as they say on the BBC. Tension mounted. At last, Ian said, 'He'll kill you!' and the urchin went westwards down the alley, while we carried on east.

A girl in a doorway in white-tasselled boots and a cowboy hat observed us on the kerb. Her legs were long and brown. Behind her through swing doors lay life's feast. Suddenly she ran up to us like a little kid trying to scare pigeons, just a yard and a half or so from her entry post, eyes hard with glee. Her legs would have been good with gravy, and a splash of bread sauce. They'd have been good in any imaginable conformation. She said hi guys, and were we coming in? When a hooker accosted Dr Johnson on Drury Lane, he said, 'No, no, young lady! This will not do!' He meant it didn't do she was soliciting; it didn't do that his breeches were jutting either. Walking away with Boswell, he'd have rolled himself, pawed the stones like a bull with his foot, body flaring up against the resistance to appetite. Boswell thought it was St Vitus's Dance, Johnson's twitching and strange tricks of movement and his weird noises. 1754. We know better now, don't we?

I would have liked to go in. What if Laura was there beyond the swing doors, as she was that time on the green hill? Soon there was a shout behind us. The girl with the Stetson was now accompanied by a man in a suit who was waving; we went back a little way. The man had a sultana face with a lot of forehead, and shiny brown tired eyes. 'Hey brother,' he called to me, scooping the air with his right hand, 'where you from? Come in here a moment or two, you and your friend. I could show you something.' He was desperate for trade. 'Come and have a drink with me! C'mon, come in here!'

'He just wants to skank us,' Ian said behind me. 'Leave it.' But on the principle that I'd had enough of negative adventures in my time, I took us down the steps behind the swing doors where the air smelled of old cigarettes and talcum powder, the man in the 550-wool Bond Street suit with slimline trousers asking us to watch our way. In the VIP Lounge, he poured us a couple of vodka and tonics and moaned about this and that, business, the girls, the cops, drug dealers, immigrants, patting me on the shoulder now and then as if I knew how it was. Maybe I was being mistaken by him for a neighbour in the same line as himself. We were dressed alike.

'Look,' he pointed at the bar, 'Saturday afternoon. Can't even get anyone to handle the drinks in here. Might as well be in Tehran, you want a damn drink. They all know about Minimum Wage nowadays.' We sat by a stage under a blank plasma screen with what appeared to be cubicles or changing rooms along the wall to our right and a dark corridor leading off mid-way. Beside the stage there was a large PA, unplugged. 'I asked my cousin to mind the bar.

Her name's Sheherezade. She's a cookie. "Oh no I got to focus totally on my courseworks." Our friend mimicked his cousin with a fanatical grimace. 'Between you and me she's an asshole. University girl. She wants to know about the world, she should come down here and mind the damn bar Saturday. I'm not trying to put her on with the guys. Here, here's an ashtray. Her father, he's just a shopkeeper. After the revolution, my father took us to the States, his brother came here. He sells pomegranates. He wants her to go somewhere in her life. Like where? Every kid's in the university nowadays. They come out of university, they think they're gonna be Foreign Secretary. There's only *one* Foreign Secretary, yeah?' He shook his head. 'Sooner or later, they're gonna learn this. Then they're gonna come down here and dance.' It appeared that none of them were going to be learning this soon enough for us to set eyes on them, when our friend glanced to the left. A girl in Ugg boots was approaching. She had dark, clever eyes and a round face; she was at least my height; over her shoulder was a little rucksack.

'Hey, Naz!' our friend cried. 'You're going to work?'

'Yeah,' Naz said. 'Suppose so.'

'What you done to your hair?'

'I ain't done anything.'

'Where's your headscarf?'

'I ain't wearing it.' Naz took a slim pack of Marlboro Lites from her rucksack and lit one.

'Ah come on, baby! The guys love to see that. You know how it is!'

Naz tapped her cigarette in my ashtray. On her brown index finger was a silver ring with the world embossed on it. I wondered if she was a student too. She went off towards the dark corridor in her soft boots as if she were heading for the Pole.

'Guys'll fill the pot, they see a girl in a hijab,' our friend said with an air of reminding us of a verity that allowed for no sentimentality. 'On the crux, they'll pay for a drink what she tells em it costs.' Picturing Naz getting changed in the dark corridor, I wondered what exactly the crux was.

'What's the crux?' Ian asked, finishing his vodka.

Our friend looked at me knowingly and said, 'This guy could tell you. Isn't that right, brother?'

'Ah, I couldn't tell him anything he doesn't know already.' I patted Ian's arm and our friend laughed with bitter joy and said we should all go up and get some more drinks with him, even if he had to manage the bar himself.

We sat on stools that had no backs so guys could swivel easy to see whatever was happening on the stage, and swivel back the way they were facing in the first place. Rear of the bar there was a sandwich fridge that had no sandwiches in it. Maybe a guy could get a sandwich elsewhere in the establishment. The VIP Lounge was austere, even ascetic. Without bar staff, snacks, or dancers, our slim-suited friend presided like the bitter priest of an unpopular temple. Along the little shelves for mixer bottles, unchilled Britvics and so forth, someone had once stuck for purposes of classification that thin sticky tape with embossed letters about which you could say no more than that you never saw it nowadays. Maybe our friend was behind the times in certain matters of detail that could mean disaster for business. Perhaps he'd been advised by a design consultant who'd brought in an installation guru with a retro passion for 1974. Still, his suit was good; and discernibly cleaner than mine, for all Ian's laundry work.

'Hey,' our friend raised his glass, 'seen you with that blonde babe. Once, twice, at least. Pair of you!' This included Ian. 'Champagne bar, Broadwick Street, where it crosses Berwick. I've seen you. You're a lucky guy. Respect, brother!' He raised his glass again, watching us as a conductor seems to examine his orchestra before the off. I understood now that my apparent fame with him had to do with the fact that he thought *I* was Laura's man. Marvellous irony! If she'd been mine, would we have been down here at all? Would I have been in this state?

But what did he want? Just to bask in the glory of buying me a couple of vodkas in his VIP Lounge? Or was there something he knew?

'This is her man,' I indicated Ian, before our friend had the chance to involve me further in error. With barely a movement of his head, he considered Ian's section of the orchestra, nodding in approval.

'Sure. Your wife yeah? You married?'

'Not really,' Ian said.

'Still, you're a lucky guy,' our friend said solemnly.

'Not so lucky,' Ian advised him.

'Why is that?'

'Because she's done a runner.'

Our friend sipped at his plain tonic water and cried 'Damn! – you're fooling me?' In accordance with his talent, Ian said nothing. 'Where's she gone? Why d'you let it happen?' our friend urged him.

'I dunno,' Ian said.

'But you been to look for her surely?' Naz came out of

the corridor wearing a headscarf and – oh fucking hell. When she bent down to plug in the PA I experienced an uprush that married the sensations of nausea and starvation like an hiatal hernia. Good God she was fine. What would Dr Johnson have said? If he'd jerked himself off of a morning, he wrote 'O' in his diary.

'I don't know where to look,' Ian said.

Our friend shook his head: 'You haven't called her?'

'She went of her own accord.'

'You're trying to be cool?' our friend said with a shrewd nod.

'I don't think so.'

'So call her! – Naz, what – what is that thing you are wearing?'

'My cardy!' Naz shouted. 'It's freezing down here.'

'All right, all right!' our friend called bitterly. 'I'll put the heating on. You look like my grandmother in that thing.' From the waist up, he'd have meant.

'I want to let her do what she wants to do,' Ian said. 'I don't want to be dragging her back, man.' Our friend considered this. 'She's gone of her own accord, she has to come back of her own accord – or not at all,' Ian continued.

'If that was my attitude, I wouldn't have no girls to my name. Zero!' our friend asserted. Naz stood with her hands on her hips waiting for it to warm up. She reminded me of a robin, alone on a wintery lawn. Had she come here to dance, and do whatever else was called for, of her own accord? Was someone somewhere wondering where the hell she was these days? Would she ever go back?

'How many girls you got?' Ian asked. Naz stalked back to the corridor and away into the darkness.

'At present two, the cream of the crop,' our friend declared. 'I love these girls. Coupla cookies. Naz down here, Nadia up top. Nadia's a Ukraine. She was cleaning pipes for a living…'

'Pipes?' We took it in turns to question him, Frank Sinatra and Sammy Davies Jnr on bar stools.

'Yeah. Municipal premises. I gave her her chance, be what she wants to be. Do your friends want to see you on your homepage, polishing pipes?'

'What about Naz?'

'Ah, Naz is cool,' our friend grumbled with an eye on the corridor. 'I love Naz… Know why she came back today?'

We didn't know.

'I called her. Two days ago she was never coming back.' Our friend counted on his fingertips. 'Three days – it was Wednesday. What did I do? I called her.'

'Where'd she gone?'

He nodded: 'Luton.'

'What was she doing there?'

'Ah, she gets pissed off now and then. Runs away to her cousin's. I don't give her enough to eat. Blah blah. Cousin cooks her chops. What's more,' under the pressure of lowering his voice our friend's face shrivelled before us like a whole fruit being speed-dried, 'she's got this thing about Nadia.' He glanced at the corridor. 'Got it in her head I'm spending too much time up top. Most of the time I'm up top, what the fuck am I doing?' He regarded us sincerely, countenance filling out again. 'I am looking out *for* Naz, that's what. Such as today. Damn! The devotion

I give this – this woman, it's out of hand. Crazy… As for her – her *meals*,' he flicked another glance at the dark corridor, 'she eats like a goddamned shark. If I didn't say, "Hey, baby, enough's enough! Think of your figure!", she'd eat chilli chops from morning to night. She'd eat whole chickens, in pomegranate sauce. Rice and fried potato – by the *hill*. Took her to The Ivy for her birthday. It's that or she'll run away. She's read about it in her *magazines* – "Oh it's the celebrity eating place tra la la." What d'you think?' He stared at us in bitter satisfaction. 'She wouldn't touch a damn thing – "Oh this ain't the kind of fare I'm used to!" Goddamn right. It's English actors' fare – as her magazines would inform her, she read down a couple of lines and stopped staring at the pictures. I had to run across the street and fetch her walnuts.'

Without her cardy Naz returned. My dick hammered under my heart.

'Ah *Naz*!' our friend shouted, 'Naz, can you take those sandals off?… She intimidates guys in em. Looks like a goddamn six-foot Hezbollah. What if some Jews came in?… Do it barefeet, baby!'

'Say please!' Naz yelled, hands on hips.

'Hey! Don't make me look like a prick in front of my pals,' our friend wailed, turning his back. It was a stand-off. 'But if you call em, they come,' he concluded moodily. 'Call em, feed em.'

I began to reverse my thoughts. Naz was in a better place than she might have been, odd as that seemed. Our friend cared about her. Cared enough to call her back, again and again. So back she came, again and again. That was the game.

Though not the game Ian claimed to be playing. The first time Laura went to him, he made her drink herself sick. Gave her nothing to eat, not a thing, and made her drink herself sick. Perhaps our friend was watching in the champagne bar the time she was telling me about that visit. Maybe he even heard her complaining so sweetly about the man who'd given her nothing to eat, and one day would not call her when she ran away.

'And you gotta call em,' our friend went on for the benefit of Ian, whose expression was unresponsive. 'Forget your pride. They don't know how to handle it on their own out there. It's all, "Yeah yeah I'm an independent woman. Stop hassling me!" After two days running round with their cousin, it's "Oh my God, why isn't he calling me. He doesn't care!" Isn't that true, brother?' he appealed to me. 'And this is where they get into danger. Cos there's guys out there, they are just waiting for a lady on her own like wolves in the dark.'

The red tape on the shelves began to glow at me as if excess current were passing through it. Trade name *Dymo-Tape*. The kidnapper of the heiress used Dymo for his demand message, to avoid fingerprints, traces, recognisable handwriting or other giveaways. A hooded man. Stuck her down a field drain. There she died. The 'Black Panther'. 1974. Laura could be anywhere. Ian's care was no more visible than the light from a dark-lantern. She could be anywhere, and we were down here. And what had he contrived for me, with his dark-lantern? The Dymo was burning like the element in an ageing bathroom fire. What in Christ's name were we doing down here?...

'I'll have to slave my iPod to the PA,' Naz said behind

us. 'You haven't got the system fixed like you said you would.' I turned and she was a yard behind me, then she was levering Ian from the floor. She had rings on her toes and her toes were white from the pressure as she crouched to deal with him. Meanwhile our friend was nodding at me in anxious conciliation. I seemed to have missed some recent seconds.

Now Ian was looking up from where Naz held him like a babe who's lost the instinct for breast-feeding and saying, 'He's my friend. It's OK.'

***

He appeared to have gone over like a Soap Sam, our Ian, gone over of his own accord and fallen in the sink, though he wasn't chipped. As our friend showed us out, he murmured to me, 'You gotta look for her yourself. That's the deal here. I'm in business. Believe me. She'll be closer than you think, brother! They always are.' He felt in his breast pocket as if to give me his card, but he had run out of cards.

Our adventures weren't over. We stuck together saying little, drinking whisky, shot after shot. I wanted to lose the sensation the red tape had induced, but wherever we went it followed, or it waited.

In the Museum Tavern I started a fight with an American couple we'd been talking to about the execution of the hostage. They agreed with you, man, Ian said in triplicate as he led me away. He was my male maid. I had Marx on my mind. The day an English crowd abused him for getting involved, Marx took a boon companion on a bender. They chucked rocks at the police and smashed gas lamps, on Tottenham Court Road. I tried to piss on the tyre of a police van. Ian took hold of my face and slobbered on me. He was a bitch. At last he loved me.

For the first time in thirty years (believe it or not) I spewed; the Dymo-Tape'd been criss-crossing my innards like a devilish sadistic corset. I spewed on a pub floor, and outside the door. It wasn't the breakfast, it was black vomit, brown-black curd, 170°C. A sort of hot slurry. A middle-aged couple up for the theatre skipped aside in disgust. Wiping my mouth I told the man my puke was pH1. It'd go through his turn-ups, and straight on through his fucking fibula. We traipsed about looking for somewhere for me to buy a toothbrush and Californian whitening toothpaste. When we were settled elsewhere, a sort of red velvet pub on the latitude of Shaftesbury Avenue, I brushed my teeth in a pint of bitter. Someone laughed at me so I threw the lot over them, though most of it ended up on my thigh where it frothed like canal water from an environmentalist video before soaking into my trousers, down over my knee and into the upper elasticity of my sock. We left; yeah – we left that place, and we went on to a smart hotel, where it seemed to be even redder, as if coals were being burned on grills behind the bar. I had a couple of red drinks. Someone sat on my knee then went away. How long she was on there I couldn't judge. I kept blacking out from the shock. It was dream time. She felt nice, but wouldn't face me. All I could feel was hair. Just sat there like Frankie Dettori, until she went away. Every time I asked Ian why she'd gone, he'd explain that she'd wet her knickers. When I asked him if I'd been getting her hot, he'd explain deferently that you still had beer all over your leg from an earlier engagement. He seemed to be coming and going rather a lot, my maid, in between saying the same thing. Could scarcely keep track of the bastard. No matter…

I'm a lonely frog
Hm hm hm hm

I seemed to be singing to another girl who was watching me from a stool, in the croaking manner of Frankie Ford, the 'negro Elvis'. The boyfriend soon appeared to establish the facts of what else I was saying, leaning over me in his Jermyn-Street-surplus shirt with plastic collar stiffeners and his jewellery going ting-a-ling-a-ling. I told him I'd been advising his girlfriend to buy an electron microscope so she could stare at me properly. He gave me a look I didn't care for, said to me a thing I didn't like to hear, so I added that she might as well try and have a look for his knob-end once she'd bought an electron microscope on account of the fact she was probably sick of trying to find it with the naked eye, then it went off and some glasses smashed, I saw a left arm cross the air like a crane boom, saw a devil's head suspended…

The Day of the Lord

'I have abysses in me, Lord, and you can see to the bottom of them.' So wrote St Augustine. Perhaps he was right that there was a God who could see it all. Indeed, it wouldn't be much of a God who could not see into what He had created. Or maybe there were just abysses in that good Latin African which he so feared that he invented a perspicuous God to look after him. Perhaps there were neither, no abysses, no God; but you couldn't have had one without the other. These days, however, the one that sees and the one seen into often go by the same name: Myself.

Darkness above me, pale light behind, amid unfamiliar blocky structures, I lived something again in a hot rush, as if a screen had burst and spilled: late winter-early spring '74. The Devil glowing and rearing at a crane's end. *Quatermass and the Pit.* I had found my favourite film. The Dymo-Tape on which I clicked the words 'Marwell is a cunt', for Marwell said to me a thing I didn't like to hear, on the school field and long lane, though my libel stayed unpublished, through lack of nerve and a certain delicacy. The night I spewed across the bedroom carpet, my mother calling to my father, cleaning me up in their nightclothes: fine reward for the marriage they had made in adversity.

Say in here was the key to all my trouble, my blockages and abjection? Say my trouble had its source in these months, a more or less unnecessary trauma? Then say I was Lord at last of this truth, grown from the dirt of recent nights and days, a most complex flower?

With these words I got myself up forever... Viva psychotherapy!

Whitby

Alison Dale was wearing a queer expression, pregnant, gentle, evasive when she informed me that Patient Liaison Service wanted to speak to me. I rang Colin Sumption of Patient Liaison Service. Colin Sumption's secretary said that Colin had actually just e-mailed me; Colin Sumption's secretary paused, and added that Colin was not at his desk just now.

Was he not indeed? He'd be signing nervously at her. I wondered if he might not be crouching beneath it.

Sorry. Beneath what?

Beneath his desk. Could she check?

He wasn't there just now. Pause. He'd be writing something for her on a post-it. He'd be back in a while though.

What sort of 'while' did he have in mind?

Sorry. She didn't follow me.

A while as in five minutes? Or as in several weeks?

Sorry?

Or ever? Would he ever be back?

He was just in a meeting with the diversity rep at the mo.

Oh well done! That was the spirit. Could she tell him I approved? And ask him if he was still a member of the National Front? I put the phone down and opened my electronic mails. A patient had complained that I smelled of drink during Friday morning's ward round. Colin was sure this couldn't be the case. He was merely raising the issue as a matter of 'formlaity' (sic).

God knows how long I'd been waiting for this to happen, waiting in fear. But now it was here, I didn't know what I'd been worried about. Indeed I actually felt a sort of triumph: the truth about myself was coming out.

I was in trouble wasn't I? Alison was standing in the door of my office. I hummed indifferently. What were they after me for?

For smelling of rum.

She'd been trying to tell me about that herself.

Ah so what!

Well it mattered. Raising the cuffs of her cardigan a couple of inches, she stood watching me as steadily as a sentry in his box, or competent bouncer.

Two hundred years ago, all doctors'd smelled of rum.

Probably why they'd killed most of their patients.

Two hundred years ago, *everyone* had smelled of rum.

Had they now?

Even the kids had. Hadn't all been as bourgeois as Alison in those days.

'I'm not bourgeois, darling.' She advanced into my office. 'I'm working class. It's you that's bourgeois. And you look like a complete prat with that black eye.'

'Bollocks.' I slipped out of the other door and marched along to visit Melania who, chaste and powerful in a pale blue trouser suit, had the manners to conclude a telephone conversation as I entered.

'Oh, Mark!' She came towards me with her lips parted,

eyes wildly on my face, as if I were her lost child, or a celebrity friend she hadn't seen since schooldays in one of the modern networks of reunion. Taking both my hands in hers, she said, 'We have to talk!' I could swear her breast was heaving. Her breath smelled of coffee, with a petrolly overtone.

'Come on!' I laughed. 'D'you want to dance?' I stepped back so our arms lengthened, as if in preparation for a riotous rush across a barn or olden field, to the sound of fiddle and tabor.

'You must see' – she was coming forward now so as to cut down the distance over which fooling was possible – 'you must see what's happening, Mark.'

'I see it all, sweetheart.'

'You don't!'

'I see everything!'

'You don't see what they're doing to you!' Her eyes turned heavy and I laughed. Suddenly she broke away from me. She had a clinic. Could I meet her for lunch?

'I'll see,' I told her, strolling from her office.

However, I did not get to see my chum for lunch since I was now invited for a chat with Bernard Henderson, the Clinical Director. He had a Brummie accent, Bernie, which made him sound like a dunce, and his suits (baggy in the leg, boxy in the jacket) were uncool; though in the later 1980s they would have been cool among fellows who had no taste and ordered a lot of Moët. His shoes – ah, his shoes – were the shoes of an alderman attending a wedding who would probably not be expected to dance until everyone was too pissed to bother. In winter, he arrived at work in an anorak too short for his suit jacket, which gave him an air of unbureaucratic distraction, as if he'd just been supervising the rescue of a hillwalker.

He just doesn't give a stuff about appearances, Bernie. Like St Augustine and other wise fellows of antiquity, he's after the inner man. He thinks psychometric probing is a pile of bollocks and, privately, he thinks the same thing about diversity training. I also know that he keeps a ten pack of B&H about his person, that he smokes off NHS premises. That accent of his, he puts to good use.

'Bloody hell, brother,' he yowled, regarding my eye. 'Have you been playing away?'

'No,' I said. 'I just keep getting picked on.'

He tried to persuade me to take a week off sick, which was a kind enough way of avoiding suspension – or its preliminary phase anyway. I refused. I wasn't sick.

'I'm not bothered about the complaint, Mark. Bothered about you… We can fend the complaint off, mate.'

'Ah. Sorry, Bernie.'

'You can't get away with being pissed on the job these days, brother.' He looked at me like a sad dog. It could be wagered that Bernie Henderson had put away a few pints of M&B in his time.

'Well give me a week's holiday, Bern,' I told him. 'That'll see me right.'

'You think that'll be long enough, mate?' He'd have had in mind counselling, rehab, Vitamin B, though without great conviction; he'd prefer a man to sort himself out.

'I'll be myself after a week, Bern! I swear to you.'

'What'll you do with yourself, mate?' he asked craftily.

'Oh I've got something to sort out. And some thinking to do.'

'You'll not be off on a bender though will you, mate?'

'No, Bern.'

'Cos I know you can put it away. I was watching you on the battle cruiser last Christmas!' This was the department luncheon on the *Belfast*. 'Couldn't believe you carried on after!' Bernie Henderson shook his head, not without approval.

'You'll not see me like this again, Bern,' I said. 'I'm sorry.' He hadn't wanted to shame me so I added something positive: 'Maybe I'll go to Whitby for a few days.'

'Used to go there myself as a kid. Till my parents discovered Tenerife.' Bernie Henderson shook his head. 'Check out Hadleys.'

'What can I get there?'

'Best fish and chips outside Walsall.' There was a glint in his spectacles as I left, which prevented me from seeing his eyes. On his wall he had a diploma to say he knew about people. What on earth would he make of my friend Ian?

For all the front I'd put on with my colleagues, I was none too sure about my next move. 'On Monday game ends,' Ian said. What could I expect from him now? Monday was half gone. There was still game time, but it was running out. When a game ended, what supervened? Serious business? Penalties? Nothing? A free-for-all?... Jeers and abuse? The possibilities were many, and almost inevitably less agreeable than the game itself. It was up to me to keep it going.

This was why I decided to keep my word to the

Clinical Director and take a train to Whitby. Instinct was an unfamiliar force where I was concerned, but I seemed to recognise it now. I felt Joan Hunter would not have been lying to me, and whatever my friend had said that morning in his long living room, he'd never denied that this might be Laura's destination. What was more, I could visit my mother and father on the way.

I paused to sit and smoke a cigarette on the bed where I was getting some things together in a holdall. I should have seen them more often. King's Cross to Newark Northgate was an hour and a quarter. What the hell else had I had to do at weekends? I saw my dad's face aged to the colour of a walnut shell, at the wheel of his moss-green Rover. As he'd lived, so he drove – with thorough composure. I saw Ma's fingers, less dextrous with the peeler now, so the Christmas potatoes had planes cut in them like massy gems. She liked a gin and she liked a joke: when she beheld my eye, she'd need her sense of humour.

Ah, what was I thinking? A fine plan, to visit them in this state. All along they'd known I was – not a classic disappointment, not with the job I'd got, in a glorious, high-ranking institute of medicine; no, they'd known I was a crippled success, one who did not thrive. Quietly and patiently, they had known that. God bless them. Better for them to look down at me in a coffin, than arrive like this.

I was close to weeping for shame, all my plans dissolving, when my mobile began to pipe 'Where the Bee Sucks There Suck I'. Underneath me shirts were being squashed. The number was withheld.

'That Mark?'

'Yes.'

Decrepitating laughter followed.

'Could you tell me who you are?'

'Frank Whitby here.'

I drew my shirts out from beneath me and placed them on my bag. The sleeves limply supported each other, like a pile of shot men. I was confounded utterly. Joan Hunter had indeed been speaking true, though not with much precision.

The caller sighed dryly. 'You all right there, Mark?'

I said yeah. It sounded like *yug*.

'I understand you're acting for your friend, Ian?' The laughter resumed, crackling and zesty. Yet for all my confusion, I sensed that I wasn't being laughed at. It was the laughter of good-fellowship.

I was acting for Ian... I had to be, hadn't I?

'Wanna do a swap then, Mark?'

Certainly. I did want to. I was ready to go along with anything that was suggested to me.

'All right, my friend, here's your procedure.' Frank Whitby named an address off Blackstock Road. 'Now get yourself over there and collect him, then bring him to Devon – all right?' More laughter, devious-good-natured... I thought of Churchill and Stalin cackling, exchanging their 'naughty note' at Moscow, in which they carved up SE Europe between them, behind Roosevelt's back. Sixty years ago today.

Whitby texted in less than an hour to advise me there was a train at 16.20 from Waterloo that was cheaper and more reliable than First Great Western. By this time, I was sitting on a Victoria Line tube approaching Oxford Circus, having taken a taxi over to the address for the collection, where a man in a cardigan with glasses on a neck band, who resembled a familiar playwright, emerged from behind the dirty dark blue door of 25a Vaudeville Mews to hand me a shoe-box-sized parcel. The parcel was evidently 'him', the man having nodded and retired behind the door. Whitby's text was nicely timed: the Bakerloo Line joined Oxford Circus to both mainline stations for the West Country.

The parcel was elegantly wrapped in heavy azure paper. At Waterloo I stood with it under my arm waiting for the platform for the Exeter train to appear on the monitors. Was I losing my passivity? I lit a cigarette. Around me, the throng opened and closed. Up close, passivity is a complex matter. We all think that passivity is the opposite of activity. But what if passivity is a form of activity? What if nothing more conduces to making things happen or come about than allowing others to act on you – or compelling them to? Indeed, passivity may be a most subtle means of empowerment. Buddhists know this, as do carved things and beaten things, monuments, cathedrals, soufflés, song-birds of bronze and gold, Ali versus Foreman in Kinshasa, certain ladies, Dr Mark Malleable...

'I didn't think it was you, Doc! I was sure it wasn't!' a

voice called. 'It is though isn't it!' A man beside me was beholding me with a ribald sort of reverence. 'Cor – your eye though!' he now said as I tried to work out who the hell he was. A patient evidently…

***

'Ah!' I cried, 'Chas!'

'Yeah – it is me!' he beamed. 'Your headache clinic – I attended it.' He was in overalls.

'How've you been, Chas?' His face seemed to have lost the sweaty lour of last Wednesday. The coally eyes were no longer suetted in.

'Ah, Doctor' – he lowered his head a little, and his voice – 'life's turned round since I saw you. All down to you it is. Like you know you told me the devil was in the quantity, yeah, when I told you I was on sixty Stellas per weekend? You probably won't remember cos you see loads like me. However, I listened to you. Sat down and made a decision after I saw you at the Institute. All my mates got the same problem, yeah? So I deleted em. Wiped em off the phone. Removed temptation. That's the recommendation, yeah, for people like me?'

'Yeah – that's right.' That was the recommendation, for people like him.

'Come up the West End solo Saturday night. Blew out football. Blew out Stella-fuelled mayhem. Blew out my mates. Went for an Indian – solo. Fish molee, yeah?' He nodded, to see what I thought. 'Cinema – solo. Admittedly, I did have a few vodka tonics – but nothing like the old days. Nothing *approaching*, Doc.'

'That's good, Chas. That's the way.'

Rooting his hands in his overall pockets, he looked round the concourse. I remembered he was a track engineer.

'Busy today, Chas?'

'Just back from Clapham, Doc. Been undertaking switchgear maintenance.'

'My dad used to work on switchgear,' I told him with some pride. 'GEC: High Voltage.'

'Ah, these are only 1kV, Doc.' He looked back at me; he assessed my eye.

'What is it?' I said. 'What d'you want to tell me?'

'Came in the Belvedere Hotel.' He sniffed. 'Saturday night. Check out the girls, as you do.' He scratched the back of his neck. 'Saw you was in there, Doc.'

'Yeah,' I replied and lit another cigarette. Red light, red drinks, grilling red heat.

'You was celebrating, Doc!' He shook his head. 'You was going for it, geezer.' He shook his head, as Bernie Henderson had shaken his.

'Sorry, Chas. I think I had one too many Manhattans.'

'Ah — far be it from me, Doc. But when you started rucking —' Chas sucked in air with a dry whistling sound, to betoken anxiety. He was wishing to tell me something, but out of respect, or out of embarrassment, out of awe, or maybe contempt — at any rate, out of something — he held back; and I had no wish to push him. 'Here,' he grinned, man-to-man, switching his thoughts to a different line, 'that bird you had on your knee — mate, she was something. Something else. Trust me!'

'Oh yeah,' I mumbled.

'Class she was,' Chas averred. 'Quality.'

'I've got to shift, Chas,' I said. 'My train's going… I'd like to talk to you another time.'

'I'd be honoured, Doctor. I've joined the Headache Forum on the Web. Here!' he reached into an inner pocket of his overalls and handed me a crisp card, then I hurried away from him across Waterloo, his clean-faced revelations confounding me as much as Whitby's call. In the rear he was shouting, 'You gave me my life, Doc!'

His card said he was Charles W Longley; below his name in tiny font was his mobile number, nothing more. Perhaps he'd had them made to start his new life. The dual-voltage South West Trains 319 locomotive slid heavily by Vauxhall and New Convent Garden towards Clapham Junction, with its great steel fans of converging and diverging lines. As London closed behind me and the west opened, it was time at last for me to inquire hard and critically into a number of things, was it not? At Ian's I'd been telling myself that I must withdraw and think, and here was the opportunity. In the next carriage, I thought I heard the drinks trolley.

But when I tried to consider my friend's recycling of our mutual past in the escapades he recounted, that all seemed behind me now like the tracks that had brought me to this moment. Did it matter that he'd really been drinking with me in Camden when he said he'd been with the couple in Primrose Hill, the blonde and her dark husband? We met after he'd been to the dentist; he had an abscess like a half-lemon. Surely knowing my memory would discover him, he lied to me; he invented the clicking bracelet.

Did it matter now that he had really been in my company the evening of the Xmas lunch on the battlecruiser *Belfast*, when he was supposedly doing Joe with Irene looking on? The drinks trolley was coming. He lied to me about telling lies to Laura involving me, surely knowing my memory would discover him; he invented the Rabbit in Irene's hand.

His practice was unfathomable, but must surely have had some purpose, servant of a strange or subtle evil whose motives weren't all, or even mainly, malevolent; yet how much it had made happen was... Ah, this got you nowhere! The girl on my knee in the Belvedere, the occurrences of Chas Longley, the omnipotence of Joan, the familiarity of the Persian – these were scarcely to be questioned, at least not by me.

By half six the land and towns of the west were black: black Yeovil, black Crewkerne, black Axminster. As the train clicked, I observed my dark reflection, a large enfeatured acorn in the carriage window. The deep, bone-stiffened York collar of my costly shirt held my head secure. Two weeks before I started secondary school, my mother took me to a department store with a list of uniform requirements and recommended items of kit, such as football boots, a bottle-green sweater, a biro that wrote in four colours. On my first morning, I beheld myself in the bathroom mirror in my new stiff cotton shirt and tie and wondered what the future held in store. As I strode down the drive swinging my bright brown pseudo-leather briefcase, maybe out of pride, maybe apprehension, my ma was trying not to cry. I saw her through the kitchen window.

At last I knew what the future had in store. Laura would be returning with me. A week from the day that she went away. I said this to myself once or twice. It had a good clear bell-like resolution. While thinking rustled and writhed, this promise rang. I said it again... Perhaps the best player of the game played the game without thinking?

Say I gave up thought altogether, turned off the torch. Progressed in the manner of the poem I like, the seventh Roman Elegy of Goethe, from thought to life... Ah, symmetry in everything. As the poet went from north to south, Weimar to Rome, so I began my life in the north where the Roman Fosse Way starts. A January day in 1964, soft fenland breezes blasting a hospital above a racecourse, in my ma's account. And the Fosse Way ends in Exeter, ancient Rome's most western outpost. Perhaps I too would receive the hospitality of Jove, 'lord of guests'; and his daughter 'Fortune' would bless me. Blessed symmetry...

The trolley returned. *Tup*. I tapped on the azure parcel on the seat to my right. *Tup*. Laura would be coming back with me. One week from the day she went away. I was the knight gallant, as had been foretold. When the king and queen fell out, it was up to the knight gallant to fetch her back. In my left hand I raised the parcel. Weighed no more than the rough brown box I once carried for a week to my anatomy class. Edinburgh 1985: autumn term. It was wrapped the colour of the blue lace Ian put on the table in front of Joan. As if skating round a pond frozen mirror-clear, faster than thought, I recalled that scene, until the scene began to shine.

You could ask who wrapped the parcel. Never mind.

Harken to the train, to its dragon growl. Honiton. Whimple. Pinhoe. Names to suit old ladies. Whitby... who would have thought, after Friday night?

But I wasn't thinking. Where would I find Whitby? Would he hand Laura over, or would she just say, 'Hi!,' and put down a newspaper? Why was she here anyway? If I'd been a reader I'd have asked these questions; but I'd read enough.

Exeter Central had a grim, wartime look. As the train came to a rest, there was a text incoming from Whitby: 'Don't get off at Central. One after!' The electric doors shut with a shuddering bang and the train began to curve down a hill over a river that glittered in the dark. Whitby's timing was exceedingly exact.

Outside Exeter St David's, with my name on an orange card, a big, handsome Arab was waiting. He was called Baghdad and we were going for a ride.

I was in his hands, I said, and he laughed and took my holdall, glancing at the azure parcel beneath my arm, appraising my black eye. As we drove out of the city along the river, he told me his life.

***

What was life about but fucking and fighting? Twenty-one years he'd been in Britain. He was a civil engineer with a BSc from the University of Newcastle, but no one would give Baghdad a job at what he'd trained for. I asked what had brought him to the West Country. The girls had brought him to the West Country. He winked and hit me on the arm. Owch. At last, he married one of his girlfriends and bought a cab. One time a driver called Mal, smelly long-haired bastard who never washed, he was riding Baghdad real bad. Never let up, morning to night. The other drivers laughed at the names Mal was calling Baghdad; they were with Mal. So at sunset, what did Baghdad do? He took Mal round the back of the station to Siding No. 5 where the Shark wagon was and he gave the motherfucker the hiding of his life. That was the day he got the nickname Baghdad. The drivers had been his friends since. Except Mal. But he never came back to work anyway.

I told him he'd done right and Baghdad said yeah, he supposed so. We had to stick up for ourselves. He asked where I was from. I told him. Then he asked where my father was from. In my life, I've been asked that more than I've been asked most things. He said it wasn't his business, but maybe my father wouldn't be glad to see my eye looking like that. I said I'd got it in combat and Baghdad hummed and said was it about a woman? I said yeah and Baghdad laughed and beat the wheel. That was good. That was how it should be. Men should fight about women.

We were on the motorway. I noticed a sign for Dartmoor. Inside the rough brown box I carried across Edinburgh to my anatomy class twenty years ago, a skull smiled in dark silence. Baghdad glanced at me absorbently. You had to search for the shine in his dark eyes. He wanted to know if I had come down here for a woman too. I said I had and Baghdad said he assumed I was taking her back, and not just visiting. Because – he paused to overtake a long vehicle – because I looked like I meant business. I said I was taking her back. And what was more, I wasn't leaving here without her either. Baghdad hunched his shoulders, projecting himself forward. In my mind's eye, his cab ripped like a tin. I was glad we were pals. He must have crippled smelly Mal. He asked if she was my woman. I said no, she was my friend's.

We descended a hill and came up the other side through a village towards a squat Norman church where the road forked. This was where Baghdad was bringing me. Some young women passed in front of us from a side lane and up the right fork. With one eye on them, he swung up on the right, halting outside the Henry IVth.

'How much do I owe you, Baghdad?' I couldn't see a meter.

'That's OK, brother. It'll be paid the other end.'

I felt I understood him. We shook hands, observing the young women entering the pub. Maybe I should have said something to him about the current high jinks in the Middle East; but do we always have to crack on about each other's origins?

At first the locals were as blurred as personnel in an Impressionist painting; but as my inspection discovered that Laura was indeed sitting nowhere, they began to take their places around me, solid, animated, diverse. I had a strange sensation of being in a process: I was the last crystal of a chemical that supersaturates a solution, causing coloured shapes to appear, fantastic, brilliant, drab.

A 300-pounder in a grey sweater hooped with pale blue, dark blue, orange, green and red, silent above the dark wood and glass of a corner table; below him, three friends in counsel. This way a kind of poet in a white Romantic shirt, a salesman, hair receding, a woman in light green and glinting specs, a couple at a table: English rose, long, dusty man…

Young women left of me, hair lush, feet brown; still dressed for summer. Dogs weave and duck, a pair of them. To my right by the bar's short arm, young lads of the village, money out beside their lager. A black-bearded hearty on the back wall holding court, whispering, patting, agreeable, at others' sallies giving way as if thrown something heavy to catch…

Though I was getting no recognition, I apprehended they were aware of me with my suit and parcel, my holdall and black eye. This was part of the process. My difference had to dissolve, yet modify that into which it was dissolving. I knew that Whitby could be in here somewhere; I knew not to ask where; he'd be in the solution from which my entrance had not yet precipitated him.

As I asked for a pint of Shotten Herring, to my left began music, unannounced. On a low stage at the pub's end was a banjo, fiddle, accordion and drum outfit. Cunning and relentless swirling filled the air. The players shouted, 'Ha!', 'One more again!' The young lads didn't much care for it: they'd sooner have been listening to R&B, but kept an eye on me in case I looked sniffy. I didn't give a fuck. I'd do them one by one. Like that kid in the alley with stars on his teeth.

The band played faster, gusto increasing. Winking in open conspiracy, they roared 'Ha!', 'Wuuh!', 'Yumaaah!' 'Wuuh' was something like a near miss; 'Yumaaah' was the back of the net. Their relentless art took you on a long and winding ride, seemed to call over its shoulder, 'We aren't finished yet by a long way!' The sound ruffled me, it thrilled my heart. If I were offered a turn on the stage, I'd give a lecture on Goethe's lyrics: 'Man's soul is the water of a lake,/ The breeze that whips it up his destiny.' That breeze as it seemed was blowing in this music.

There was a break and the poet was being coaxed to join in. Bearing a curious instrument, about the size of a halved marrow, he took his place on a small stool in his flowing duellist's shirt. The instrument hung around his neck on a broad belt. In shape, it was an inverted teardrop, but with a flat front down which ran a fingering structure like a deck-house: held horizontally, rather than at an angle, it would have resembled a mastless boat. As he fingered the instrument with his left hand, the long-haired poet wound a little curved handle at the top end with his right.

He began to produce a melodious buzz and heart-stirring wail. The drummer, whacking one of those shallow Irish drums, grinned at the addition through his pale beard. It was by no means a cool sound. The village lads were smirking. It was much rarer than that. It was a sweet-disciplined skirl in light, persistent rhythm, lone drum and pipe keeping company. My private film was rolling, of death and glory, my own private film... until the buzz fell away and I was just a black eye, a bulging bladder. Leaving my bag and my parcel where I'd stood, I went along to the Gents. If only the music could have played without end, I would have been made.

Yet on returning, as if with a click, the air changed.

Laura was about to appear. This would be the time. The black-beard approached me crying richly, 'Mark! Why didn't you announce yourself? Standing there on your own for goodness' sake! – What'll you have?' This must be Whitby; after everything, Whitby was just going to be a nice version of Rab. I was thinking that maybe I shouldn't really be surprised, given my range of recreational interests, when the good-hearted fellow cried, 'Mark, I'm only Owen Salter but this is my place!' He was the landlord of the Henry IVth.

It now came about that I was distracted into the company of the locals by the woman with glinting spectacles and green cardigan, and brought to the table of the English rose and dusty man, who drew me into leisurely talk about the world, London, Devon, the train journey from Waterloo, the hostage crises in the Middle East. Did female hostages generally stand a better chance than male? We had to wonder. Laura was not mentioned. Laura was not hinted at. We were keeping mum. Evidently she was going to make a spectacular entrance. For a moment my breath caught. Surely these people were in on it? The bespectacled woman and lean dusty man smoked hand-rolled tobacco with a kind of slow enjoyment quite unlike my own suicidal emphasis. They had an old way of talking, their sentences complete, patient, unsyncopated. Phrases such as 'In any case' recurred, and 'besides' and 'after all', for measure and rhythm. I wondered if I'd ended up among a coven of unhurried witches, far from the hedonist babble of the city. Owen Salter appeared with a new drink for me. The new drink was a rum and shrub.

The woman in glinting specs twirled her roll-up in the ashtray to extinguish it, laid it on the rim and hoped Owen was not trying to get me tipsy. Owen, who was rather reminding me of the wig-salesman in Scorsese's *GoodFellas*, recoiled with the motion of catching a small, manageable boulder, protesting that shrub was only a cordial. I wondered if this little exchange had ever been played before. The dusty man, who must be a builder or stone worker, said shrub was an Arabic word, originally. How much of a ritual was I involved in here? How familiar was this process? My heart pulsed. How many visitors had Baghdad brought to the Henry IVth?

'I'm doing you a steak,' Owen Salter stooped to murmur. 'Daresay you haven't eaten. Chips or b.p.?'

So they wanted to fatten me? I noticed that the table had acquired more company: the poet and the salesman had penetrated the space between the others, or to be precise it seemed to have widened to accommodate them. With trembling fingers, the poet was rolling himself a cigarette. He smoked an unusual brand of tobacco, from a one-ounce crimson and ochre pouch. The salesman had an expression of queasy complacency. To my left, a girl in shorts was hovering in consultation with the bespectacled woman. At the bar, two of her friends were lurking. They'd be about nineteen. One of the friends pushed out her chest: she was wearing a heavenly camisole the colour of my parcel. Her hair was thick, clean, dark gold. I imagined her leaning from an upper window to dry it, face skyward. Could this be happening for the first time?

My meal arrived. I was to eat it in front of an audience of nine, including Owen Salter, now invested in a clean white apron, who stood back, arms folded. I looked down at what I'd been served and up at Master Salter, who whirred through his beard. The steak was a T-bone, a cubit in size: you could have opened the batting with it. Maybe my host was an old *Flintstones* fan. To balance the steak, he had ladled a ridge of peas onto the right side of the plate. 'We'll place Wellington's infantry here, Second and Third Battalions of the 95th and the Inniskillings!' I said in the manner of a battle enthusiast who's still allowed airtime since he doesn't look the part in any respect. Someone emitted a cackle. The chips were stacked in the middle, as thick as the planks in Jewson's yard. They were feeding me up all right.

My host went away, returning with a glass and bottle of claret. They lowered their eyes or looked among themselves: this was how they'd watched the kings eat. The girl in shorts, who'd seated herself to my left, unlidded the mustard for me, distant-eyed as a dentist's assistant. My knife was sharp; it worked the plate over with the skill of an old swordsman. Around me they were talking well. The poet led them. My assistant asked me for a chip, and nibbled it slowly. Queasily the salesman watched her. The girl in heaven blue stuck her tongue out. This was how they watched the mock king eat, surrounded by concubines. Next morning they tore out his heart. My assistant plucked open a handbag that was no bigger than a purse, withdrew a little jar and applied an ointment to my eye. It was cool.

'What have you got in your parcel, Mark? Is it a present?' she asked me confidentially.

'Oh that ain't for you, Suzie!'

For a while I'd been aware of a tenth spectator, supping quietly at the bar from a silver tankard, rolling himself a cigarette from a tin; the russett-bearded drummer from the band had been holding himself in reserve. Perhaps he was guarding against my doing a runner. Behind his steel-framed specs, his eyes were sharp with a kind of permanent alacrity, as if he were watching a race. He was wearing trousers such as you don't see in the city now, the sort advertised in the right-of-centre papers at the weekend: 100% wool: classically tailored: grey, bottle green or navy blue: two pairs for £15.99. Work boots were on his feet. He had the look of a cunning, tireless trapper or prospector; but there was something too of the boffin whose work has made him careless of appearances; yet the beard of faded gold and bright attentiveness of the eyes made me think of a captain, shrewd and unsinkable. To complete his outfit, he wore a swarfy blue-green jumper-cum-sweatshirt. It was he who'd spoken now, grinning at my plate.

'Come and sit down, Frank, for goodness' sake, instead of lingering up there!' the woman with spectacles told him.

'Don't mind if I do, Liz!' laughed my captain and took a stool between that lady and Suzie; once again, space seemed to expand to make room around the table. 'Frank Whitby,' he said, holding out his hand to me. 'I'd have joined you earlier, like, but I don't care to disturb a man while he's eating.'

Whitby's face was tanned, forearms cabled with sinews beneath the flesh. 'Pleased to meet you.' I offered him my hand.

'Pleasure's mine, Mark. Did you enjoy your steak?'

I declared the steak was excellent.

'Like death with his scythe you were, way you set about those peas!' Wheezily Whitby began to laugh. As I accompanied him, I wondered where he had Laura.

I laughed until my jaw ached with the kind of dull pain that sets in for spans of thirty or forty minutes at a time in omen of an abscess, before things really turn critical and the face assumes a bestial character. Whitby, as I already knew, liked to laugh. He also liked to laugh for a long time; the wheezing was merely the sound of his lungs getting going, it was no impediment. I mustn't stop till he was just about to, and therefore kept an eye on him while he rejoiced. Just as we appeared to be approaching the last bars of the movement, the salesman joined in (not without malice I thought); we were compelled to carry on.

'Ah,' Whitby exclaimed finally, 'Owen's been trying to offload those peas since St George's Day!' This brought on another outburst, in which all participated. This time, the poet kept Whitby company up to the closing moments. I intermitted earlier, since I wouldn't be expected to appreciate the esoteric aspect of this, and Suzie paused with me and had a drink of my claret. Under the table, she was trying to do something to me with her bare foot.

'So,' Whitby gave me his bright look and grinned with strong teeth, 'what have you brought, my friend?'

I put the parcel on the table where my plate had been amid the glasses and ashtrays. Did he wish to open it, or should I?

'Oh I think you should, if you'd be so kind,' Whitby said.

So I undid the azure parcel with their eyes on me and inside was a shoebox which contained nothing but a smaller box of dark pink. Lifting this from its tissue paper, I undid its clasp and raised the lid. A tinkling filled the room as if an ice-cream van had just parked outside then a little female figure rose to a standing position and began to rotate in front of a little oval mirror. In her left hand was a blue bird. It was a musical vanity box, with room in front of the rotating figure for jewellery and trinkets. The tinkling song was 'Some Day My Prince Will Come', but the figurine's hair was blonde, tied in a pink bow.

The locals looked on in enchantment. 'Ah!' Suzie sighed. 'Ain't she lovely!' The figurine rotated and the music tinkled. Whitby stroked his beard and nodded. I fancied that the English rose had tears in her eyes. The poet seemed to be trembling with pleasure. Whitby stayed stroking his beard and the tiny song repeated itself. Presently the mechanism ran down. Raising the box, Liz wound the small key at the back and music resumed and the little blonde figure with the pink bow turned. Again we sat and stared... But when the box had been wound for the last time, what followed?

Had Ian contrived this in his subtle heart, free drink, food, female attention, Laura's body in a field grave, soon to be joined by mine? Or was Laura just the lure to the sacrifice of a man like me?... What were these folk I'd come among? How much went down in England, of which we had no clue? I looked up. Liz glinted. What were these folk? Utter innocents... or white connoisseurs of a strange and devious order? How much longer were we to listen to this tinkling toy, which had now been wound for a third time? If I told them it was a piece of trash, would they slap my back like the boy who shouted at the emperor – or finally turn on me?

Suzie whispered. She wanted to know what I thought; her breath dissolved my thinking. Perhaps manners were more important than taste here. When in Rome... the cliché was felicitous, was it not?

Later, Whitby touched my arm and asked me to go to the bar with him for a minute. 'Looks like young Laura doan it?' he murmured.

I said *yeah*, because in a way it did, depending on how much significance you allowed simulacra. Then Whitby glanced into his empty tankard and said it was myself I'd delivered her to, if the truth be told. All the way from London. I smelled a rat here and quickly asked this humorous host about the real Laura. When was I going to be able to see her? Regarding me now with a sort of iron grandfatherliness, Whitby patted my shoulder and assured me she was safe and sound. His fingers were like little hammers, shocking the nerves as if they were carrying live current. I was assured.

As for the little lady in the music box, well that was a sign I'd made it. What I'd brought was what I'd come for. It symbolised she'd been in my arms, so to speak, or in my possession long before I arrived here. That's what it symbolised. Owen Salter handed Whitby his replenished tankard. I grinned as if my driving instructor had just revealed I'd passed, regardless of my actual performance in the test. Nor was Whitby finished with his revelations: 'As you'll no doubt have guessed, Mark, Ian's my brother's boy.' He paused for me to virtually stick a Rothmans up my left nostril. 'You ain't surprised are you, Mark?'

'I don't always spot the obvious,' I muttered, wondering if this might not be one of my major problems.

Whitby was hard put not to laugh till the cock crew. At last he cried, 'Well what must you have been thinking with all this palaver I do not know! I am sorry, my friend!'

I tried to tell him it was all right, though this was far from easy. Then Suzie waved at me. She wasn't laughing. I supposed I'd been enjoying myself.

'Good!' Whitby put down his tankard firmly. 'You deserve to enjoy yourself too, from what I been noticing. Your enjoyment ain't over yet either.' Suzie crossed her legs. The salesman was trying to make up to her. 'What it comes down to basically – speaking as an ex-services man – and I think you're somewhat interested in army matters yourself, Mark – what it comes down to is this. Ian – ever since he were a very small fellow indeed – he's took his time over things. Always, he has done things in such a way as to obtain the best result; or some advantage at least. Even when he's made a mistake, or worse. I'll give you an example. When he was a schoolboy, him and his pals, larking around, they contrived to set a barn on fire. Substantial amount of damage to property they caused. All the other boys owned up to it pretty immediately; he wouldn't. But they all tried to drop each other in it and

241

blame each other for having the paraffin; he was in trouble, but he was saying nothing. At last, he told the truth to the police, and he told it straight – in his own time. He was the ringleader. Well, he got off with no more'n a row, whereas two of the other boys were sent to the detention centre.

'Now militarily speaking, that's a form of tactical withdrawal.' Whitby rolled a cigarette, sealing it lightly with his hammer-hard forefinger, then looked at me. 'One of Napoleon's great techniques. When he's in a tough spot, he pulls back so as to take the fewest casualties on his own side. That's his first aim. Second aim: to disorder the enemy's front by drawing him forward into an area where it's no longer to his advantage to be. With me?'

'Yeah,' I said. I was fascinated. Once again, I had so much to think of that I needed to make a withdrawal of my own in order to get any of this into some sort of order … if only I'd not opted out of thinking.

'This is my way of looking at it anyhow,' Whitby continued, lighting up.

'And you've known Laura some time then?'

'Oo yes… Came down here with Ian for one of their first holidays together. Years ago. Loves it. Seen her swimming in a tarn like a water baby. Loves nature, Laura does. And what better place to find it than Dartmoor!' Whitby cried as if hosting a Sunday night TV programme. 'So when things go hard between herself and Ian, she rings up her Uncle Frank and asks if she can come down for a while.'

'So she is here?'

'She's been here this last week.'

I was perplexed in the extreme. How much of this was set up, and how much of it was just happening? Or how much of it was in between? *Between* in the way that although orders of battle are set up, or directed from a centre of command, the battle itself is very apt to happen in its own way, driven by its own forces. Furthermore, whose side was who on? Obviously, I was benefitting from Ian's 'tactical withdrawal' if Laura was going to end up as – I could scarcely think this – as *mine*. Obviously. But what was I doing down here 200 miles west of him? And what about the disorder effected upon *my* front in the last week?

'I know what you're thinking,' Whitby grinned. 'You're wondering where you stand. Well here's what I've learned from my own experience: when you're confused what exactly's going on around you, best thing to do is look after your own position; dig in till the confusion clears. What you *don't* want to be doing,' Whitby was doing his best to avoid sounding as if he was giving me orders, 'what you don't want is running this way and that trying to clear up what the hell's happening. Cos all you do then is lose track of your own position. Then you are utterly vulnerable to enemy fire, *and* to fire from your own side.' Whitby refreshed himself from his tankard. There was a whiff of cold fire and swarf from him. 'D'you know,' he informed me, 'I can feel another set coming on!'

He strolled away towards the pub's end, where the poet joined him on his curious instrument. They began to produce a buzz that filled the air in many places at once with solemn, redoutable jauntiness. Over this was a sound of pattering rain, thunderous rumbling, rain re-pattering.

On and on they played. Spirits must be playing among them: they made enough sound for two dozen. I saw the dusty man crouching before them with the music box, balancing a mic on its front edge, withdrawing. It began to tinkle through the rainy buzz, courageous, sentimental, then shrieking with feedback, till he returned to make it better. Its waltzing melody reminded me at last of the noise Ian said he heard last Monday morning, of Germans carousing. That noise which had something to do with an omen.

★★★

In a jet-black 4x4 we were swooping through high hedgerows in the early dawn, Whitby having offered to take me to the wars. Three and a half centuries ago, Cromwell's men clattered down these narrow plunging lanes to subdue the county. Devon was easily subdued, passive territory. Whitby, steering with the careless professionalism of a driver on a rough road in Armagh, Basra or Kandahar, sung a shanty; the rest of us did the chorus, which went something like this:

> The first mate's in his cuddy,
> The doctor's on the piss,
> The first mate's in his cuddy
> Oh there's nothing gone amiss!

For want of space, Suzie sat on my knee, inclining herself backwards; my dick felt useful, full with potential, like a chisel in a soft case. I held her waist to balance her.

There'd been an incident late in the khazi of the Henry IVth: she'd sneaked in and offered to go down on me. When I said *No*, in the manner of Dr Johnson, she asked if I was saving myself for the 'other one'. Because if I was, I might be interested to know she'd been through half the lads in the village. Oh ho! She was making this up, from jealousy no doubt. I'd never had as many women coming on as this last week. Even Liz Whitby was leaning hard against me as we took the bends. I forgave Suzie, who'd healed my eye and had been bestowing upon me since she introduced herself strange and felicitous sensations of what might still be possible.

With a final chorus of the shanty, we turned off the road down a track into a meadow, where we left the cars. Dew was on the grass and the light hadn't developed enough to turn the tree lines down either side, the copse in the middle and the woodland 100 yards away at the meadow's end, from black to their natural colour. Behind unbroken cloud, October sun was rising. In a quilted sleeveless jacket, a man stepped out of the grey air and Whitby cried, 'Hoy! Here already, Don!' Don dragged his left leg as he walked. He was in the early stages of muscular dystrophy. Behind me I heard a snap of metal and shivered slightly. Perhaps all this had indeed been a complicated lure to put me to death in a green meadow, a fatal charade from beginning to end. How much went down in England, of which we had no notion?... Were these folk about to enjoy my terror?

With marvellous speed Whitby was assembling a machine on the wet grass. It consisted of a spring-loaded arm on a low stand, with a small seat on the left of the arm and perpendicular handle on the right. At the back of the 4x4, the poet was mixing a maroon liquid from a medicine bottle with sherry in a row of little shot glasses on the lid of a biscuit tin.

'This gentleman first!' Whitby laughed. I swallowed mine and as the rich aniseedy liquor coated my oesophagus, I knew nothing could terrify me more than the thought of the life I'd led – and failed to lead. The poet was murmuring something to me about a chemist of the county who still sold paregoric when his words were overmounted by a louder voice, a whirr, a blasting crack.

Turning I saw smoke on the brightening air, Whitby seated at his little machine, the ruddy-faced countryman Don watching the sky above the copse, breaking open a shotgun which sagged obediently; producing two yellow cartridges from his pocket, cocking his gun with a cry of 'Pull!'

Whitby pulled and pulled again the arm on his machine sending two black disks whirring high above the copse. The countryman following them with his gun as they rose and hovered, shot the left-hand disk in half and clipped the second; a spray of fragments spun beyond it as it began to fall. Smooth as a wooden signal rising, the countryman did it again; and again.

'Don's the champ,' Whitby told me presently as I examined Don's over-and-under shotgun. There was silver plating beneath the lower barrel, intricately engraved with flowers and volutes like an Italianate fashion shirt from the Seventies. 'Shoots crows, Don does… Farmers pay a fiver a dozen.'

'Pull!' Don shattered two more then stood aside and lit an Embassy.

'You shall have a turn in a minute,' Whitby said. 'Ever shot before?' I shook my head. I'd only dreamed of it. Whitby rose from his machine, pulled a long zip-up case from the back of the 4x4 and produced my gun. Speaking ever so softly, as if I were a prince of the realm, he showed me the ropes. 'Never point him, right? Hold him downwards – at all times. Till you want to fire him. Safety catch, he's off like this. Keep the sight on the clay – it'll just be the one for you, Mark! – sight on the clay, see? Follow him as he rises. Try and hit him while he's still climbing, all right?' He opened a box of red cartridges, laying it by my feet. Picking one out like a fat tube of sweets I slid it in. 'When he clicks, he's cocked.' Whitby watched me, then squatted at his machine.

Pull!

The clay whirred and at seventy feet, I blew his arse off. Softly the shotgun cracked and kicked, requiring nothing.

'Shot!' Don said.

Pull!... Pull!... Pull! I shattered two more ascending, then hit one as he began to fall beyond the copse. And another. And another. Over there, Liz, Suzie and the other women were sitting with a thermos of coffee, courtesy of the provident Owen who was now fussing with a rug which slipped off their knees as they jiggled and applauded. I blasted away, shot spreading, hot smoke rising. The black powder charge stuffed and soused the air. This was eminently better than thinking. Rear rank fire! I shot down my thoughts like owls, portly brown abstractions.

Shot! the poet was murmuring. Oh well shot... Handing me another glass of his potion, he brushed from

247

his eyes his long hair, unzipped his own piece from its brown case and began to blast the clays like Byron on a duck-hunt, left eye shrewdly cocked. Then in turn the English rose shot the clays, and Owen Salter, the dusty man and Suzie. And the way they shot had for each of them her or his own character in it, reminding me of when I had first observed them. And the dew on the cold grass washed Suzie's feet clean from the pissy floor of the khazi of the Henry IVth. And woe betide anyone who came down to fuck with their corner of old England, because they were as accurate as the English squares at Waterloo when the French rode upon them in their glittering cuirasses and their plumes. They were accurate and they took their time; and they were beginning to glow at me with a sort of fuzzy vividness, something like an order of angels, enstationed before the cars.

I went with Don to collect the unbroken clays from the meadow beyond the copse. It was daylight now, though overcast and still. A flight of dark birds rose cawing from the woodland. At my side, Don paused to watch them, then stooped to gather a clay that glistened in the grass. I wanted to say something to him, this man who shot so sweetly and dragged his foot as he went. But my profession stuck in my mouth, with its diagnostic questions and its enervating labels. What had I been doing for twenty years drooping over the sick? *I* of all people? Here was where his therapy was, blasting crows from the black sky.

'Got em all now, I would think,' Don said, face slightly averted. We turned and began to walk back to the cars.

'What you see with Frank, it ain't all you get like,' he told me, face still averted, 'not by a way.'

'He's quite a character, Don,' I said.

'Oh he's a character all right… He's been around too.'

'Really?'

'Oh he's been around, Frank has.'

'He's a local man though I take it?' I said to be polite. I was intent on not drawing Don. I wanted people to stop informing me of things for a good long time, maybe forever.

'Yes. Local man, Mr Whitby. But he's seen a bit of the world.'

'Really?'

'Oh yes. He has been around.'

I hummed politely. 'Where's he been then, Don?'

'Oh he ain't really disposed to talk about it, Frank ain't.'

'Ah.' This was very quaint. I grinned at my shoes; the fine matt leather was dew-glossed, in spots and tiny runnels.

'He's turned his hand to a good many things, old Frank.' Don looked across at me, left eye partly closed as if something were lodged in it. His face was raw and shy. Then he said something else and I carried on in silence, looking at my feet. It must have been something I was thinking tangling with Don's words, because what I thought I heard him say was *and he would kill his own nephew*. By the time I'd untangled the words from the thought, we were back at the cars. What he'd said was, *And he has been a lot of things too*. I seemed to be tripping again; this must be an effect of the maroon potion administered by the long-haired poet, and the sleep I'd missed in recent times.

Next Whitby showed me something long wrapped in a green cloth, which he began to unfurl. '.303 he is,' Whitby explained. Silver and brown he shone, with a black telescopic sight. Whitby produced a little box of brass-coated bullets, loaded one, aimed casually at the woodland and fired. The meadow beneath my feet rang with the sound which then vibrated shockingly up the body and out through the skull, as if lightning were ungrounding itself. 'Quite a recoil on him!' Whitby laughed above the twanging air. At last, I knew how war once sounded. That sound multiplied by many thousands. How it must have blasted the souls of men, weeks and years of that sound! In me it rang on with the reverb of acute nerve pain, from teeth to spine, up and down and along the bones, embarrassing my death-and-glory cinema, shaming its pathetic images.

Then Whitby seemed to take me up to a high place where I could no longer see the others and the wind was blowing hard from the west. He asked me all I'd feared, and when I told him Whitby pointed at a cloud which seemed to swirl nauseous and abject yellow in a trough of air. 'Out with fear!' this curious captain called above the wind, gazing at me with alacrity, then raised his .303 and shot the cloud and I swear that it dispersed like a slick of grease at the contact of detergent. Next he asked me why I held back and when I told him, 'Well,' cried Whitby, 'you should reckon yourself four times the man you are. Not reduce yourself as you have been doing. You've been living as neither half, you fool! You've been given the gift of double nature. What have you done with it? You have been denying yourself nature entirely. From what I have heard, you been living as no man.' A deer broke into the field below us, maybe a quarter of a mile away. Whitby dropped to the floor and seemed to be humping the grass; at last he settled, still as death, took aim and brought the deer down. 'I'll have him dressed and sent to your mother and father,' Whitby said, and we seemed now to be back in a wooded place, Whitby carrying the deer over his shoulders. We came to a clearing and sun broke through the cloud wall and slanted across a tree stump covered with ivy. 'Who's there now?' Whitby asked me, and I saw the stump as the golden-bearded countenance of my friend Ian. I couldn't speak, and Whitby said, 'If he don't identify himself, you know what we have to do!' And still I couldn't speak, then Whitby gave me his hunting rifle and said, 'Take him out, Chopra! That's an order. Take him out now… It's all for love!' So I raised the piece and fired into the light and as the air screamed, the sun went in and the dark stump was no longer a man.

Then we were back by the cars. Someone had switched on the stereos and Owen was uncorking a couple of bottles of sherry, which were passed round and swigged from the neck, as we began to dance in a circle like a field full of old witches, Don leaning against the back of the 4x4, watching us, watching the sky. By God could Whitby cut a caper! Even as he danced he smoked a roll-up, grinning, throwing high his knees. Round and roundabout we spun, cackling and wheezing till the ground began to tilt and we all fell reeling, sick and hilarious on the lumpy meadow grass where we sat with spread legs like wounded troops awaiting evacuation.

'I fancy,' Whitby said at length, looking at his boots,

then leaning towards me, 'fancy Laura'll be ready now.'
And so we rose and scattered.

Laura

Above the fireplace was a photograph of Whitby in uniform, clean shaven, holding a beret, eyes alert; he was without glasses. In another photo a cloth dragon with foiled face and snout observed the camera; this was Whitby in the mummer's play for St George's Day. He'd now sped upstairs on an errand; I trusted this was to fetch Laura, who'd not been waiting for me in the flower-wreathed door of the Whitbys' cottage. On the lawn outside lay the corpse of the stag he'd shot. There was a copy of the *Daily Mail* on the settee. 'He's had a stag home and dressed by nine in the morning before now,' Liz Whitby said. She was standing behind me. 'Carried him quarter of a mile on his back.' Whitby was hardly any bigger than me, and a confirmed smoker of hand-rolled cigarettes. He was not of our time, this strange figure of activity. A black cat came from the back of the living room and peered up the chimney. Yet he knew how to pass for nothing exceptional, concealing himself in the present.

'Come away now, Pan!' Liz ordered. 'Silly thing's been stuck in there several times.'

The cat vamoosed at the sound of stamping on the stairs which led from the corner of the room beside the mantelpiece, where Whitby suddenly appeared to be dangling raggedly in the opening beneath the lintel. He emerged fully examining a piece of paper.

'What's this now, Frank?' Liz enquired in her green cardigan, which seemed to have acquired a thistly texture.

Whitby smacked the paper lightly with the back of his hand and said, 'Oh nothing.' There was a black iron frame on the hearth from which a brush, shovel and poker dangled like knights on a gibbet. This ground against the tiles as Whitby edged it with his boot; his trousers were rather old and grubby, in the light of day. I suspected that this document had something to do with Laura, who Whitby'd positively said would be ready now. Yet having gone upstairs to fetch her, he'd returned with a piece of paper. What trickery was this?

Well I was staying put until I got what I came down for. This was my resolution. None too politely, I succumbed into an armchair facing the fireplace. Immediately an unwelcome weariness took hold of me. As if they were behind a door like parents of a sick child, I could hear Liz and Whitby murmuring. The weariness was uncannily yet pitiably malevolent, as if a damp, cold wraith had crept into me and zipped itself secure. My parents murmured on. I could scarcely see them. The wraith was in fact myself, seeking me out as my aims began to fade. The couple at the room's edge were now asking me something, or just mentioning me. The disappointment was as paralysing as nausea. I hadn't got what I'd been promised; I wasn't going to get it either. Outside the window, Whitby hoisted the stag on his back and disappeared. Which was what I should have done with Laura. The visions Whitby'd showed me, on the hill and down in the wood, were nothing now. I was going home alone.

And at last it began to hit me hard that I'd maybe lost my job; I'd certainly lost the respect of my colleagues. Yet Whitby was dressing a stag to send to my parents. What the hell for? As a sign of triumph? A sign their boy had done well at last? An ash of black irony settled round me, a failure's confetti.

At last I rose creaking from the leather armchair to ask Liz, who now appeared to be in a kitchen adjoining, if I could smoke. The discarded piece of paper lay on a side-table, evidently left for my inspection. It was a fax headed 'Priest's Farm', politely informing Mr Frank Whitby that an order for two new gates had to be cancelled due to insurance advice that the ones in use were still serviceable.

When I came down from the shower, Liz was fussing with Pan. 'Frank's in the forge,' she said without looking at me. 'Go and see him, Mark.'

'The forge?'

'Yes. Through the back door, down the drive.' As I stepped outside, she called, 'Frank's the blacksmith.'

Beyond a large roofed wooden frame like a well covering, from which the stag hung bleeding into a pail, I came upon Whitby alone in a little room that resembled a domestic garage in his costume of the night before. There was no leather apron, no great dray horse waiting to be shoed: over a small fire of coals, half the size of a domestic hob, he was twizzling a slim iron rod.

Fifteen hundred centigrade he is... Whitby withdrew the rod from the coals, began to beat out the end that was grey from the heat on a neat, table-shaped anvil, then re-inserted it into the coals, which were no bigger than croutons. A haze hung over them. He twizzled the rod, removed it and beat it again, tapering the end, re-inserted it in the coals, twizzled, took it out and began to curve the end he was beating.

I'd get what I deserved, provided I followed my instincts. Whitby went on with his work until he had curled the rod round and round on itself for half its length, leaving a straight section which he now began to heat on the coals. Faster and faster he seemed to be working, yet his body was almost still. He made these to calm himself down.

Now he began to beat the grey rod, flattening it then applying delicate taps to bifurcate the head. Did I know what he was?

I thought he was starting to look like a snail.

Whitby winked and heated the creature on the coals again, then raised the bifurcations to make its horns, glancing out of the forge up the drive. Finally, with a sound of chips hitting hot oil, he plunged the black iron creature into a boxy bath of water with his long pliers.

'So long then, Mark. Taxi's waiting on the lane.'

'Thanks for everything.'

'Here, have a souvenir!' He pulled the snail from his bath, dried him in a rag and handed him to me. I almost dropped him with the heat. Whitby began to laugh. He was still laughing when Baghdad leaned across and opened the passenger door for me.

Baghdad was unimpressed to see me coming home with an iron snail rather than a living woman, after all the bravado of last night's journey to the moors. Tactfully he absorbed my failure, with his shineless eyes. But as we left the village behind, I began to gather all I'd seen and heard, done and been shown; and then I wondered if I maybe wasn't a kind of special failure. Put it this way, how many common failures got the treatment like that from Whitby and his kind? His was a free and open nature such as I'd only come across in reading: had I not benefitted from my encounter with the thing itself? As for the souvenir which I was passing from hand to hand – it was still as hot as hell – well what if my instincts *were* snail-like? We all resemble some beast or other, and the snail... I began to cackle in the fashion of Whitby. The snail always reaches its destination in the end, like any other beast. It just takes a fuck of a long time about it. Baghdad laughed too, and said it reminded him of a devil with a fat belly when I held it vertically. Moreover it was an iron beast. Did this mean my instincts were iron? That certainly sounded good. I had iron in me, and eventually I would arrive. By the time Baghdad dropped me off at Exeter St David's in good time for the 2.35 to Waterloo, I was cheerful enough.

I mean I'd not got Laura... but had she ever really been the issue? I was traipsing down the hill from East Finchley to the house now, bag over my shoulder like a demobbed infantryman. Had she been the issue at all? My self had been the problem, and the visit to Whitby had helped me to sort it; indeed, the whole of the last week, no matter how debauched it would have looked to any objective observer, had been, in some strange but exact way, curative, salutary and good. What had love got to do with any of this? A half-moon of apricot yellow shone over the cemetery. Had I ever really loved her? Thinking back, what would you say? Was it love, or the drooling of a nitwit? The North Circular hissed in the distance, as the sea hisses at night. Perhaps Whitby'd cured me of her too. I'd not drunk since we left the meadow; I hadn't smoked a cigarette for hours. Autumn was going to be all right and all other things would be well too; I would see to it − on my own, thanks. I was my own man − at last. I'd loved her even less than she'd loved me, which was saying something. Ha! I knew what she thought of me. Had enough of her tricks that time at the swimming baths in Covent Garden. *I was delighted to see your cock!* Who knows she didn't set that old fruit up to humiliate me? Who knows she *hadn't* been through half the lads in the village, on her country breaks?

There was light in the house, the Venetian blinds were down and the door opened to me. Laura was behind it laughing. Was this her fetch, an apparition such as Joan Hunter told us of; or one of those phenomena Whitby had showed me? Hadn't I already caught sight of her once or twice lately in places she should not have been? But what did *should* mean by now? There was a smell of baking. I would have laughed as well, but a sensation of triumph buoyed by superfluity was choking me. She wore a short black dress and some jewels. 'Viva, Mark!' she cried. I had a sudden desire to check my mail which I saw she'd placed on the little mahogany table by the front door, beneath the convex sunny-haired mirror in which we both looked as if we were subject to an alien order of gravity, two stretched beings, dark and gold, but she had her hands on my shoulders and was saying, 'Your house is full of old things!' She'd been drinking wine. 'What have you been doing up here? All these years?' She'd have been making me feel sorry for myself, if her eyes hadn't been shining at me greenly as I'd never seen them before. 'How have you managed in a place like this, Mark? It really is like you said it was!' Her jewels were fake diamonds. Fake diamonds for honesty, real ones for corruption. I tried to explain to her how easy it had been, I tried to tell her this was all unnecessary, that this was in excess of requirements.

But she was laughing and the words would not materialise... that what I really wanted was to stay as I was – it struck me strongly now that this was of the essence – if only she'd leave me alone for a minute instead of jumping, a golden hound upon a visiting boy. What I really wanted was to persist in my chronic, solitary dream. By the sunny-haired mirror which she was now cutting off, I wished to stand and reconsider my life. She was wearing a vanilla-based perfume; it seized the senses like a dessert laced with brandy. Everything that might have seemed a problem was less than one. I needed to make this clear. Owed it to my history. There was actually some value in the way I'd been! It was as close as someone like me could get to art. If she'd cut it out with her finesses, if she'd let me breathe – her lips were as cool as cucumbers, and as slippery – I'd tell her I'd always meant to be the way I had. How the hell did she know how to do this?

How has anyone ever known?... To Nietzsche with his hopeless love for Lou, the practice of chastity'd been creatively vital: no philosophy, no word palaces, without it... she was at my belt grinning, oldly, freshly... To Yeats with his sunny-haired idol, a secret hero of mine, it was the same. D'you think he made all that fuss about Maud Gonne just so he could get laid? No sir! Turned him into the noblest-sounding poet of our time, the lack of satisfaction. So how the hell did they think it stood with me, a man who couldn't hope to write a thing that anyone would stop to read. Could they not see what it meant to me to refuse physical enjoyment? It was the sacrifice I made for the art I lacked... that's what it was, damn it! It was satisfaction of the spirit, such as attained by the fakirs and the christs...

If only I could explain myself in the golden mirror which had been my grandparents', the one furnishing I'd brought here with me, the glass would flatten, taking with it the alien distortion of my face. If I could stay standing and explain... if I could just explain to her that sex was for everyone else... but she had the better of me; because – just because she was someone else. She was someone else, and I was nothing but my idea of myself. She had yellow hair like Colonel Custer in the book from the adult library, the last but one to die. The science of it – the science of it was... I didn't know as much as I thought, down here on the dusty stairs where she dragged me on to the carnival.

'I was going to buy a lobster and champagne. Then I decided it'd be much more welcoming to make something myself – and better for you,' Laura explained. I was dumb, with the rapture of a chronic boy. When my father gave me my first wristwatch as a prize for top marks in school tests, I was so delighted that the sensation overheated into a kind of embarrassment that suggested to me that I had not deserved this. Was the pie in the oven a similar reward? She'd used a little plastic brush she'd found in the drawer among the old people's kitchen apparatus to glaze the crust with milk.

I was dumb with humility, a peasant who'd landed in a future adept in billion-year-old practices such as his own age prohibited. Modern life was much grander than it was cracked up to be. She bent over the oven. She was a phenomenon, a golden human phenomenon in azure pants with fluttered edges. Damn. Such things were possible. I was dumb too in the hope of seeming at ease, fearing I might squeak if I opened my mouth. Jesus Christ. She must have practised bending like that. The geometry of it. Wasn't even pornographic technically. It was real for a start. When did women practise these accomplishments? Now she came over and patted my dick. When did they practise? I had my trousers on again, though she'd been all for a naked feast. I swaggered in my chair like a goodfella. Surprising how quick we learn these things. As she fashioned some green beans in black mustard seeds for an accompaniment, she chattered lightly to me.

She was very accomplished, handling that frying pan with the seeds fizzing in hot oil. I hoped she was being careful. Was this how it was generally, in the kitchens of the land? When she was gone I was going to have a good think about her breasts, which seemed to turn her into three.

'You can look, you know!' she cried suddenly, left hand on her hip; in her right she held an ancient pink-handled spatula, its brown blade glistening at the edge. My eyes dazzled. I was dumb as a beast. When she'd gone, I'd take it all in. For the time being, it was some order of carnival extravagance, to enjoy by the passing moment. It was a holiday.

So with dabbing movements of her spatula, she chattered as one on holiday of matters that back home would be getting everybody down – or worse. Ian had slipped a disc. He'd taken some days off work. Apparently he'd incurred the injury falling off a bar stool. He couldn't expect much sympathy could he? I shook my head slightly, for holiday's sake. Mary'd passed away. It was tragic. Her lungs couldn't cope with the operation. The cardiologist said her lungs were black as… (I couldn't get her next words. She was trying a bean for tenderness.)

Poor Mary. I'd been fond of her.

Well that was life. *C'est la vie.* Didn't I think?

Yeah. I wondered how I could find out about the funeral. I wanted to be there for her. Poor Mary.

I should be careful though. Really I should. How many did I smoke a day? Honestly? Me being a consultant too! (I had a qualm here, regarding my career prospects.) Twenty-five or so? Oh yeah! She smiled at me with her hands on her hips. The three of her. I saw Mary in her crimson cardigan, pushing at a bathroom door, I saw her creature's eyes.

With the food I drank water flavoured with a dash of Rose's Lime Cordial. The pastry was as gold as her hair. I was living for the moment. Her green eyes on me, she lolled at the table in her knickers and jewels like Baudelaire's darling in 'Les Bijoux', chewing fragments, beans, a mushroom. That is one hot poem. I was in the bordello now. She put her blonde foot on my dick and her jewels flashed. Old Dutch Bishop was on his own outside, whittling on a stick. Ah, what had been the point of that solitariness, on the eve of death? Chastity was for philosophers and priests, and them alone: Nietzsche's bitter knowledge. The rest of us had to get it on. Even Yeats did in the end. What in God's name had I been up to? Trying to talk to that hooker on Easter Road, eighteen years ago. Asking her about *existence*; recommending the National Gallery. All she wanted was twenty pounds for a gram of H and a pack of Lambert & Butler. Velázquez' painting of an old woman cooking eggs was neither here nor there. Yes, even Yeats became a shagger in the end… once he'd got the big blonde off his mind.

'You're thinking again, Mark!' she cried and rubbed with her foot. 'It's so naughty to keep doing that!' She was a teacher after all.

Presently we went upstairs holding hands like Hansel and Gretel, to look around my funny old house. Who came in here? This was the back bedroom with its two stripped single beds that smelled of army, or some form of harsh existence.

No one.

Never?

Never.

But why hadn't I made it cosy?

I'd been waiting for her to visit.

We could both have had tears in our eyes after that one as we went back out onto the landing to look at the round brass wall barometer, which as often was between *Settled* and *Change*.

She'd put some of her things in here. She indicated the box room. We went to examine her things – *some* of her things. Light from the apricot moon was falling on the boxes I'd never unpacked. The twenty-two-year-old calendar of showdogs shone darkly on the wall. In the pub car park beyond the garden fence, a youth in an old Datsun performed a handbreak turn on the gravel. I wasn't alone anymore. Downstairs the landline was ringing: Melania's voice entered the air. Two suitcases lay beside my crates, three holdalls, four giant plastic lunch-boxes that held her books, photos, emptied frames, cards, CDs, jars, vases, a herb-rack. She'd moved in, hadn't she? She wasn't going to be gone. What sort of holiday was this?

In the main bedroom, she'd hung dresses and blouses in the wardrobe – if this was all right with me. I'd never had a woman's things besides my suits. I stared at the arrangement until she began to show signs of anxiety beside me; it was the feeling that I could never have made this happen on my own that was arresting me. I went forward and stroked her clothes like a kid touching a donkey or other beast of the field across a country fence. She must have installed herself... when? When indeed?

I turned in haste because I'd thought of the stained pillows on my bed – but she'd already changed the cases. Settled in, changed the bedding, constructed a most handsome pie of steak and stout and mushroom, hung up her things in next to no time, for she couldn't have been back in London much longer than I had – could she? Not to mention all the packing. Wonderful.

She was wearing a silver grey slip for this tour which gave her a mermaid sheen, and which I now had my hand up from behind. I didn't want to seem a greedy lad about this, though I was hoping she'd probably experienced so little greed from Ian in recent times that she might be thoroughly glad of some on my part. I had a hope too that she might have been inclined since I came in through the front door to mistake callowness for a kind of seasonal deprivation common enough in fellows of my age, as when a van driver stuck in traffic engages you in a pantomime dialogue about the babe in the miniskirt who's giving you both the ballache. Yeah – if only she'd drop something, brother! Maybe age levels us all off, veterans and tyros... Bloody hell. She was being free enough now. Wonderful it was – cool, real, wonderful, with a slight lack of ideal smoothness.

God this was – I'd have said astonishing, but what was so fantastic was the factuality of it. The manifold factuality. Could have made a career of this, as a poet say, crossed with one of those culinary presenters who go around country areas checking out the flavours. Bloody as Merlot, syrup-sweet, with a note of hay; then the land itself in thundery weather. First impressions. Ah – but fundamentally, leather streaked with salt, riding boots crossing a salt marsh, or an Irish bay. Now and then I caught her watching me as she must have watched her pupils, if only there weren't laws against teachers watching the kids like that.

So she wished to live here with me, live here and grow old and save me from dying. This is what she had set her heart on. We were down having more to eat now, and she was sipping a glass of Viognier, of which she'd brought a bottle. Was it much to ask?

'But you wouldn't want to live in a place like this. You're a modern woman,' I said carefully. I had some memory of what Ian told me when this all started. This really was a house for shrivelled natures – as mine had been. By God, if *I* hadn't known something about being shrivelled! I more than anyone. 'I mean look at those!' I indicated the rack of porcelain thimbles painted with the heads of royalty, on the wall beside the fridge. Laughing she took my hand to go and look at them. They were obviously very naff. Pointing at the tiny portraits one by one, she asked who was my favourite. I must have loved them all really, never to have taken them down. She was as pert as could be with me as we stood before the porcelain pseudo-antiques, but she didn't exactly split herself with irony. She even seemed a little sad as she drew me back to the table and the brown-streaked plates. Perhaps it was the thought of old things being taken down and slung out, chipping and cracking as they hit the bin. Perhaps she was frightened for herself. Perhaps she was sorry for me.

She asked if we could share a cigarette, so I went into the hall to get the Rothmans from my discarded jacket. I found the black iron snail in my pocket and brought it back to amuse her. Of course, she wanted to know where it was from as I pushed it heavily round the plate emitting a motoring sound, *brrrrm brrrrm*. Next I held it up in the fat-bellied devil posture. She asked if it was my good-luck charm. Why had I never showed it before? Who made it? It was very sweet – though a bit sinister. Why wouldn't I tell her? She came to sit on my knee to punish me for being naughty about my pet snail. She bit my ear and neck and whispered tell me. Oh why wouldn't I? Her curiosity was taking hold of her, principally because I was saying nothing. I had no wish to deny her. But I couldn't say the name.

I mean we obviously had lots to talk about. Foremost was the 'Whitby factor', though this was only the starting point. There was so much more to analyse than that. Yet on the Don Quixote principle of not looking too far into the nature of the lady by whom you've been enchanted, I was preferring to play dumb than risk a conversation... here the landline rang again and Melania asked if I was there, and on my knee I felt Laura begin to cry, fearing all would be spoiled by the phone, red light flashing on the console, and by my silence, so I told her some baloney about how I'd acquired the snail from an old man in La Rochelle. I'd said about that before once, hadn't I? Something about a film? Indeed I had. Could she remember when? Was it a long time ago? Yes. How long? Oh, right at the beginning. She seemed to like this, so I jiggled her up and down on my knee until she started laughing. And would I take her there? Perhaps I would. Perhaps I'd take her there soon, in a hot-air balloon. She bent round to kiss me; her eyes were grey.

Then we had a cup of tea and listened to the John Peel show; and so to bed.

★★★

What we looked like I don't know, sitting there on a bench in Cherry Tree Woods on a still grey October afternoon, but we were both men transformed now. I hadn't drunk in four days. You wouldn't believe what a devilish unhappy cast drink gives the face… or perhaps you would. I was wearing a slim-fitting black suit with pale blue shirt (tieless, untucked), a carnation in my buttonhole, Laura's idea this before she left for work. Chas (or as he'd now notified *The Times*, 'Charles W Longley') was in charcoal jeans with brown Italian shoes like roughened, elongated peanuts, a black Versace shirt, a really fine silver wristwatch that couldn't have been more than 1.75mm thick, a solid Roman-looking silver bracelet and eye-catching silver ring on his left hand, with the countenance of something like a satyr. He'd lost a good ten pounds since I saw him in my clinic. His complexion was good, his smell was top cologne, unisex if I wasn't mistaken. I'd called him up to see me for lunch, and yarely he was with me, clutching a bag of Braeburns for health. We'd kept clear of the pub and brought chips from Bar Neptune to this sylvan park at the bottom of the High Road.

Chas was eager to discuss multiculturalism: he'd been filling in the monitoring form for a college course before we met. So I'd told him about all the times in the English Seventies and Eighties when I observed my own mother silently check my old man wasn't getting disrespect, from a traffic cop or shop assistant, or hearty at the occasional functions we attended with a beer tent or bar.

'Easier for her if she'd been same skin colour as him maybe?' Chas suggested. 'As opposed to white British.'

'In a way... I think it made me cautious about expressing myself too.'

'I can see how that might be, Doc.' Chas crunched his apple. 'When you're one thing, you know where you stand. Mixed race,' he continued carefully, 'ain't so easy – necessarily.'

'I certainly made it difficult for myself.'

'However,' Chas hurled his apple stump at a grey squirrel, 'my old man did not expect me to pass exams. He didn't expect me to do nothing; whereas yours *did*. That's the benefit. From what you say, your school wasn't greatly superior to mine.'

'True.'

'Yet you become a doctor, whereas I become trouble. Yeah?'

'Yeah.'

'That's where you express yourself. Your profession.' He was worried I'd been inclined to throw it all away. This really fazed him. He'd had his suspicions when he came into the headache clinic last Wednesday, which were unpleasantly confirmed in the Belvedere Hotel on Saturday night. Even now he was a little concerned I wasn't in my place of work. On the Headache Forum on the Web, him and some other lads had been organising a whip-round to get a Sri Lankan over for a consultation. Vim Vapappaty was just a farmer's son with V12 headaches and suspicions of a benign tumour. How was he going to make the air fare? Well, Charles and the other lads were hoping Vim might get to be seen by me, on Charles W Longley's personal recommendation.

I said yeah, I'd see Vim as a priority, and patted Chas W Longley. If he was shaming me, he was also looking up to me. It was as simple as that. So much now appeared simple. Laura'd already surmised she'd conceived my child – after two days this was – and introduced plants to the house. Simple.

'But I mean,' Chas persisted, 'that wasn't like your *normal* way of carrying on was it? What I saw, wasn't like *typical*?'

'Ah, I'd had tendencies for years. Last week was a crisis.'

'This thing about your mate's bird going off?'

'Yeah – basically.' An Indian woman passed in front of us singing to two identical boys on small bicycles.

'But he could of ruined your career,' Chas said sternly. He was well down on drinking friends these days. 'Should of thought of that – *he* should of I mean. Keeping you up and all that, night after night. You go in looking like a bag of smashed crabs in your profession, it's suicide. What was he trying to do to you?' Chas began to bite another Braeburn, in Ian's effigy.

'I believe he was trying to help me.'

'I'd need convincing, Doc,' Chas crunched shrewdly.

'Well the proof of it is I feel better. Look at me!'

'Simple as that?' Chas pushed up his shirt sleeves a little. A Charlton tattoo emerged on his forearm.

'Better than I ever have.'

'Cos you took his bird off of him?' Chas stretched his legs out on the long grass.

'Yeah.' Behind us wood pigeons called.

'That the sum of it?'

'Well I sort of got activated in a variety of ways, if you know what I mean.'

We thought together for a while, until Chas said, 'You was certainly activated in the Belvedere.'

'When I got smacked?'

'Yeah – well you was having words first, you and the geezer. Then he hit you.'

'What happened then?'

'Ah, you dropped him, Doc.'

'Literally?'

'Yeah.' Chas sniffed. 'He called you *babu*. You did not like that, Doc!'

'I should fucking think not either!'

'I confess I never heard that one, Doc.'

'It's fucking one century out of date that is. Went out with Rudyard Kipling.'

'What's it mean?'

'Means an Indian who's read too many books… Why did you not tell me this when I met you at Waterloo?'

'Ah,' Chas looked at his feet, rooting in the pockets of his jeans with his fists, 'didn't want to worry you.'

'How d'you mean?'

'Well you being a top neurologist and that.'

'Cos of my position?'

'Well, that included,' Chas laughed without cheer. 'They got closed circuit in there, Doc. But I mean, you fucking hurt him bad. He was not moving afterwards.'

I realised that he thought I'd care ethically about causing a head injury to another man. I cared as much about being too pissed to remember it clearly. Damn. My finest moment quite blacked out. 'Hey,' I said, 'I felt sure I saw your arm hitting someone though, Chas. It's coming back to me… That devil ring you're wearing.'

'I was just trying to pull you apart from him, Doc,' Chas explained.

'Ah.'

'Funny thing was,' Chas went on, 'I previously seen *your* mate, your mate *Ian* – he's got the beard, yeah? – seen him talking to the one you hit. From where I was standing.'

'When?'

'Well you, Doc, was singing like a frog to the girl that was at the bar, and your mate was talking to him. *Then* it was. In his ear.'

And what would my fair-bearded friend have been saying in his ear? What word?

'What about the other girl, Chas, the one who was on my knee?'

'She'd already gone. Before the mayhem commenced.'

'Ah.'

'But come to think of it, I saw your mate talking to her too; followed her down to the Ladies after she got off of your knee.' He was one sharp spectator, my man Chas. This was what coming off sixty Stellas per weekend gave you: eyes like a hawk. 'Saw him give you something too – like he was picking your pocket in reverse.'

This must have been the returning of my keys, which I'd already been speculating Ian might have taken from my trousers on the Saturday morning after the pie skirmish, in order to make my house in East Finchley enterable. He must have been having them cut while I was on the settee thinking about thinking. I nudged Chas: 'He was trying to get me out of *otium* and into *negotium*!'

'What's that mean?'

'In the Renaissance, they thought it was no good sitting around thinking: you had to be active, make your mark on the world.'

'I reckon thinking's all right,' Chas declared hoarsely. 'There should be more of it. And I should know too: created enough mayhem in my time. I've left my mark on the world for sure, number of people I've damaged, things I've destroyed… 1996 I done six months' Marines training. They discharged me cos of my attitude. I thought they'd appreciate an attitude like mine, in the Royal Marines.' Raising his face to the sky, he laughed slightly.

'Yeah well it's all right for you, Chaphistophilis. Spare a thought for the bloke who's done nothing but think.'

'You've *cured* though.' He shook his head. 'What I can't understand is why you don't regard that with the respect it deserves.'

'You don't express yourself through curing.'

'You expressed yourself to *me*.' Chas was adamant. 'Give me a new life… And now we've become friends.' I was silent. 'I mean I know there's nothing quite the same as sex and violence,' Chas continued. 'I *know* that. But a dog knows that. A man, he has to know more than that.'

'Yeah, but he has to know that too.'

'To an extent he has to.'

'To be a man.'

'Well I suppose your friend got you started.' Chas sniffed. 'Regime change so to speak.'

A shrewd phrase. He was a shrewd fellow, my friend Chaphistophilis. 'D'you want a look at her?' I said evilly.

Chas said, 'Sure,' and cleared his throat. Pulling out my phone, I showed him a close-up shot of Laura's golden face. 'Lovely girl,' he said somewhat bashfully, looking away as if he wasn't surprised.

'She was making me a pie when I came in from Devon the other night.'

'Cor, lucky man!' Chas cried.

'Yeah.' I'd discovered a strip of cardboard from a Waitrose pie carton when I was putting the rubbish out yesterday morning. I'd taken the Don Quixote line on this. An evil enchanter must have planted it, to make it look as if Laura, how shall we say – was not exactly all that she seemed? But who cared anyway? Everyone cheats on cooking nowadays, particularly busy professional ladies who *juggle* several pursuits. Everyone does. Everyone…

'I better go,' I said. 'She'll be coming home soon.'

'Still owe you one, Doc,' Chas growled wistfully as we stood up.

'Ah, talking to you has been good,' I told him. We walked across the rough grass through the trees and past the children's play area in silence, Chas, clutching his bag in which two apples remained, wanting to say more before we parted. On the roundabout, the Indian mum and her twins rotated watching us. Then we arrived at the underground, where Chas tautened the underside of his throat and set his shoulders back. He was a large man.

'I would kill for you, Doc!'

'Don't be daft!' I laughed. 'You've given up mayhem. Go and study, Chastopher! Go and read!' Then I walked away up the hill past the library and the cemetery to make Laura's tea.

Epilogue

The expenditure of cultural resources on treatment, cure, regime change, persuasion and the like is in excess of measurable returns. That is a verity, derived from historical and recent experience... Discuss.

What the Third Reich gained from the production of the most expensive Technicolor film in history to that date, *Kolberg*, for which the Propaganda Ministry withdrew 187,000 desperately-needed serving troops from the Eastern Front to act as *extras* in nineteenth-century costumes – this at a time when division strength in the *Ostheer* stood at 2-3,000 max (an 80% reduction from the war's beginning) and the Red Army was coming on with a momentum and in numbers unprecedented in conventional warfare – what the Third Reich gained from the production of *Kolberg* was nothing more than a laugh in its face. For when the film was shown to the garrison of La Rochelle on 27th January 1945 to inspire them with the heroic example of the resistance of the Pomeranian city of Kolberg to Napoleon in 1807, the garrison cheered loud and pledged unswerving resistance to the Allies to the last man, then raised their glasses and toasted the Führer. At lunchtime the next day, they surrendered *en masse* to US XX Corps – like 'Fuck you, Goebbels!' Which could be interpreted as a commensurate gain only by a culture utterly, ruthlessly dedicated to irony. Ja?!

What the Yanks and the Brits gain from 'Shock and Awe' and the subsequent intervention will never appear to balance the expenditure, the output of force or the collateral damage, politically, economically or morally. And this is because at the very best their actions can bring about nothing more than an imitation of their own polities, a shadow of their nature that hates them with the self-consciousness of the chronic adolescent whose slogan is that he didn't ask to be born.

What Britain and the NHS gain from setting to work Functional Alcoholic No. 1 to cure the headaches of Functional Alcoholic No. 2, when FA1's training alone cost in real terms maybe ten times the annual salary of FA2, not to mention what FA1 has been paid by the state since he qualified – well what's on the bottom line here? Not that it may not have been well worth it personally between me and Chas Longley, yeah? But was the state apparatus really required for the production of one happy effect? Did we really need all that in order to become friends?... Ah, as you get closer to the personal, the less clear the issue of expenditure becomes.

For was it not worth all the efforts of Ian, that excellent secretary, all those hundreds of pages of notes compiled in backward-flowing pale blue ink to get me here in the armchair with a cup of strong tea, Laura Blake over there in her glasses with *The Observer* and selected bits of the *Sunday Times*, my edition of Goethe's poems lying somewhat to her side? Lord what a wealth of resources he dedicated, in cunning, time, invention, observation... Wealth? Damn it, this was a surplus, surely, a massive surplus? Far far in excess of requirements. Couldn't he just have said like any man, 'You have obviously got a thing about each other. Fucking take her!'?

Maybe, if I'd been any man. But it wasn't any man he was dealing with. As Whitby explained when he took me to that high green place, I lacked nature; and such a man will resist what the normal fellow will put out his hand to as a matter of instinct: here a quadrant of pork pie alone on a plate, there a stripper's butt with a neutron bomb tattooed on it. Such a man may combine in himself resistance and passivity in a negativity so dark and chronic that he barely knows the one from the other. He may bring down empires, like the Christian priest or Mahatma Gandhi. He will baffle all his friends. Dealing with him is bound to call for surplus effort, the target being narrow to an extreme. So, just as from a long roll of thick cloth a tailor of the old school may cut a suit exactly to match the shape and caprices of his client, wasting quantities of material in the process, this was a plot designed exactly for me… Was that it?

Or were they more like a pair of alchemists, Ian and his golden partner, dedicating themselves to a physical transformation that seemed impossible? Then Ian's handwritten sheets and his notebooks were their experimental notes and recipes, from which they devised me a phantasmagoria, outsize and shaggy, woven of total unselective realism, accident, untruth, coincidence, not to mention melodrama and kitsch (calling to mind certain episodes, such as the séance in The Green Man and the music-box). Maybe the hero of modern life has to put up with bad taste… Look at her now with the Money Section. Those specs were a well-kept secret.

Come here, sweetheart!

Why are you laughing like that?

Put down the paper. Keep your glasses on. Turn your eyes on me, like you're running me down! Ha… Now we see you. *Formidable*!

But was it worth the expenditure?

***

And so in to work. Monday again. Nineteen days now past the Equinox.

'Someone looks better,' said Alison Dale.

'Thanks, Alison. The good spirit found me at long last.'

She nodded decently, no doubt thinking I'd begun some sort of therapy; bending her broad back over her computer she told me I'd had them worried with my antics. I said I was sorry, and Alison Dale said never mind, they all wanted to sit with me and her at the Christmas lunch this year. There you are, I said. They know celebrity when they see it. I got her to contact a colleague who could give Ian a scan for the slipped disc so he could avoid a seven-week wait for a consult. If that disc was in position C5/6, it could paralyse him. I asked the colleague not to mention my name, then went along to visit Bernie Henderson, who was expecting me.

'Smell my face, Bern!' I invited him, closing his office door behind me. 'I'm off the hooch.'

He blushed slightly: 'Only wanted to ask you how your holiday went, mate. Did you go where you said?'

'Yeah,' I said. 'I visited Whitby.'

Bernie Henderson looked glad. Had I checked out Hadleys for fish and chips? I said I was afraid I'd missed out on that pleasure. I'd gone hunting venison instead. Ah, Bernie yowled, fuck off out of it, squire. I had an impulse to shake his hand. On his wall he'd stuck a poster-painting in black, yellow, dark green: it looked like a cross between Napoleon and a duck. Underneath, it said 'Dad'.

Melania was wearing an ultra-professional shirt by Thomas Pink, in variegated royal purple, arterial purple, mauve, grape, pale blue, royal blue, indigo, thin beige and fine black stripes when we met for lunch at the Bramah Centre.

'You look so much better!' she cried. 'God what have you been doing, Mark! Look at you!' She made a performance of inspecting me in the manner of a kid messing round with a statue; all was far from well with Dr Morgan. 'You've turned the corner.'

We sat down at a table with a vegetarian savoury and a diet coke apiece. 'We're still meeting for liver and bacon sometimes though aren't we?' Melania said. 'And talks about neurology and Western culture?'

'Yes.'

'Well don't sound so eager!' she yelled. 'Why haven't you returned my calls? Hey? Why haven't you answered any of my messages? What a cunt you have turned into!'

'Ha! Think of your rep, Mel!' I warned her. This place was frequented by our colleagues.

'I don't care about my fucking reputation!' She was showing a lot of forehead today: her hair was extra barbaric, as if she was riding a fighting pony into a gale in the hills of Anatolia or ancient Cym, a necklace of the skulls of beasts around her throat. She has some Turk in her, Melania Morgan, a little of the wild Azarbaijani north, a slice of Silurian Celt; it's a fierce genetic combination. 'You're with her now aren't you? Don't argue. I *know* you are.'

'I wasn't going to argue.'

'So smug. What a creep you've become!'

'It's a regime change!' I laughed.

'If only you knew!' Mel whispered. 'You wouldn't be laughing if you knew.' The whispering, taut and dry as a pit-viper's rattle, was drawing still more attention than the outcry. 'They've been playing you for years.'

'I know they have.'

'You don't know they have at all. You *so* don't know they have. I know who they are. It was that Catweazle with the wispy beard that was at my thirty-third birthday. And the Aryan bitch. *Christ* she was so fucking coming on to you – disgustingly. We all saw it. She's been after you for years. They've been playing you the pair of them.'

'I know they have.'

'So common. Makes me want to vomit to think of it. Both of them playing you.'

'I know.'

'You don't know a thing! I've been watching you destroy yourself year in year out because of this pair. God the greatest regret of my fucking *life* is that I ever invited them.'

I said we'd better go and sit outside on the wall and smoke a cigarette.

'Now listen, Mel,' I told her. 'I've always known. It's just I play a long game.'

'Pathetic! You're with her now.' We carried on in this vein for a while, she insisting I knew nothing, me maintaining that I knew it all, till Melania cried into the

281

grey October air of early afternoon, 'She even used her aunt! Got her aunt involved, scheming Aryan slut!' Her breast was heaving like a diva's, in her tight technicolour shirt. Across the gardens in the middle of the square passed Ulrich Uhlmann in a hurry.

Melania now disclosed as fact that Joan Hunter and Laura were related as aunt and niece, or more likely as cousins – I was trying to interpret her diatribe – but with enough age difference for Laura to know Joan as 'Aunty'. The source of this information was Felicity Makepeace, to whom Mel had been speaking on the phone when I came into her office last Monday morning with a black eye, Felicity of course being a blood relation of the Laura clan. Now Felicity knew from her mother that Laura sometimes met Joan (who'd actually been in prison at least once for stealing jewels, *and* on a 'documentary' on Channel 5 about criminals – that was the sort of company my new girlfriend kept) for a pizza; it wasn't approved of, but Laura was a grown woman – apparently (who shared genes with a convicted criminal by the way). Anyway Laura (Mel was having difficulty pronouncing this name with contempt owing to its phonetics) had been meeting Joan for pizzas rather regularly of late, and there'd been a plan – yes a plan – to trick me into going away for the weekend and meeting Laura without Ian, so desperate was Laura to fuck me. Here, Mel's information ran out. But this was what she'd been ringing me about. They'd been getting me worked up on false pretences. The bitch hadn't really disappeared at all.

Yeah. I knew all this. (I'd absorbed quickly that information about Joan's TV history, which probably accounted for our warm welcome back to Ian's local on the night the three of us were barred.) I knew all this. I knew better than this. In fact, the plan had been to get me away from London in order to make time for Laura to move into my house. Which couldn't be accomplished until Ian had obtained by stealth my keys. So Joan had been jumping the gun trying to get me to go away, since Ian hadn't yet had a chance to get my keys. Moreover, she'd not been well briefed, because she was all for sending me to the wrong Whitby – the place in Yorkshire, rather than a blacksmith of that name. Incidentally (I was improvising now) Joan, being a trifle bent, was indispensable to getting my keys cut, since one of them was a Banham, which was illegal to copy. This was something Ian probably wouldn't have been able to manage alone. However however – however, it wouldn't have mattered if I *had* gone to the wrong Whitby, if only Ian had had the keys. In a way it wouldn't have mattered… yet in another way, it would have mattered a millionfold, since the Whitby I ended up visiting had had such – ah…

I'd said enough. I couldn't explain Ian's alchemy out here in the grey air. It wasn't to be explained. A light rain was trying to fall. Yeats believed in alchemy. Maybe he was a fool. He was still worth two gross of wise men. Alchemy lets loose forces. I could feel them in me. Melania had ventured now to lean against me on the wall. Ian's doing: my forces…

'I dig your shirt,' I told her. She leaned differently from Laura. Her spirit sprung out like a nettle. It stung me. She had a savage spirit; luckily she had a mind to contain it. It differed from Laura's; really it differed; perhaps differed as much as two spirits can.

'I've just got hold of some new research on Lenin,' I told her. 'State-censored neuropathology.' She said nothing. Technically she hadn't finished being furious; she accepted another cigarette. 'He's like Nietzsche in reverse,' I continued. 'He did die of a syphilitic brain, but the Soviets passed it off as something else – arteriosclerosis to be precise. Some of his doctors played along. Others refused... Bet you wouldn't have signed a fraudulent death certificate.'

'What's the point of any of that any more?' Mel stared at her feet.

'Come on!' I rallied her. 'We can branch out. Communism's the only alternative to Nietzsche anyway.'

'But there aren't going to be any more lunches... They were all I had to look forward to – our conversations. You never realised.'

She had her arms folded in front of her breasts now in that manner I remember from Angie Alexander and the girls of my schooldays, who wouldn't wear a coat or cardigan in the bitterest weather of a Lincolnshire winter when Russian easterlies commanded the air. I fancied getting my head in her pussy. She was wearing ladies' trousers from Joseph. I fancied getting it in there *schnell*. Her husband hadn't touched her since the last World Cup – I knew this for a fact. She regarded our lunches together as tantamount to an affair. With her this was not bourgeois over-sensitivity, it was savage superstition. I knew this for a fact. She loved me as well. We sat in silence like two generals on the heights. In a minute I could ask her to marry me and she'd say she would divorce him. Then we'd walk back across the gardens hand in hand to tell Alison Dale. We'd go and live in the woods the two of us, and never come back... And here was the rain.

So long my friends, if you've made it this far.

Michael Nath was brought up in South Wales and Lincolnshire. He is a lecturer in English at the University of Westminster. *La Rochelle* is his first novel.

For further information on this book,
and for Route's full book programme
please visit:

www.route-online.com